ARISING FROM DARKNESS

THE RIFTRIDER'S RETURN SERIES BOOK 1

C. N. PINCKARD

Arising From Darkness
The Riftrider's Return Series Book 1
C. N. Pinckard
Copyright© 2015

This book is a work of fiction. Any and all events, people, things are also fiction.

Edited, formatted, and typesetting of the cover art by Jennifer Oneal Gunn

Cover Illustrated by Katerina Ventova

This book can be purchased in all countries.

Print and digital

Printed in the United States of America.

04/09/2015

ISBN-13: 978-1494468798

ISBN-10: 1494468794

The publisher would like to thank all contributors of this work.

Dedication

To James, thanks for being my rock in a rocky life. My love is with you always, the pain of your loss may fade, but will never go away.

To my friends and family who have supported me through all of this. This was a labor of love and I thank you for being there for me. Jennifer, you have been there for me from the beginning. Leslie and Diana, thanks for helping me to keep the ball rolling. To my mom, Wanda, you are an inspiration in perseverance who told me to never stop trying. Thank you.

PREFACE

In the land of Yeverdin, the region of the snow elves, precious metals used to make the beautiful armor and swords needed to guard kings came from the caves of the vast region. While blacksmiths smelted the ore found in the caverns into useful metals, the gems were used to encrust the hilts of the weapons.

In Herium, the largest trade city in the realm, the snow elves learned to use some of the metals to conduct electricity. As well as his riches and false claim to power, Gavid wished to take the entire town for his own.

Gavid worked with the forces of evil to break King Ledric's kingdom to the ground, little by little, destroying those who get in his way. Meranda, a snow elven woman, was in his clutches until recently...

CHAPTER 1

S he jumped as thunder clapped overhead. Gavid, the one who lorded over the lands, kept her captive. She finally had enough and escaped. She heard the king of the realm was in town and she needed to get to him to report everything she learned days ago.

Distracted, she ran and tripped over an elven man's fruit stand. As she stumbled, she did her best to try to clean up the fruit and he helped her. He didn't recognize her and spoke gently, "What has gotten you so upset?"

She cried as she spoke, "I heard King Ledric was in town. Do you know where he is?"

He could see that her body was not in any condition to see the king and tried to help her, but she pushed him off. Her wet curly hair was matted to her face and her lavender eyes sparkled from the tears as she looked at him. He sighed. "The king is at the Hunted Fox Inn."

She thanked him in a quiet voice then ran off to finally see King Ledric. She began to run toward him when she heard a voice behind her speak. "One more step and it will be the end of you!"

The elven woman paused as if in thought for a moment and shook her head. She darted toward the king.

The king, in turn, looked at the man who spoke to her. "This is what you have been up to," he said as the sneered at the man.

The man laughed as he watched Meranda. Ledric commanded the guards to arrest the man as he began to wave his hands. The dark elven man knew he had to get the spells out before he was captured and was successful, he shocked the woman before him. Then he vanished, laughing, which made the entire town shake in fear.

Before the king, the woman shook in a frenzy and fell to the ground. He quickly ran and caught the poor child, looking up at his guards who stood still in disbelief. Ledric grumbled and screamed at them, "Capture that man! Go to the keep and get him! I don't care how you do it, just do it!"

The guards left to find the keep as Ledric picked up the woman. He looked around and shouted to his aids to find a healer then took her up to his room. Gently, he laid her down, seeing an arch in her spine. He turned her over gently, questioning her, "What did he do to you?"

"More than I care to think about," a voice behind him spoke.

Ledric turned around to see an elven woman with soft white skin, bright blue eyes, and soft gray hair. He turned back to the woman then replied, "Who is she? The lady of the lands?"

The elven woman sighed. "This is the daughter of a lord, yes, Meranda. She has been treated poorly by Gavid for years. He knew there was something different about her, but couldn't place his finger on it. There were times I would heal her while he was away, yet there were times she had healing from someone or somewhere else I could not explain."

Ledric continued to stare at the girl when the woman spoke again, "Help me get her healed up this time. Perhaps we can get her away from here and get her some training. She is a Riftrider."

"What?!" he shouted loudly. "She is a Riftrider? Where was help when she needed it? Where are those who are like her when she was crying for help?"

Erissa touched his hand. "My dear, where were you? We sent several messages about her and you never came. She was in need of you and you didn't even send someone to see if the rumors were true."

He jerked his hand away as if she shocked him and looked down at the girl. This was just as much his responsibility as it was others.

She smiled as she glanced at him. "Come on, we can fix this. She needs it once again."

Ledric snapped from his thoughts and nodded. "What do you need me to do?"

He thought for a moment and she looked down at Meranda then spoke, "Flip her over gently then hold the pin. I have become practiced at healing this out of her back."

He contemplated what was said and gently flipped her over. Together, they healed Meranda slowly.

As the pin came out, Ledric's rage slowly set in, not only at himself but the desert elf who did this to her. He silently vowed he would fix all of this and help her get what she needed in training. Once the healing was done, Erissa covered her up, glanced over at him, then spoke, "Get her some clothes and you need to find some way to get her to Elmwick. That's where they train. She had some training, but it's all been unconscious. Now, help her get back on her feet and make things better."

He watched as she gently healed the girl and noticed other scars on her back. He turned to her. "How are all of these scars possible?"

She finished spells and sighed before she answered. "Some are unexplainable, but others are from Gavid, he really did terrible things to her."

Anger, once again, clouded anything Erissa had to tell Ledric as she spoke, "She needs to get to her father as well, your majesty." She looked at him. "Sire, are you okay?"

Again, he suddenly looked at her. "Yes, whatever she needs to do, I'll help her do it."

Erissa touched his hand and spoke quietly, "See, she knows that she's safe this time. Speak with her and find her some clothes as well as some transportation to get her to Elmwick and to her parents."

"What about her father?" he questioned to her. "Surely he is dead."

She took a deep breath, let it out slowly, and replied, "She'll know what to do. Just let her know it's okay." She stood up and continued, "Now, if you'll excuse me, I must go check on the healer area and get prepared for the trip."

He watched as she walked out of the room and looked at Meranda. Ledric then thought to himself, *How could I not see it sooner? How come I never followed up on those rumors? Something more has to be done. This is just as much my fault as anyone else's.*

With that, he sat on a chair and watched her. Thoughts ran through his mind and soon he was fast asleep.

Gavid cursed silently as he arrived back at the keep, his dark hair flowed about his shoulders as his cooper colored eyes surveyed the area. He looked around and saw nothing out of the ordinary. He quickly made his way inside.

He opened the large door; he walked in and took in everything. He needed to get rid of the keep and the evidence against him. He kept the daughter of Gervis captured there. He knew who the girl was and he was advised to keep her secret.

The plan was to take over the lands that surrounded the kingdom of Yeverdin. He was part of the plan, there were others, but it seemed he was the hardest working and already took control. Once he fled, after Meranda went to see the king, Gavid knew the plan was altered slightly, but not changed.

Quickly, he gathered up a few things, but noticed things were out of place. He paid no mind to it as he made his way out of the keep. He heard guards not far away and knew time was of the essence. He ran carefully through the forest then hid in the trees within eyesight of the keep. As he watched the guards approach, he pulled out a couple of components then waved his hand. He stared at the keep, Gavid intently watched it explode in a ball of fire. Immediately, he rose and walked into the keep as he heard the guards while they screamed and shouted about the fire.

He rapidly made his way into the forest and soon found his way into the desert. His luck hadn't changed nor had the plan. He escaped, Meranda was dead, and the wives of her brothers would soon be dead. He simply would have to wait to return. Once things settled down in town, he would make his way back as if nothing happened.

The important thing was to return to town. The land outside of the keep was full of resources that helped the entire continent function. Some metals allowed the conduction of power to every home in Herium and others surrounding them. Some resources were sold to other towns, like in the desert, to help towns flourish and grow. Controlling all of these would be important to Herium and once Gavid did that, he could possibly take over the continent.

Soon, he was in the desert enjoying the warmth. The summers in the snow region were far different than here. The weather was mild and it constantly rained. He did not know how to handle the weather as those who lived there did.

He made his way to the city of Quarden and walked to an inn. The Quiet Breeze was a small charming place that didn't draw much attention to itself. It seemed to be out of the way and in a quiet area of town.

Paying for a weeks' worth of rent for the room, he smiled at the lady. She gave him the key and smiled back. He spoke with a soft charm, "My dear, when will dinner be served?"

She smiled happily and replied, "Dinner will be served later this evening. Take some time to enjoy the markets and the sights. I can tell you are not from here."

He shrugged and spoke, "I was raised here, but it has been a while since I have been here. I will just stay in my room and enjoy the time in there. Thank you, however."

She looked at him and touched his hand. "I'm here, if you need anything else." The clerk was certainly attractive, her dark brown skin glistened in the sunlight as she looked at him with her piercing light brown eyes.

He gently took his hand from under hers and smiled. "Thank you, but I will not be needing that kind of company this evening. Just dinner when it is ready."

Slowly, he took the key and made his way into his room and unlocked the door. Things certainly hadn't changed much, but his heart secretly belonged to someone else. He hadn't heard from her in a long time, but he knew why.

He sat on the balcony and listening to the town winding down. There was laughter and happiness. The sun was starting to set on the left of him and he admired how it reflected on the forest of the region of Yeverdin.

Slowly he closed his eyes and tried his best to contact the woman that had his heart. When he got no response he opened his eyes and continued to listen to the town. Not long after, there was a quiet knock on the door. He stood up and saw dinner had arrived. Gavid smiled and let the porter in.

The man left his meal and held out his hand. Knowing what he wanted, Gavid slipped a little silver into the man's hand. The elven man grumbled and walked out, talking about how cheap people were.

This was the first time Gavid enjoyed some peace and quiet. The town was full of life and there weren't people begging him for money or food. The snow elven people seemed to take it harder than most when life got them down. There were those who were willing to work for Gavid even if he paid them little to nothing. However, there were those who were spreading rumors about the girl and her family. He had to put them out of their misery and make people believe what they were saying wasn't true.

Not long after, he sat and ate his meal, the food was hot and wonderful. It brought memories back of his childhood. Although it was a happy one, he always remembered wanting more. He knew he was nearly there and his plans were not too far off balance. Soon, he would be back in Herium controlling everything. He finished his meal and left the tray outside. He was back to the balcony and enjoyed the peaceful sounds, which made him drift off to sleep.

CHAPTER 2

Earlier, he stood in disbelief as he watched from the crowd in Herium, a small woman shaking in agony. He felt every tingle that went through her body, but something told him she wasn't dead. Now, he was with the guards that he sent to investigate her anguish.

He stood out amongst them; tall, muscular, long red hair pulled back behind him, with dark skin and green eyes. He wore a leather vest with a green shirt underneath. The guard walked up to him. "Sir, you don't have to be here."

"The name is Treidon and yes I do. I have witnessed a murder and you know how the Riftriders feel about those kinds of things," he said matter-of-factly.

The guard nodded and let the man be. Treidon looked around at the destruction. The rain doused out most of the fire by the time he arrived. There was something about her, he felt connected to. He couldn't resist her helplessness. He arrived in Herium a day or so before the girl was hurt. He heard the commotion of the desert elf and made his way through the crowd when he saw her and felt the same things she did. She looked battered and bewildered, he wanted to find a way to help her, if she was alive.

He called to his pet and knelt down to him to give him a scratch between the ears. The pet was a forest leopard. Dark brown with lighter brown spots and green eyes. He smiled as the leopard purred. "We need some help. Looks like a woman was murdered. We can't have that, now can we?"

The leopard nuzzled up to him in response and began to sniff the ground. Treidon followed him and looked for any signs around the keep as to where she could be.

Soon, he walked and heard a clink of metal on metal and looked down. He noticed a rusted iron chain blending in with the dirt and melting snow. He followed it to a large tree the chain was connected to. He soon found the end, which was a hook.

Treidon looked around and stared in amazement. There were tools scattered on a tree stump, placed there to implement pain. There were dried blood stains on them. Treidon's eyes began to water as thoughts began to race through his mind. Thoughts about her being connected to the tree. *Why would someone use these on this poor woman? How long has she been like this?* The more he thought, the angrier he got. He noticed what appeared to be a run-down shack not far from the same tree.

Dropping the chain, he walked to the shack and opened the door. It didn't look like anything from the outside, but the inside told an entirely different story. There were nice hand crafted stairs leading down into the darkness. He whistled for his pet, who quickly responded and ran to him. "Let's see where this goes, Quein."

Together they walked down, feeling the rough wooden walls, soon they were at the bottom. Treidon felt around to see if there was a light switch and soon found it. Flipping the switch, he gasped as he looked around.

The walls were lined with shelves of books. A desk with a small lamp, scattered books, and more tools. Treidon wiped a tear from his eye, the pain was more evident this time than before. As he turned, his body was full of anger, then he noticed the blood stained sheets.

His hands were shaking from being enraged as he touched the sheets. Suddenly, he heard a woman's voice through the darkness. "Help me."

Jumping, he turned around and looked at his pet, who tilted his head to one side. "Can anyone here me?" the voice questioned again.

Treidon responded out loud, "Where are you? I don't see you around me?"

His anger seem to subside when the response came to him. "I was at the Hunted Fox Inn when my master shocked me and left me for dead. Now, there is something in the darkness wanting to kill me. Can you help me?"

Freezing in his steps, he looked down again to his pet. "You're alive?"

"For now," she said with a quiver in her voice and he noticed the fear in his own body.

She was alive and still in danger. He took the stairs inside to get outside the shack as fast as he could and responded, "I will be on my way to help you. What do you hear around you?"

"Other than my pet growling to protect me, snarls and roars," she said in a hushed voice.

He realized she was mentally talking to him and she also mentioned her pet. "Wait, you have a pet?"

She tried to make a joke as she responded, "Doesn't every Riftrider?"

He could tell she was scared, but his mind raced. She was a Riftrider like he was. Why didn't they come save her? He was soon racing to his horse, only stopping to speak to the guards about the shack they needed to see.

He left them in a dash, climbing on his horse, riding out. Quein was keeping up with him easily and Treidon looked down at him. "She needs protecting, keep her and her pet safe."

The pet vanished in a blue light and Treidon continued to ride as hard as he could. He felt a scratch across the back of his leg and screamed in pain. Then he realized it was against his leg and spurred the horse toward the town. "Hide, my pet will be with you soon."

"Where?" she said. "The area is pitch black and I cannot see anything in front of me."

He finally arrived when he heard her scream. Unmoved, Treidon contacted her. "Is everything okay?"

"Yes, your pet and mine are trying their best to keep me safe, please hurry," she said, the desperation in her voice was apparent.

He stopped at the inn, climbed off the horse, ran to the inn keeper. Out of breath, he spoke to her. "Where is King Ledric's room?"

She was a beautiful snow elven woman, light green eyes, light brown skin, and brown hair. She shook her head. "I was informed not to let anyone know."

Treidon looked around and then spoke again, "Look, the woman he brought up to his room. She needs my help."

He winced and looked down at his hand, her eyes widen. "You're bleeding for no reason. How did that happen?"

Treidon was frustrated, but kept his cool. "The woman with him. I need to save her."

She finally pointed up and spoke. "He's in the third floor, he has taken the entire floor."

Treidon sprinted to the stairs and the climbed them swiftly and effortlessly. He opened the door quickly.

King Ledric jumped up and looked at the man who just intruded in his room, but before he could speak, Treidon pointed to the blackness where Meranda was. "She's in danger."

Ledric turned and was shocked to see the room in pitch black and nodded to him. "Go."

Treidon darted into the darkness and appeared in Meranda's mind. "I'm here. Where are you?"

She appeared out of the darkness, her beauty was unmatched. He gently held out his hand and she grabbed it firmly. He heard the roars around them and the subtle growls. Instantly he knew what it was and spoke. "Hold on, my dear, it is going to get bright." She buried her head into his vested chest and closed her eyes

All she heard were screams of terror and the word 'sleep.' She felt relaxed and finally drifted into a deep sleep.

Three men sat and stared at the fire. The news from the grapevine trailed down to them in a twisted way. Gavid fled after his attempts at killing the king. There was no way Gavid would do something that insane.

One elven man was regarded as the oldest; he had long white hair, pale lavender eyes, and soft gray skin. The middle one looked almost identical to him, but his hair was shorter. While the youngest brother had the same eye color, short white hair, and darker gray skin.

"What are we going to do, Linden? Has Gavid really left town?" the middle one questioned.

Linden stared into the fire and shrugged. He didn't know. "We made that promise to our wives, but this is different. If he's not in town, Davignon, then we should have no troubles going back."

The youngest looked at the pair of them and stood up. "I think we should go out there in the morning. We've been gone too long."

"Jayidus, we can't just walk into town like that. There are a few that seem to think we're dead," Linden replied.

Jayidus started to speak up when they heard a horse rushing up toward them. The other brothers stood up quickly and turned in the direction. A young snow elven male with black hair and light green eyes approached them.

"Good, you are still awake," he said softly, looking around. "Erissa has sent word. Your sister is alive and you need to come into town. Gavid tried to kill her, but he did not succeed."

They stared at the young elf blankly and then shook their heads in unison as Linden approached the young lad. "That's impossible, we don't have a sister."

The boy shrugged. "I was told to come see the three of you and tell you that you do have a sister. She will be on her way out to get training, once they find a Riftrider. Your sister is with King Ledric. With Gavid gone, the three of you can take the town. I must be getting back though, you know how Erissa can get."

Davignon started to hand the boy some gold, but he pushed it away and turned. "Just get to town when you can. It needs you more than you realize."

He rode off and left the men in thought of their own treatment of their newly found sister.

"She can't be our sister, can she?" questioned Linden.

None of them had an answer. Jayidus finally replied, "There is no telling what happened while we were gone. Our parents could have had a baby and it could be the girl that we treated so poorly.

If that is the case, she's going to be irate with us, for one. Two, she's going to be scared of everyone. Each one of us turned her away and gave her back to Gavid. If this is true, I have to find that miscreant and show him how to treat a lady and how *not* to treat our sister."

Staring at Jayidus for a moment, Linden shook his head. "You have room to talk, dear brother. We all treated her poorly in some fashion."

Jayidus nodded and looked down to the fire. They continue to reflect on the time they spent with their newly found sister. Soon, the daylight began to peek over the horizon and their wives walked out of their homes. They all looked nearly identical, blonde hair, green eyes, and dark skin, but their facial structure set them all apart.

They sat beside the men and Jayidus' wife spoke, "My dear, what has kept you all up tonight? The sunlight is coming up, please come to bed."

He took her hand gently and pulled her into his lap then brushed a blonde hair from her face. "Dear Terian, do you remember the frail woman that was with Gavid?"

She looked at him, concerned, she nodded. "We all had some hatred for her. We tried several times to kill her, but Gavid said that was for him to do, not us."

Linden looked at his wife. "Do you feel the same way, Saraj?"

She nodded and gave a smile. "I do, my dear. We were told by Gavid not to kill her. He was doing things that he wanted to finish."

This was colder than all three brothers remembered. They would have defended her, normally. Davignon was tired of it, he stood up and walked to his wife. "She is our sister and that's not what you would have done in the past, my dear Jilian."

Jilian waved her hand like she was someone of high power and rolled her eyes. "My dear husband, she wanted to take you away from me according to Gavid. She is not your sister or I would have not wanted to do so."

"Lies, every single last bit of them were lies. What has Gavid put into your head that made you believe him? Jilian, I expected you not to believe anything that he put out there against us or our family. Here you stand now, defending him?" Davignon spoke loudly.

She shook her head and tried to back out of it. "That's not what I meant."

The others stood up against Davignon and the brothers. Terian spoke against him. "You don't know what Gavid is like. He's kind, compassionate, and concerned for us."

Linden grumbled and got into his wife's face and stared her deep in the eyes. "What has he done to you, my dear Saraj? Something is different and I don't like it."

Saraj laughed and walked away from him. "Believe what you want, dear husband, but I am telling you what I know. She is not your sister."

The three of them sashayed off, leaving their husbands to wonder what just happened. The three of men sat back down, focused on the fire, and how they could not have seen the facts sooner. They sat quietly together for most of the morning.

CHAPTER 3

Treidon emerged into the room and looked at King Ledric. Ledric stood in amazement and shook his head. "How did you know she was here?"

Treidon sat comfortably on the bed next to Meranda and looked at him. "I was standing in the crowd when I heard a commotion, as I arrived, I saw her being shocked in front of you. I went to go check out the keep with the guards and found some disturbing things, that's when she contacted me."

Gently he ran a finger though her white locks and sighed. "She's a Riftrider, but I believe there is more to it."

As Treidon turned, Ledric noticed a few of the scars on his arm that Meranda had on hers and cleared his throat.

Treidon looked up to him. "What is it, sire?"

Ledric was curious. "You are bleeding for one. Another, can I see your back? Just curious is all."

Treidon had forgotten about the wound on his hand and the back of his leg. He took out a potion for healing and drank it then gently took off his vest, lifting his shirt to show his back.

Being subconscious of his scars, he looked at Meranda's body and his eyes widened. "How long has she had those scars?"

Ledric observed his back and then said to Treidon, "About as long as you have had yours, I'm guessing."

Treidon put his shirt down and stared at him in disbelief. "What do you mean by that?"

Ledric gently pulled down the blankets that covered Meranda and touched her back where his exact scar was. "This was where an eye pin was in her back."

He walked into the living area and picked up the pin, bringing it back to him. "She had this in her back?"

Treidon covered her up gently and stood up. He took the pin and walked into the living area. Sitting in a chair, he reflected on what was before him. "There was always a constant pull as I trained, in my back. I knew the moment it was out, I was free to train, grow stronger. However, this," he said balancing it in his hand. "This piece here would be my bane."

Ledric listened to him and looked at the pin. "The lord of the land put that in her and kept her outside."

Treidon nodded and took a deep breath. "There was a long chain outside that he probably kept her on."

Memories and facts about the matter flooded to his mind. Anger rushed to the forefront and he gripped the pin as Ledric spoke. "Why would he do something like that to her?"

"I know," a soft voice spoke up behind them. "But can we cover all of the mirrors in the room please. Gavid is able to check on everyone through a communication spell."

They both stood up and looked at her. Although she looked healthy and muscular for someone who was tormented, she also gave the appearance of a frail woman.

Treidon and Ledric covered up the mirrors and any other reflective surface that could be used to see in the room.

She relaxed and sat back on the bed, wrapped up in blankets. Her skin was dirty from falling in the mud earlier, but she was still beautiful. Treidon gently put his hand on her back and she gave a slight shudder as the butterflies developed in her stomach.

Ledric sat in the chair in front of her. "So, what can you tell us? Why did he do this to you?"

Meranda looked at Treidon and then at Ledric. "There were some questionable things that would happen to me that he wanted to explore."

Ledric looked at her concerned, "Like what? You are a beautiful snow elf, but what would more could there be?"

Meranda took a deep breath and shrugged. "There were unknown things, like my body healing without him touching it. My health was not deteriorating despite his efforts, not feeding me for months. I was growing stronger and he knew it. When the shadow elves freed me this time, instead of running to my parents, where he had always caught me in the past, I ran here."

Treidon touched her back again and turned to notice the scars. "I have the same ones, here," he said as he ran his fingers over her scars. "This one my father didn't understand. It was the first one. After that, when I would get one, I would just go to the healers quickly."

She shivered at his touch and closed her eyes for a moment. His touch felt like a light feather than daggers, which most touches felt like. "That was the first one, after the pin he placed in me. He said it was for my own good."

He noticed a birthmark which looked like a long sword with three slashes on the end of it, on her shoulder and gently brushed it. "I don't have this one. Do you know what it is?"

She shrugged and closed her eyes once again. "Gavid constantly would want to cut it out. He said it was a hideous thing. I don't understand why the shadow elves didn't just kill him when they had the chance."

"That's because they work with evil," Treidon said as he removed his hand.

Meranda shook her head, but Ledric asked another question. "My dear, why would Gavid want to control this town? There isn't much to it."

She looked at the king. "There's more to it than you could image. He talked to me and did things in front of me, because he thought I didn't understand. Like talking to people in the mirror. He didn't think I was understanding what he was saying. Someone in the plains was giving him commands, but I don't know why. This town is rich with resources and he wanted to control them. Controlling the people and controlling the resources would choke out the entire realm. Also, we are the largest trade town for the desert. We are the only passage through the mountains to get to the desert, so trade is strong here." She gave a soft yawn and looked at Ledric again. "I am aware of a lot more than he realized, so trying to kill me off might have been a good thing."

Treidon noticed the yawn and moved to get a shirt for her, since he hadn't noticed any clothes yet. He gently handed it to her. "Here, I will get you some clothes."

She got up, took the sheet with her and walked to the bathroom. Treidon looked at Ledric who spoke softly, "You two are bonded. Those scars are on her."

Treidon nodded in agreement. "Every scar, except that birthmark, are on me. I wonder about that birthmark, such an odd one." He let it go though and watched as she came out. She certainly looked better in his clothes than he did.

He looked away as she climbed back into the bed. She gently laid her head on the pillows, satisfied that the mirrors were covered and Gavid wouldn't see them. He leaned down and kissed her forehead. "Get some rest. I'll take you to Elmwick for training."

She nodded and closed her eyes and was soon back to sleep. Ledric looked at him. "So, you'll take her tomorrow?"

Treidon gave a smile. "Yes, she will be in a trial to see what she knows. We will leave in the morning."

Ledric nodded in satisfaction and Treidon sat in the bed beside her to watch her sleep. Ledric spoke, "I will get her some clothes and have the arrangements made before you get ready to leave."

Treidon nodded in thanks and Ledric sat back on the couch, closing his eyes for the night.

Gavid tossed and turned while the images of the woman dying in front of him played out. However, those images also told him she was alive. This did not settle well with him. He sat up and looked around.

He needed to know if Ledric was able to save her and keep her safe. She was certainly getting stronger, despite what he tried to do to her. Starve her, cut her, or beat her, it didn't matter. She was starting to show signs of resistance and fight as well.

Soon, he got up out of the bed and grabbed a few spell components he needed.

He walked to the mirror and waved his hand over the spell components and then over the mirror. It glowed and swirled until the images around Herium appeared. Gavid remembered the last place they were was at the Hunted Fox Inn. He focused his thoughts there and then waved his hand. The images moved to the inn and to the mirrors that might be within.

He flipped through images of lovers, dark rooms, those sleeping or unimportant to him. He concentrated on those rooms, which weren't many, that might pique his interest. He only found one room and a bloody set of sheets, yet there was no indication it was King Ledric's room. There was no window where he could see the position of the room. There were no other clues to know what happened in that room, just the sheets. He finally gave up and determined that they tried to save her and failed. Soon he curled up and went back to sleep. The sleep was peaceful.

The morning light was upon him and he woke up with a stretch. He climbed out of the bed and got ready for the day. He wanted to see what changed in town since he was last here. It certainly was a thriving place.

First, he remembered, he needed to find out how the goblins and orcs were doing with preparations. He strided to the mirror and cast the spell again. The first image that appeared was of a small goblin. His skin was dark green, his eyes were small and beady, and his hair was dark and long. "You called, my lord?"

Gavid nodded. "I wanted to see how things were going."

Jael, king of the goblins, stood up and walked to the mirror, he was hunched over like all goblins were. "My lord, things are going well. Ores are separated as are gems and other items. We toss the dirt out when we are done."

Gavid rubbed his head. Dirt was important to other regions like the desert. "Don't throw the dirt out. It can be sold for some nice hefty gold in the desert regions. Keep it in a good place and I will deal with that when I get back."

Jael looked confused and shrugged. "Your call, but I don't see why we have to keep it."

Grumbling to himself, Gavid gritted his teeth as he spoke, "Just do it. Don't question me."

Jael did his own mumbling of dissatisfaction and looked at Gavid who was frustrated, then he spoke, "I will do what you ask. Now if you'll excuse me, I need to take care of the changes in orders."

Gavid watched as Jael left the room and he waved his hand to the orc. Dark green in skin tone with bright green hair and dark green eyes, the man looked up at the mirror. "What do you need, my lord?"

He liked the orc and wondered how he got to be so well-mannered. "I need you to save the dirt, Ugex. I know most of your orcs are working on the armor and weapons and that Jael's group is the miners, but make sure he saves the dirt."

Ugex gave a slight nod. "Is there anything else, my lord? The mining is going slow and I don't think Jael is telling you the entire truth. We keep running out of iron for the weapons and armor. He has found other ores, like gold and mithril, but he seems to keep that to himself. My clan has reported to me that this is happening."

Gavid nodded. "Let me handle him. If you find any black rubies, let me know. Save them for me, please."

He looked behind him subtly and then to Gavid. "I notice you are not home. Where are you, my lord?"

Gavid turned and sighed. "I had to kill the woman that was outside. She was gaining momentum and nearly got to the king this time. Usually, I can rely on her trying to flee in another direction and catch her before she gets too far. This time she ran straight to the king. Such a pity."

Ugex gave a nod and replied, "Well, stay safe. I am sure things will fade in people's minds soon."

Gavid agreed and then heard a knock on the door. "That is my breakfast. I hope you can do what I ask."

Standing up, Ugex was a tall muscular man, which was not odd for an orc. "I need to go check on the rubies that you asked for, my lord. Just know, we are doing our best to keep things progressing."

"Thank you, I will be in touch later," Gavid said with a wave of his hand.

He went to the door and opened it, the porter walked in with his food and expected a tip. Gavid grumbled and handed him a copper coin. This did not please the porter and he walked out complaining about how cheap people were again.

Gavid shut the door behind him and took the food to the table. Gently, he sat down to eat breakfast. The eggs were fresh and steaming, along with the other bits of his food. As he ate it, it went down warmly and freshened his soul. After he got done eating, he stood up and walked out the door, down to the town to enjoy the sights and sounds.

CHAPTER 4

s Treidon and Meranda slept, Ledric called one of his aids into the room. "I need you to get her some clothes before the morning, she will need them on her travels."

The aid looked at him. "Sire, why do you treat this woman as those she were of some importance? She, from all appearances, was a slave to the lord."

Ledric closed his eyes to cool his anger and opened them to the puzzled aid. "She is not a slave and he is not the lord of this land. He was someone who took the place while others were gone. Gervis and his wife have not been seen and I think their boys are nearby, but she is no slave. She is my subject and part of this town.

No man, woman, or child should have to be subjected to what she had done to her."

The aid looked at her and the man laying by her. He then turned to Ledric. "I still don't see why I should help, sire."

Ledric finally had enough and grabbed the aid by the arm with force and spoke in a harsh tone. "I am the king. She has been mistreated by someone who should and will be dead, if I ever get my hands on him. Now, do as I tell you. Get her those clothes and whatever else you can find for her. Do not question anything else I have to say, do you understand?"

The aid was fearful of the king and gave a gulp which showed he was afraid. "Sorry, sire. I had no idea she was important to you."

Ledric let go of his arm and looked at the aid. "She's very important to me. Because of her, I am learning that this town is in deeper trouble that I thought and I need to fix it. The elves of this town were enslaved by that desert snake and I need to help them. Now can you get her some clothes, please?"

The aid gave a nod, looked at the girl then walked out of the room.

Ledric grabbed a blanket and laid on the couch. He thought to himself as he closed his eyes. *Why do people have to be forced to do things around here before they will actually do them?*

Soon, he was drifting off to sleep and dreaming of his own family.

Treidon slowly rose and looked at the woman before him. She was certainly attractive and had the strength to pull a bow if it came to it, but there was a lot of damage. She was damaged

and physically. He walked over to Ledric and gently
him on the arm.

lric stretched to see him there. Treidon smiled and spoke,
"Did you get everything ready?"

Sitting up, he noticed two full outfits ready for the girl and
then over at Treidon. "Those are for her. I believe the carriage is
ready. I was informed that Erissa will be coming with you."

Treidon shrugged but he heard Meranda speaking behind
them. She seem to have a knack for waking up silently. "That's
good, always having her with me makes me feel a bit safer. Not
saying that you wouldn't make sure I was safe, but I hardly know
you."

Treidon gently handed her a set of clothes and smiled. "I
think, in time, you'll see that there are things that are meant to be
and people that are meant to be."

She stood up and glanced at him for a moment, taking the
clothes from his hands. "Excuse me while I get ready."

He watched her in amazement, heard a clearing of a throat
and turned toward Ledric. "Sorry, she's beautiful, but those scars
are all over, in the same places I have mine. She is going to have a
long mental road ahead of her and most of the Riftrider training is
mental."

Ledric nodded and watched Treidon for a moment. He was
certainly enamored with Meranda and for good reason. "The
carriage is ready to go and they will take you through the quickest
way. Quarden then to Tanisworth and then to Elmwick."

Meranda walked out in a dark blue long sleeved shirt with
black pants. The shirt had slight gold trim to it and fit her
perfectly. She was shaking her head and spoke her concern. "We
can't go through that way. That is where Gavid has gone. I want to
remain a secret and get out of here as quickly as possible."

Treidon picked up the other clothes and agreed with her.
"We'll have a talk with the others, come on, daylight is waiting."

She nodded and thanked King Ledric. The pair went down stairs to meet with Erissa. A snow elven man with light peach skin and long dark hair was standing with her.

"Are you ready to go, my dear?" Erissa questioned.

Meranda nodded and gave Erissa a concern. "We can't go through Quarden, we will have to find another way."

Erissa smiled and looked at the woman. "Perfect opportunity to see the rest of your family. Come on, let's go. I'll explain in the carriage."

They all climbed into the carriage and were off. Elves in the town did not concern themselves with who was in the carriage as Meranda used her new cloak to wrap herself up and hide from the eye of everyone.

Treidon looked at Erissa and was not happy when he heard Meranda had three brothers in the town not far from them. It also did not sit well that her father was still alive. Erissa mentioned something about her mother, but she really wasn't her mother. Meranda continued to hide her emotions as she was experiencing something Treidon was, anger. It did not suit her well. Treidon noticed the uncomfortableness of Meranda and sighed, trying to let the anger go for her. He wasn't sure yet that they were bonded, but something seemed to be telling him they were. The carriage continued down the trail toward her brothers' city in the darkness.

Linden and his brothers sat as they continued to reflect on their own time with their sister. Something was not right with their wives, but they didn't know what. Everything seemed out of place. They didn't know who was who any more. The woman they allowed to be tormented was actually their sister, not a slave. This fact didn't settle well either, there were laws that kept people from owning people in the snow region, but it didn't stop Gavid from owning their sister. No one seemed bothered by this fact, until now.

Jayidus spoke up finally. "I can't believe that we allowed this to happen. We shouldn't have allowed him to own her, but we did."

"We didn't know she was family," Davignon said.

Jayidus shook his head in disagreement. "That shouldn't matter, no snow elf should be owned."

They suddenly heard hooves in the distance. With the rumors being different, the brothers all feared Gavid returned to kill them. They had to defend their sister and take care of him.

They quickly ran into the street to stop the horses from continuing or stopping them. The carriage came to a stop, it was non-descript and the driver shouted at them to move, they were on important business.

The brothers quickly ran to the carriage and gasped as they saw Erissa. Linden opened the door of the carriage and took her hand. "I'm sorry, we thought it was Gavid coming to kill us."

Erissa took his hand and climbed out of the carriage along with the other three. Erissa frowned and shook her head. "Gavid is still out of town. Why would he come and kill you? There are others that are around you more than capable of doing so."

This fell on deaf ears as they didn't understand. They recognized Ivadian, but not the other two. The woman seem to keep the cloak over her face, but her soft gray skin showed she was snow elven.

She stayed close to a forest elf. Erissa grabbed their attention. "We are on our way to Elmwick. Treidon, here." She gestured toward the forest elf. "And your sister are on their way to get her some help."

They turned to the girl and walked carefully up to her. As they approached her, she pulled her cloak away from her face and looked at them.

All three stopped in their tracks and stared at her. Jaydius quickly picked her up. "You look like our mother. How could we have not recognized that?"

She pushed him off, tears flowed down her face in confusion and anger. "Does it matter? I'm your sister. I am a snow elf. I should not have been in anyone's control."

Turning to Treidon, she held out her hand. "Do you still have the pin?"

He reached into his bag and pulled out the long iron metal pin with threads and a claw at the end of it.

The three men winced at the sight as she shoved it into their faces and spoke to each of them. "This is what he had in my back. This is only one of the torments I went through."

She lifted her shirt sleeve and the scars were evident. "He cut me, he scrapped my skin from my body. Where were you when I was screaming for help?!"

By now she was yelling, anger fueled the facts of who she was, it should not have mattered. She winced as her shoulder burned. She turned around and noticed the three women looking in her direction.

Quickly, she threw the cloak hood over her face and walked back into the carriage and cried. Treidon got in with her and touched her shoulder, she winced and shrugged him off.

He looked hurt and she looked at him apologetically. "I'm sorry. I shouldn't get angry at them, they should have known better though."

Treidon sat in silence, he knew something was different about her. Erissa finally climbed into the carriage. "Is everything okay, dear?"

"No," she said in an ugly tone. "Those women, there is something not right about them. Every time they came to see Gavid, my shoulder burned. Just like the woman I saw lying next to my father. Something is not right here, but I wouldn't know why my shoulder is burning."

Erissa looked at her with a curious glance and then at the women. "I have seen them with Gavid, haven't I?"

She nodded and Erissa asked Treidon to move, he did and then she sat beside her to look at her shoulder. Meranda allowed the touch and Erissa sat in amazement, but didn't say anything about the birthmark glowing a vibrant blue.

Quickly she put her shirt down as the brothers knocked on the carriage door. "Sister, we're really sorry. We should have done something more."

She took a deep breath. Meranda had to forgive them to figure out why those women were so important to her. She slowly uncovered her face and whipped her tears, she looked over at Treidon who was quickly doing the same before she saw him. Curious, she smiled and let it go.

She then stared at her brothers. "I must forgive to move on. Things like this should bother me, but the way you treated me will not be forgotten."

Jayidus took her hand then hugged her tightly. "I'm Jayidus, this is Davignon and Linden."

The others hugged her tightly. They should have taken care of Gavid and freed her. Linden whispered in her ear, "Your brothers will protect you from now on and make this right."

They walked her into town and announced to everyone they had a sister. The town smiled as they realized how much she looked like her mother, telling her as much.

Treidon held her hand and gave her the confidence she needed to continue deeper into town. Although the occasional wincing made him wonder what was hurting her.

They decided tonight was a celebration of freedom. Gavid was gone and they could claim the town in the morning. People liked the sound of this idea. The sisters seemed to be put off about it, but kept by their husband's side.

CHAPTER 5

Ugex was fuming when he learned Gavid had killed the woman they were sworn to protect. He stood up, walked to the door, and slammed it shut. He locked it and walked to the mirror.

Quickly, he changed his appearance, he was no longer the green orc that Gavid knew, but an elven man with soft gray skin, long white hair, and lavender eyes. He looked into the mirror, mumbled a word then touched it. The mirror swirled until the image of a soft white man with light green eyes and white hair appeared before him. "What is it, son?"

"She's dead," he flatly said. "The woman you asked us to watch over is dead. How could you allow this to happen?"

The man behind the mirror looked at him, confused. "She is alive according to Erissa, son. She has left town and is on her way to Elmwick with Morida's son, Treidon. She's very well protected now."

Ugex's body relaxed, the tone in his voice was softer too. "How do you want us to proceed here then? Gavid wants us to save the dirt and eventually attack the town. I want to stay here and do my best to slow them down. Also, I want to send Quesep and Derix to check on the town and come back and tell me how they are."

The man on the other side of the mirror nodded. "Go ahead with that plan, just keep me informed of what is going on down there. I would hate to see Herium fall to the hands of the goblins."

Ugex shook his head. "It won't happen while I'm on watch."

There was a knock on the door and a voice behind it. "Is everything okay in there, Ugex? We could hear you down the hall."

The elven man behind the mirror nodded and dismissed the image, Ugex changed his appearance again to the orc form, unlocked the door, and opened it. "Not really. I'm tired of Gavid telling me how I should run things down here."

Ugex sat down and nodded, he couldn't help but smile as Jael sat in the large furniture. He looked like a child in a grown up chair. His feet couldn't even touch the ground. He sat there helpless as he looked at Ugex smiling. "What are you grinning about? I am just as tired as you are about that desert elf. Who does he think he is to control us like that? I thought we agreed to take over the mines and he could have the town."

Ugex gave a slight nod and dropped his smile down to a smirk. "I'm sorry. You're right, he has no right to tell us what to do when he's not even in town."

Jael looked surprised. "What do you mean he is not even in town? Where is he?"

"Apparently, he fled to a desert town. If you had noticed, he was in an adobe room. I inquired him and he said he killed that woman that was outside at his home," Ugex said relaxing a bit, as if not bothered by anything.

Jael grumbled softly. "She did nothing to him. Why would he kill her?"

Ugex was actually surprised at the kindness he showed toward the woman and shrugged. "She was close to telling the king everything, possibly knew of what we were up too as well. He had to take care of her."

Jael's anger seem to boil more. "How can you sit there casually and pretend you didn't know she was just an innocent child? So what, she told the king, perhaps he would have been taken care of and she would not have been included in this."

Ugex leaned forward and stared at him coldly. "And what if she would have told the king we were here? We would have been flushed out without a second thought. My good goblin, you have grown soft for the woman. I surely thought you would want the taste of elf blood on you as much as I do."

Jael scooted out of his chair and stood up then jump on Ugex's desk. He then leaned forward and stared into his eyes, anger filled them. "I love the elves who can give me a fighting chance. What Gavid did to her is wrong on so many levels. She had been growing strong because we were helping her. I wanted her to flee from him. I wanted her to share all the information with the king. I want to bring the fight here. We are ready for him."

Ugex nodded in satisfaction. "I was just testing you. It makes my blood boil too about how he treated her. We helped her as well, I was glad to hear she fled. Sad thing that he had to kill her."

This was all a lie to Jael, but he knew no better and relaxed. "So we plan to attack the town despite Gavid telling us to wait?"

Ugex nodded and smiled. "I like the sound of that, but you don't know how much the woman was able to tell the king before she passed away. They could be here soon."

Jael shrugged as he walked out. "That doesn't matter, we're ready when they do come. Aren't you?"

Ugex grunted as Jael shut the door. He then stood up and locked it again behind him. He slumped in the chair and relaxed. How to slow the progress down to keep the goblins from attacking the town was something entirely different than working with him in the cave. He needed to contact his father later and his brothers to see how the town was doing.

He sat up and began to work on a plan to destroy the plans of Jael, yet keep him from figuring it out.

Soon, he stood up and walked out of the room to find his brothers. He was frustrated with the way goblins and orcs, which were secretly elves, worked together. He wondered how many times someone wanted to kill a goblin when they had the chance.

"Help me! Can anyone hear me? Please, help!" a distant voice screamed in Meranda's mind.

The party was now in full swing; there was laughter, roasted venison over a fire pit, music, and happiness.

Meranda looked around then over at Treidon. "Did you hear something? Someone's calling for help."

By now, she learned to ignore the burning pain in her shoulder, but it was still there.

He shook his head. "What are you hearing?"

"Someone calling for help."

She noticed the wives' faces were blank and she concentrated on Terian. "Please, help me. I know someone can hear me."

Another voice replied to her. "Shut up, you fool! Once we kill your husband, you are dead as well. Can't believe he was unable to kill that girl as well. We will have to report to Gavid about this."

Meranda quickly pulled out and her lavender eyes sparkled with shock. Treidon looked at her and touched her hand in concern. "Everything okay?"

"No, my brothers' wives are entrapped by Gavid. How could I not see it?" she questioned and thought back on her own time with their wives.

He nodded and ran a nail over her hand and was amazed that he actually felt the sensation on his hand. "Anything we can do about it?"

"Anything we can do about what?" a voice said beside them. Erissa looked concerned and then up to the women. "What's wrong with them? They don't seem to be enjoying anything."

Meranda turned her attention to them and sighed sadly. "It seems that Gavid has deceived them and they have something inside them. I heard someone say they were going to kill my brothers and their wives."

Erissa mumbled something and then nodded in agreement with Meranda. "They have temptresses in them. I hardly see them so I didn't suspect anything."

"What are we going to do?" Meranda said with concern. "They really don't deserve this to happen to them. They need to be free and not trying to kill my brothers or alert Gavid."

She got Ivadian's attention. "We need your help."

He touched her arm lightly and smiled. "Whatever you need, my dear love."

She smiled. "We need to get the wives alone. I also need to get to Gervis and wake him up. Meranda, your mother isn't your mother. She needs to be taken care of as well."

Meranda shook her head. "That would explain the words she used toward me. Worthless, stupid, non-existent, and my favorite, slave. She tried to put me down constantly."

Treidon sighed and rubbed her forehead. "So, you are telling me, her father is alive? Why didn't he inform us that there was trouble?"

Erissa gave a long frustrated sigh and looked at him. "Because we were stupid to believe stupid things. We can discuss that at a later time. Right now, those women are ready to kill everyone and probably tonight."

Meranda sent a thought to the women and she grabbed Treidon's hand. They all quickly left, darting into the forest. Once there, she touched the ground and mumbled a word. Treidon watched as the ground glowed and sent out veins of blue.

She grabbed his hand and followed Erissa and Ivadian to the cave. Erissa and Meranda walked in while Treidon and Ivadian watched. As she walked in, she winced. Erissa looked at her with concern. "Burning again?" Meranda nodded and looked as a large bear stood over Gervis, watching over him. The woman beside him seemed to have not been as well taken care off.

The bear walked up to Meranda and began to sniff her and then lick her. She laughed and pushed him off. "Easy there, Marix. We need to get Gervis."

She leaned in and kissed his forehead and woke him up. The first wolf howled and she froze. "They will be here soon." Erissa nodded. "I'll take care of this thing here," she said as she poked the woman before them.

Gervis looked at her. "Why are you doing that to my wife?"

Erissa and Meranda stood before him. Erissa shrugged and gave an ugly remark. "If she was your wife, she would have treated her daughter better."

43

There was another howl. Erissa spoke. "We don't have time. The brothers' wives will be here soon. We have to take care of them. They were entrapped with temptresses."

Gervis sighed and walked out with Meranda. Treidon looked at her. "There were wolf howls."

"I know, they are letting me know where the wives are. They will be here soon. What's the plan?"

Treidon looked around. "Where is Erissa?"

"Taking care of something, she will be here to help soon. So what is the plan?" she questioned while looking into the forest.

Ivadian folded his arms and tightened his muscles. "I say we just beat it out of them."

Gervis took a deep breath and replied as he heard screams from the cave. "I think we could tie them up and take care of them that way. Erissa is the only one who can manage demons."

Meranda bit her lip and the pain shot through her shoulder and knelt down. "They're here."

Treidon looked up and noticed the women coming out of the forest into the clearing. He grabbed some rope from his pack and tossed some to Ivadian. They wrapped the three of them to the tree while Meranda knelt paralyzed in pain.

The women wiggled and screamed at them. They cursed as soon the demons floated out of their bodies and screamed. Each temptress had purple skin, long black hair, and black eyes; tattoos riddled their bodies. They stood looking at the four of them. Before they attacked, however, they found themselves bound together and unable to move.

"Get a jar!" Erissa screamed behind them. Treidon scrambled through his pack and quickly found a jar and threw it out under the demons. Luckily it landed with the opening up and Erissa placed them inside, closing it quickly. She touched the glass and they danced, trying to escape the fire. Finally, she opened a chasm and dropped the jar in, the glass found the molten lava at the core of the realm.

Gervis looked at Erissa. "So what did you do with my wife?"

Erissa looked at the three wives who were limp and nearly lifeless. She quickly untied them and healed their bodies and souls until they were breathing normally again. She looked at Gervis. "That woman was not your wife. I don't know where you wife is, but that thing was not her."

Meranda stood up as the pain subsided and then looked at Treidon with a smile. "We need to get back to my family. I am sure they would be more than happy to see my father and their wives back to their loving selves."

Treidon nodded and gently took her hand, they walked back to the party to celebrate more.

CHAPTER 6

Laughter and happiness could be heard down in the tavern below. As the sun set on the town, Gavid watched people laughing and having fun. He decided it was time to go down for dinner and enjoy himself as well.

The tavern in the inn was bustling with people. The clerk at the desk noticed Gavid and gently took his hand. "Come, sit and enjoy the meal tonight. Fresh duck brought in from the town of Herium. They sent it today. They are nice people."

He knew it was probably a lie, he hadn't authorized anyone to send anything to a town without money, but he smiled and graciously accepted the invite.

She placed him near the fire and the bards were playing happily. The music was soothing and inviting. Soon, his meal was brought to him and he thanked the server. He poked it a moment and then delved into it. There was an unmistakable gaminess to the meat, but he knew it wasn't duck. He continued to eat until it was gone and asked for a nice desert ale. The server brought him a glass and a bottle then another brought him some dessert. He dove into the dessert and the ale. The musicians played happily and lightened the mood in the tavern.

People were dancing on the nearby dance floor. There was happiness all the way around. Like he remembered as a kid. Soon the party was slowing down, but it seemed like the music wasn't going to end. The bards continued to play the happy music and a few sad songs. He drifted away in thought, thinking of the woman he was with in this plan. He had not heard from her since she and Meranda's father went missing. He closed his eyes and tried to contact her. When she doesn't respond to his many attempts, he finally decided she had perished for the greater good. He shrugged it off, it wasn't like he had really fallen in love with her. She was just a pawn in the plan. He continued to listen for a moment for any return contact, but then decided it was for the best. He continued to listen to the music for a brief time, then tipped the waiter and the bards. Slowly, he rose and went to bed for the night.

After a peaceful night's sleep, Gavid rose out of the bed and remembered he hadn't contacted the wives. He reached in his pack to get the spell components he needed and grumbled as he realized he was out of ingredients for the communication spell.

He walked down to the tavern and ordered breakfast. The waiter looked at him and smiled, then left to get his food. Gavid looked around, it seemed that people were a bit more sluggish today than they were the night before. He smiled as most were probably hung over and then his waiter arrived. He handed some tip money to the man and proceeded to eat his meal in peace. After he was finished, he stood up and walked over to the clerk, grinning. "Where is the best place I can get a cheap price on spell components?"

She pointed out the Nightshade Emporium was a nice, reasonable place. He smiled, thanked her, and left the inn, quickly finding his way to the shop. He walked in and the bell rung. A small elven man walked up to the counter. "Can I help you?"

The man was smaller than a normal desert elf, but looked normal; long black hair, light brown eyes, and dark skin. Gavid gave a simple nod. "I need these things," he said as he handed him the list he needed.

The man looked over the list and then returned the gesture. He looked him over for a moment. "Anything you need right away?"

Gavid paused then said, "I need the components for a communication spell. I have to contact my employer."

The man gave Gavid what he needed then left him to fill the rest of the order.

He walked away and sat in a quiet area amongst all of the strange oddities the continent had to offer. As he sat down, he pulled a mirror from his pack and conjured up the spell. A plains elven man with green eyes, long blond hair, and dark skin sat down in a nice soft chair and looked at him. "Gavid, how are things on your end?"

Gavid smiled and gave him a nod. "My lord Siebrien, everything is going smoothly. The woman I had outside is dead, soon the brothers will be."

Siebrien smiled and leaned forward. "Excellent. Now only if those elves in the surrounding areas of Elmwick could show some improvements, we would have this finished. However, they don't seem to be ready in the least. They will at least take a year."

"A year!" Gavid exclaimed. "That is far too long."

The plains elven man nodded. "I understand, but I cannot control them."

Gavid sighed in frustration and rubbed his forehead. "Fine, but keep me informed of what is going on."

Siebrien heard a knock on the door and turned to Gavid. "I have to go, just remember you have the resources, so perhaps we could choke out Elmwick."

Gavid simply nodded and waved his hand. A year was far too long. He put the mirror in the pack then stood up and looked around for a moment. He began to think and realized he could do a better job and control the entire plan. That's what he would do, go to Rishmede and kill Siebrien.

The clerk handed him a box of components and spoke, "I need two thousand gold."

"Two thousand! That is far too much for what I asked for."

The man shook his head and shrugged. "I'm the only one that has a few of the things you asked for. It's hard to get them in stock these days. I am actually cutting you a deal."

Gavid grumbled and paid the man. He took the box and walked out of the room. After that, he went to a cartographer to find the quickest way to Weisbech. Soon, he was back to the inn for a fresh meal then off to bed for the evening.

The evening was in full swing for the brothers and the rest of the town. The air smelled like roasted venison as the snow elves celebrated. They were clueless as to what actually happened in the darkness of the forest, until Gervis and the others walked through the trees.

The brothers; Davignon, Jaydius, and Linden glanced up from what they were doing and quickly ran to their father. "Where's mother?" Linden questioned.

Gervis shifted the weight of Linden's wife in his arms and looked at Erissa. "Apparently, she was a monster."

Erissa shook her head as the three brothers took their wives from Treidon, Ivadian, and Gervis then spoke, "That woman was no monster. A monster would have been nicer to Meranda. She was a demon."

Gervis looked at his son in relief and then toward Erissa. "You are saying the woman that was beside me was a demon?"

The brothers started to leave and Meranda spoke up. "You want to make sure that the mirrors are covers. I know Gavid has been talking to them in that way."

The brothers gave a quick nod and left to put their wives to bed. The rest of the town had gone back to celebrating the fact that Gavid was gone and Gervis was still alive.

Gervis walked into town and several people pushed everyone to a table for a meal. Soon the plates were filled and Meranda was not use to this, she began to shrink away from them. Treidon gently grabbed her arm, he looked at her. "Might as well get used to it."

The people left, feeling how uncomfortable she was. Then Meranda began to eat. Treidon finished his meal and looked over at her. "Slow down, you act like you haven't eaten in a while."

She covered her mouth and watched him for a second. "I might have eaten, but nothing warm."

He sighed and gave her a slight smile. "You'll be eating warm from now on, so slow down."

The brothers arrived back at the celebration and sat with Gervis, looking around at the rest of the group. Linden glanced at

Erissa. "So, what had my wife? She is peacefully sleeping, she hasn't been for a while."

Erissa turned to Meranda who was trying to keep to herself. "Talk to *her*, she was the one that heard the cry for help."

"I knew when I heard the call for help that I should have known something was wrong," Meranda said, not lifting her head to regard them. She then continued, "Gavid always had them checking in to see what you were doing. He always knew how things were."

Davignon stared at his sister. "So you knew this. Why didn't you inform us when you were around us?"

Erissa nearly spoke up when Meranda gave a cold reply as she stared him in the eyes. "Because you were too busy trying to push me off of you. Every time I came to you while you in were in town, you pushed me away. You told me that I would never be as good as you."

He felt a touch on her arm and glanced down to see her father's hand. "It's in the past. We have to let it stay there, dear daughter. We can't let it get in our heads, that's how Gavid and others win. They allow things to eat away and make us lose focus."

Davignon was intimidated by his sister. He was showing that he was scared as she sat down and grumbled. "Father, they allowed evil things to happen and then accused me of not talking to them about what was going on?"

She felt Treidon gently touching her arm and the sensation was cooling, peaceful, calming. "I just want to be away from him. If they capture Gavid, they better make sure they break his fingers."

"Why would someone do that?" Jayidus questioned.

A voice from the forest spoke loudly, "Because he's a mage and to do that would take all of his abilities away."

They turned and all stood up as Ledric walked into the area. The town stopped once again and bowed. He raised his hand to let them know he acknowledged them and to go about their business.

As the town did so, he sat down and was presented with a plate of food. Linden looked at Ledric and then nodded. "So he would suffer more if we just simply break his fingers?"

Ledric nodded in response and then covered his mouth. "He would just be a normal person without any ability. It would be the worst case for him. Oh, Meranda." He looked down at a bag and handed it to her. "Gavid thought he had destroyed the entire keep, but there was a room I guess he magically protected. A lot of artwork was saved, as well as a few weapons and armor."

He picked it up and gently handed her a bag. "It has a lot of things I thought you might use."

She stared and smiled. Meranda then dug through the bag and gently pulled out the black bow with emerald encrusted gems on the sides. She placed it on the table then pulled out two swords.

Gervis looked at her. "Do you remember what to do with them?"

She grinned and gave a nod. "I do, Father. Can't wait to cast magic through them. Oh, King Ledric..." Meranda seemed to have a realization, despite the happiness, her mood changed. "There are goblins in the cave south of here, but," she spoke and then leaned in and whispered knowing the sensitivity of the people around. "There are Aqudens watching us too. They helped me grow stronger and helped free me every time."

Gervis stared in amazement. "What did they look like?"

She gave a long yawn and then replied, "One looked just like you. I was confused at first, but he said it really didn't matter."

Letting out a long groan, Gervis rubbed his forehead as he watched Meranda yawn again. "Where are they, so we can stop them?"

"They are in the cave between the snow and desert, you won't be able to miss it once you arrive," she said with a long yawn.

Gervis grumbled and focused his thoughts on her. "It's time for bed for you."

She nodded and then slowly rose. "I agree, it is bed time, so everyone have a good night."

Treidon stood up with her and together they went to their room for the evening.

CHAPTER 7

Treidon stared at the woman that laid in another bed next to his. He watched her sleep peacefully. Meranda had been in his life only a day, but for some reason he seemed more attached to her than any other woman. His sisters, his mother, and grandmothers, all did not feel as important as she did.

Could they really be bonded mates? How could that be possible when he never met her? He was finally starting to believe he had not yet met his bonded mate, until he saw her scars. They were in every place on her as they were on him. Every wound she endured, he felt like he did as well. Curiosity got the best of him and he needed to check out something that would confirm she was his bonded mate. He gently lifted her blanket and looked down at the bottom of her foot. He gasped as he saw the scar on the arch of

Meranda's foot. He remembered stepping on a metal shard that went through the entire foot. He winced, wondering how this pain felt to her. Treidon covered her back up carefully and stared at her. There were many other visible scars that were on his and her body. Gently, he sat on the side of the bed and looked at her. She was facing away from him and he knew there were other scars on her neck that he received while training.

Suddenly, she began to fight in her sleep. He stood up in shock and watched as her arms flew around, trying to hit something invisible. Soon, he winced and looked down to see his arm bleeding. Meranda was running her nails down her arms, cutting herself. She was bleeding as well. She rolled over, grabbed her leg, and began to deeply scratch herself again. Treidon groaned painfully and grabbed her arms to stop her from doing more damage.

He mentally called for help from Gervis and anyone else who could hear him as held her down. She fought and kicked him, all the while, fighting whatever was going on in her mind. Gervis ran in with Erissa and Ivadian behind him. They all noticed he was bleeding. He turned to Erissa. "Heal me, she will heal."

Meranda got lucky and kicked him between the legs before Erissa got to him. He grunted but would not let go.

Erissa touched his bare arm and began to chant as her hand glowed a soft pale green. Soon, the wounds on Treidon healed as did Meranda's. Erissa then chanted a different type of spell, but did not lose her touch on Treidon. Her hand changed colors to a pale purple and went through Treidon's arm to Meranda. Meranda opened her eyes and let out a loud scream that made the dogs bark outside, waking up some of the town.

Treidon gently let her go and she plunged her face into his chest and cried. "Why do those things want me dead?"

He wrapped his arms lovingly around her as Gervis, Erissa, and Ivadian looked on.

"What things?" Erissa asked out of curiosity, but in her mind she already knew the answer.

Meranda let go of Treidon and he sat beside her in a protective manner. She glanced up at Erissa and then back down. "Demons, one called herself Irisa saying I will not live until I have reached my potential."

Gervis stared for a moment and shook his head. "Irisa was what my wife said she changed her name to."

Erissa nodded and looked at Meranda who was still holding back tears. Treidon held her tight as Erissa regarded Gervis. "She was a demon. After Anmylica left, this woman came and claimed to be her. She was just a demon and I was more than thankful to put her to sleep at the request. Knowing I could kill her at any moment."

Gervis sighed and looked at Meranda. "I should have known something wasn't right when she asked me to leave you with Gavid. That was a mistake and I am sorry, my dear daughter."

Suddenly, the door opened in a rather loud fashion and everyone turned to see Meranda's brothers and King Ledric standing there.

"What happened? Is everything okay?" Linden spoke concerned. "We heard the screams and the dogs barking."

The three of them stood and watched Meranda who had apparently been crying, curled up in fear with Treidon. Jayidus gave an angry glance. "Did he hurt you?"

Erissa stood up. "No, he didn't. She was attacked by demons in her sleep. We are going to have an around the clock eye on her until we reach Elmwick. My dear, you are destined for greatness, we just have to make sure you stay safe."

Treidon nodded and regarded the family. "I will be here with her. We are bonded mates. I didn't believe it at first myself, as I don't remember giving the kiss that would put us together. However, she and I are bonded. I have scars on my own body inflicted during training then I have others that were unknown until tonight."

Davignon gave a glance to his father. "Is this true?"

Ledric spoke up. "I remember a young forest elven boy and his family coming to town for the Serime Festival during the spring while Gervis' wife was pregnant, but that was many years ago. Treidon's father is Pagues, his mother is Morida. He has three sisters. They were in town during that time before his sisters were alive. It is possible that young elf was Treidon."

Treidon looked down at Meranda who was now sound asleep in his arms. Her breathing was normal and she appeared to be peaceful. He glanced up and nodded. "I remember that time in town very well. I remember meeting your mother, and..." He stopped himself and remembered.

Then Gervis nodded. "You kissed Anmylica's stomach. I remember that too."

Ledric smiled as he glanced over at Meranda. "Look, she's sleeping. They need to get going to Elmwick, I am sure they can discuss that later. We should probably leave her alone now."

They all agreed and left the room. Treidon held Meranda tight. He remembered that day very well. Kissing her mother's stomach, saying he would marry her someday. Most just brushed it off as a kid being cute. However, here they were together and he swore to protect her.

The next morning, everyone got ready and made it to the carriage before the town woke. She closed her eyes and touched the road to the next town then looked at them. "Let's go."

They gathered into the carriage and were soon on the road to Derlwood, the plains elf town.

The night was a restless one for Gavid. Every time he turned, the bed creaked so loudly he thought the entire town could hear it. He finally laid on his back and grumbled. Soon the sun broke through the horizon and through his window. The town began to smell of fresh smoke as other taverns and inns opened up for breakfast. Sitting up, he knew he had a long road to travel before he got to Weisbech. He climbed out of bed, freshened up in the bathroom, changed clothes to something more loose fitting, and then walked out the door with his stuff.

After checking out, he looked at his map and found the road that led out of town and toward Weisbech. He didn't travel by carriage because the price was too steep, however, this trip wouldn't be safe either. He looked in his pack, pulled out his long walking stick and began his travels. The desert mornings were always the coldest, so making the trip in four hours on foot could be possible. He walked without any incident for two hours. The sun was still rising and he knew the town would be within sight soon. The temperature was cool, but he could tell it was starting to rise slowly, indicating the desert heat.

Knowing he needed to pick up the pace, Gavid pulled out a few spell components and mumbled a word then touched his feet. This helped him to walk faster than the carriage might be able to take him. In casting the spell, it took an hour off of his time. He was almost into town when the spell ran out and he heard a low growling behind him.

Slowly, he turned to see a desert panther ready to attack him. She looked hungry and ready to kill. He grabbed more components and swiftly mumbled out the spell, when she leapt in the air to attack him, he touched her fur and sent the spell through her. She fell dead on the ground instantly and he continued to walk on, leaving her to the other hungry animals to clean up off the ground.

He walked casually into the town of Weisbech. It was a fairly small town that laid deep in a valley, a river fed into the town by a waterfall then carried further along to the ocean. Trade here was mostly crafted goods from metals and gems. However, this town was also a good farming town. Small gardens here and there helped the town thrive.

Slowly, he walked to his favorite place. When he saw the sign, he knew where he was. The Burley Branch sign hung high on the roof. As he walked in, the bell chimed, indicating the door opened.

A spice skin colored elven woman with lime green eyes looked up at him with a soft smile. "Well, welcome back, Gavid. What brings you here?"

He gave her a cheerful grin. "I want more of your wonderful packing. I hope you have grown enough since I was last here, Serina?"

Serina gave a charming smile and nodded. "We have, thanks to that dirt you sent us. Come see."

They walk out together to see a full growing house of the packing he so richly loved. He grinned and took a glance around. "Well, I see you are doing well for yourself. Will you be open tomorrow? I just arrived and need to get settled in. Also, you are about to close."

She gave a nod and looked at him. "We will be open as soon as you arrive. I have a few things for you. You will not be disappointed."

He gave her a nod and a firm handshake. "I will see you tomorrow."

Serina returned the handshake and waved good bye to him.

He walked out of the building and to an inn. The Viridian Goblet seemed to be a wonderful place that was off the beaten path. He walked in and a woman with beautiful onyx hair and golden brown eyes smiled at him.

"Can I have a room for the night? I am traveling to Rishmede and I need to stay here until the morning," he said quietly.

She gave a slight nod. "The payment will be ten gold."

He slide her the gold plus a little more and looked at her. "What is for dinner? The road was long and I am hungry."

She gave a sweet grin and nodded. "For dinner tonight you have several options, roasted mutton and soft cheese, stewed mutton and stewed vegetables, or pickled boar with mashed potatoes."

The sound of the menu made Gavid's mouth water. "Sounds delightful, put me down for the pickled boar and mashed potatoes for the evening, please."

The woman laughed, which was beautiful, then gave him a nod. "That'll be up to you when the time comes. Dinner is in an hour. Should give you some time to check in and clean up."

He did notice he was a bit dirty after his travels and excused himself to go tidy up before dinner.

The room was quaint and small, but it had a table, a sofa, a bed, and a nice balcony with a beautiful view. He put his stuff down and walked out of the window onto the terrace, admiring the sunset. The town was a peaceful one and it didn't seem to be one of those included in the plan. People were happy and carefree.

He took it in for a moment. Gavid noticed a few things that seemed out of place, like the way the town was laid out, but it wasn't his business. It was nearly time for dinner so he got up and went downstairs for the evening meal.

CHAPTER 8

A dark carriage drove past the townspeople as they woke. It didn't occur to them of what happened the night before. Linden, Davignon, Ledric, and Jayidus all stood in the center of town as Terian, Jilian, and Saraj walked to their husbands.

Saraj touched Linden on the arm, he turned and smiled. She smiled back and glanced around the town. "Where is your family?"

Linden looked in the direction that his family had gone and then back to her. "They are on their way to Derlwood," he whispered softly. "There have been some things I will never forgive myself for."

He hugged her tightly and she returned it. Terian looked at Jayidus, "Still would have liked to have thank her. She saved us.

We could not have done anything without her. We would all be dead."

The other wives agreed with the statement and soon they were surrounded with people from the town. One lady spoke to the king, "Sire, is it true Gavid is gone?"

Linden gave a nod and then spoke to the rest of the town. "Gavid has fled, because he murdered our sister and then fled like a cowardly dog."

"Your sister?" someone questioned in the crowed.

The three sons of Gervis knew that wouldn't be the last time they were asked.

Taking a deep breath, Ledric spoke. "The woman that was entrapped by Gavid was Lord Gervis' daughter. However, we can't reflect on that, we need rangers to meet us in the forest west of here."

The seven of them walked to Herium. It didn't take long for the people of the town to come from their homes. Linden, Davignon, and Jayidus shook their heads. The town they once loved so much was deplorable. There was an apparent poor side and one that was more extravagant.

Several snow elves came out and ran up to Ledric. "Your Majesty, is it true that Gavid is gone?"

He gave a nod and grinned. "My dear townsfolk, he has fled like the coward he was. We are here to find rangers then to prepare to protect this town. There are goblins and orcs to the south of us and it looks like this town isn't even ready for survival, much less attacks."

Several women cried in fear and ran off to tell their husbands, other people suggested going to the ranger guild on the west side of town. Soon, there was a masculine voice behind him. "We'd be willing to help you, sire, but who will be here to protect the town?"

Linden turned to see three men in camouflaged clothing with bows strapped to their backs. "Well, kind sir, we plan on building the defenses and I hope that together we can work to defeat those that are coming."

"Pay is also not a problem. We need to find that cave soon before it gets too far into the darkness," Ledric said. "How many rangers are there?"

The man turned to the other two and they walked off. He then spun back around and responded, "The name is Seirian, sire, and there are at least thirty of us. We can leave at least ten here and the others can go out to the cave with you."

"We need to get going. Can you come with us?" Davignon spoke.

Seirian gave a nod. "We can wait on the others, they will be here soon."

Once that left the man's mouth the others arrived. Seirian spoke for a moment to the ten that would stay and then the rest. Linden, Ledric, Davignon, and Jayidus left to investigate the cave. It took a better part of the day, but they finally arrived at the location Meranda spoke of. It didn't look like much and they wondered if Meranda had given them the wrong location. As they started to turn, Linden noticed something running out. A goblin had run out of the cave with a bucket in his hand. He ran to a pile of dirt, dumped it out, and then ran back in.

Ledric turned to the rangers. "We need some sort of system to get the word out before they arrive."

The rangers stepped aside with Ledric and discussed a plan while the three brothers sat and watched the cave in amazement.

Jaydius, who had been quiet most of this day spoke up, "There is no telling how deep this thing goes or how many are in there. We are going to need an army to protect our town."

Davignon agreed in silence as he wondered what they could possibly do to protect the town when Ledric arrived back. "The rangers have plotted out a path that the monsters in that cave are likely to take all the way to town. They will rest in the trees and rotate out and wait them out to see if they attack. We need to get back into town and get started."

They all agreed and returned to town. Herium had been setting up a celebration of Gavid's flight and the return of Gervis' sons. Ledric sighed. "This is not going to be an easy announcement is it? They are clueless as to how big this thing is. From the size of that pile of dirt I saw, it looks like they have been there a while."

Linden agreed and slumped his shoulders. "Sire, let them have one day, because the next day will be a busy one."

The brothers walked to their wives as Ledric walked on. One of the aids came to him. "Sire, what do you need us to do? Isn't our duty done?"

Ledric shook his head without taking his eyes off of the town. "No, our duty isn't done here. Please, go to Yevidin and tell my wife I will not be home soon. Also, please tell Sir Celore that we are in need of many soldiers to come and help this town. This is a town ripe for the picking and we can't let them take it."

The aid gave a slight nod and then walked off to find the stables to get the carriage and horses, getting ready for the trip.

Ledric walked with the other aids and decided to help the town get prepared for the night's celebration.

Treidon sat with his arms crossed while Meranda was sleeping comfortably with her head on his lap. "How could you do this to her?"

Gervis knew that the anger was well placed, but spoke anyways, "We were all duped by the woman who pretended to be my wife. She told us all that it would be okay. Then suggested that we vanish. Erissa put us to sleep and I guess made a mistake when it was time to wake us. I hated every moment of the torment she went through. I tried my best to train her in my abilities of a Riftrider."

That answer did not please Treidon as he continued to stare hatefully at the other side of the carriage. "Erissa, you and Ivadian should have kept her safe."

Erissa sighed sadly and shook her head as she stared at Meranda. "I should have told Ivadian to keep her in his home until Gavid had done what he did, but she was so fearful after I brought her back to life, that she would run away toward him."

Ivadian was so sad he could barely keep his emotions in check. "I should have done more. Taken her from town, kept her hidden until they found out more. I wish Ledric would have followed the leads we sent to him. I personally told him of a few and he simply said he would check into it."

Treidon was not happy with the way snow elves handled their business, nor was he happy with the way the Riftriders and Dragons handled this. He started to speak up when Meranda's eyes flew open and she sat up. "Stop the carriage!"

They all looked at her and she held her head out the window and screamed again, "Stop the carriage!"

The carriage came to a stop and Gervis sat in confusion. "My dear, why are we stopping?"

She opened the door and grabbed her weapons then turned to her father. "Bandits up the road. They are on either side waiting."

Treidon started to protest, but Meranda had gone into the trees. He kept a protective eye on her, but soon he lost her.

They had gotten out of the carriage and wondered what was going on. The driver looked down. "What's going on?"

Soon, they heard two men screaming in panic as they were suddenly dangling from a tree not three feet away from them.

Gervis walked up to them while Treidon was still shocked at what he saw before him. The bandits started to squirm when they saw Gervis, believing him to be a ghost. "Please don't harm us, ghost! We don't wish to be sent away."

Giving a haunting smile, Gervis leaned in and spoke, "Only if you stop robbing those who are traveling. I realize that Gavid has Herium and the surrounding towns begging for him, however, he is not home."

Gervis dropped a bag of gold on the ground. "Now go." He waved his hand and the limbs dropped the bandits, they grabbed the gold and ran screaming about ghosts into the forest.

Walking back to the group, he smiled. "Well done, Meranda. It's a good thing you were watching ahead to keep an eye on the roads. I am glad I taught you that."

"You are welcome, Father. I am sure Treidon will get over the shock so we can get back on the road," she said standing behind him.

Jumping and spinning around, he was amazed to see Meranda before him. "How did you do all of that?"

She smiled and slipped back into the carriage along with Gervis and Treidon.

Treidon was still amazed and angry about what he saw. "How did you learn that? That's an Elder stage spell."

Gervis leaned back and stared at him. "Ever thought I could be an Elder too? If not Esteemed?"

Shaking his head, Treidon grumbled. "That's impossible. An Esteemed Elder would have known to inform us about what is going on. Besides, she couldn't know much while she was with Gavid."

Meranda let out a long, frustrating sigh and glanced at him then back at her father. "Father is an Esteemed Elder, but they were all tricked by that demon. He trained me while I was unconscious and recovering. Don't beat them up. They have had it hard enough knowing what was going on. I am just thankful the king finally came into town to investigate."

Treidon was still not happy with this and sighed heavily. "I'm sorry, Meranda. I really can't allow them to get away with not helping you to escape from such a terrible thing."

Meranda gently touched his leg. "My dear, we can't just focus on what has happened. We have to know that there are things that we can't change now. We have to see what the future holds and right now, it holds the pair of us."

He gently ran his fingers from her face to the back of her hair as he gazed into her eyes. "I know, my dear, but we could have been happier sooner."

She took a deep breath and leaned into his touch and laid closer to him. "I realize that, but there's no need to dwell."

He held her tight as they road quietly to Derlwood, checking in to a nice quaint inn for the night. They ate a meal and enjoyed the time together, then went to their rooms. Meranda did a little bit of training and practice, then she decided to freshen up before bed. Together they laid down and Treidon watched her. Soon she was sleeping, but Treidon was still fuming over the fact that she could have been training much sooner. He remembered something that caught his eye and knew he needed to talk to his father about it.

She had skills he hadn't seen in an untrained Riftrider. Could it be possible people could train subconsciously or was that something Gervis said to make him feel better? As she slept he thought about talking to his father.

CHAPTER 9

He heard the morning arriving as the birds started to sing. He knew the time as the mirror reflected what was going on outside. He sat up and grumbled, because he hadn't had a decent meal or a bath. Rising out of the bed, he rubbed his forehead and waved his hand to dismiss the image when he heard a knock on the door. He went to it, changed his appearance, and then unlocked it.

Once he opened it, Quesep and Derix walked through and he closed it behind them. He looked at the pair then spoke, "We need to figure out a way to sabotage the armor."

Derix grinned and replied, "We can always have the shadow elves steal ore, gems, and armor. That should slow things down a bit."

Ugex liked the idea and gave a nod. "They could also help us get out of here and continue to sabotage the mines. That would allow all of us to get to Herium and help those elves protect the town."

Quesep glanced around the room then spoke, "Heard anything from them?"

Ugex shook his head and sighed quietly. "Not in the longest time. I do hope they are okay. Last I heard, Hariton was telling me, they were on their way to Elmwick."

Derix spoke again, "We best change our appearance too, especially you, Ugex. We don't want the town to be confused. Do you need us to go out and scout ahead?"

Ugex nodded and looked at the pair. "Just be careful when you get out of the cave. I am sure the woman has told them about all of that which is going on now."

Derix and Quesep gave a quick nod.

"How will you get in touch with the shadow elves?" questioned Derix.

Ugex smiled and looked at his brother. "We will just simply talk to the darkness. I am sure they have been here for some time."

A pewter skinned elven man came out of the shadows and smiled. "We have been here a while. Hariton told us you might need us soon. What do you need?"

The man stood with pewter skin, long ink black hair, and eggplant colored eyes. Ugex looked at the elf and smiled. "Good to see you again, Weisgar. Can you help us?"

Weisgar gave a grin and nodded. "You know I can, my friend. What do you need us to do?"

Ugex thought for a moment. "I need you to take out all of the ores, gems, and armory, take them to the storage in Herium. Report to Ledric or Linden if they are in charge. I am sure by now the woman has told them about what is going on."

Weisgar stared and then smiled. "Meranda has told everything she knows, they have come outside of the cave and watched a goblin taking dirt outside. Linden and Ledric are both there as are Davignon and Jayidus. Meranda is still on her way to Elmwick and they stopped for the night in Derlwood. Now, do you need us to take care of all of the gems, ores, and other things, and put them in storage? What about the goblins? We can take care of them just give us the command."

Ugex shook his head. "Not yet, my friend? Just for now, take the things that they need, the ores, gems, and armory then put them in Herium's storage. We will discuss what to do later because I want to make sure Meranda has gotten to Elmwick safely and we can leave, go to Herium and help those people."

Derix spoke up. "Do you need us to go check on the rest of her family? And then come back to you?"

"Yes, be careful though. Leave now while it's early. Then get back here quickly."

Weisgar looked at the other two. "I can get you there outside of town to change your appearances, then get in and see everything, and get you back here if you want. I need to discuss these plans with the other shadow elves about the goblins, but for now, I can get you there."

That sounded like a good idea and the pair agreed. Weisgar gently took one of the arms of each brother and vanished.

Ugex turned to the mirror and frowned for a moment when there was a knock on the door. He opened it and Jael walked in. "Sick of being down here. When can we attack? Gavid hasn't reported to us in a while. I am anxious to get out."

All of his whining was getting annoying, but Ugex walked to his chair and sat. "Well, we can sit here and wait until all of the armor and weapons are done or we can just go out there unprepared. Have you thought of how you would attack the town?"

Jael sat in the large chair and grumbled. It was apparent he hadn't thought of that and looked at the orc.

Ugex sighed and shook his head. "We need to have the same plan of attack. We can't just go in and attack without some sort of organization."

He really didn't like that idea, but it made sense. Jael slowly climbed out of the chair and looked at him excitedly. "I'll get on it now."

Ugex gave a nod and Jael left the room. Ugex dropped his shoulders, stood up, and locked the door. He was ready to get out of here as well as the others in his group. He sat back down and stared at the mirror. It was a matter of days, if not moments, before he would get back to Herium and help kill the goblins that would attack the city. He liked that Jael was totally ignorant as to what was going on. Ugex slowly rose and walked out to check on the progress of the armor and ask if his tribe was ready to change plans.

Weisbech was a pleasant town, it was thriving with excitement and joy. It was one of those towns that was out of the way enough hardly anyone bothered them, but close enough to be an important part of trade.

He watched the town below enjoying their wealth and happiness. Gavid always loved this town and decided when he had had enough of Herium, he would abandon them and come here to kill the duke. Once that was done, he would simply take over. Right now, he had the town in demand of the cold soil from Herium, he had a monopoly on that.

He was wealthy, he leaned back and enjoyed his time here. There weren't people demanding anything of him or a woman crying at his feet. Gavid reflected on her for a moment. He really enjoyed raking those tools across her skin. Even killing her, he didn't understand how she always managed to heal or come back to life. She was loyal up until a few days ago.

He took a deep breath, he knew he hadn't talked to the wives of her bothers. He pulled a few things out of the nearby box and picked up his handheld mirror. Sprinkling the spell components on the mirror, Gavid mumbled, then the mirror swirled in a rainbow of colors. Soon, the colors faded and he found all three mirrors in darkness. They were black. Perhaps they were indecent or they were sleeping, but this was the normal time they should be talking. He dismissed the spell and looked back out of the balcony. The town was soon shutting down for the evening. This gave Gavid a good idea, it was time for bed himself.

Standing up, Gavid made his way to the bed and changed. Soon, he was lying comfortably in the bed and studying the spells he might possibly need for the next leg of the trip. The night time called him and he was soon fast asleep.

The night was eventless, soon the morning peeked through his window. He got up and went to the bathroom, freshening himself. Next, he went back to the packing shop. The Burley Branch didn't appear to be open, but as he approached it, Serina opened the door. "Welcome. Come on in. I have a few things for you."

They walked in together and she showed him many things, like several pipes. She pulled out one more. "I thought of you when I saw this one."

It was extravagant and was etched with ivory. He ran his fingers over it and nodded. "I'll take it and three pounds of your packing."

Serina grinned then started wrapping it up. "I hope you do plan on returning soon. Three pounds is a lot."

He gave a slight shrug and grinned. "Well, it was a while since the last time I came out here. I am going to be out a while once again."

She understood and handed him the pipe and the packing. "That'll be four hundred gold."

She always gave him a deal and he willingly handed her the money. They said their good byes and he left with a light bounce in his step.

Once he left from the packing shop, he walked toward the carriage station to pay his way to Beaumarion, the next town over. The woman smiled and took his money then he was on his way to the next town. He was the only one in the carriage so he decided to contact Siebrien. He picked out the spell components and cast the spell again. Siebrien looked up at the mirror and sighed.

"We're still not ready, Gavid. And where are you? You look to be in a carriage," he said as he noticed the carriage in the background.

Gavid looked around and nodded. "I am going to see a few people in Weisbech. Herium will still be in turmoil while I am away. It'll only be for a few days. Besides, those people rely on me too much and will soon forget what happened."

The lord gave a nod and grumbled. "Well, just be sure you are back home when I give the word. I cannot have you out of town when it's time. So do me a huge favor and be there."

Gavid shrugged and looked at the man in charge. "You act like this is going to happen tomorrow. We both know I still have plenty of time. I could probably see the entire realm in the amount of time that the order would be ready."

The lord rubbed his forehead and shook his head. "That shouldn't matter, but I agree. I just want you to be ready when the time comes."

Leaning forward, Gavid replied, "I will be more than ready. Just have your ducks in a row when it does. Herium is already ripe for the taking."

Siebrien took this as good news then heard a knock on the door. He leaned in and whispered, "Just make sure everything is ready. The Dragons are already on my tail about everything. I don't want them to learn of this any time soon. I have worked my hardest to keep this quiet. I'm glad you're one of those who hasn't told anyone. There are others that seem to be willing to spill the secret. Now if you will excuse me, I need to go take care of some business."

Siebrien dismissed the image and left Gavid to contemplate what was going on.

The trip was going to be a long and unadventurous one. There were no monsters or bandits in this part of the area. The lack of hiding places made sure of that. Still, the caves surrounding the path did make him wonder. It didn't matter, he could handle it. Soon, he was drifting off to sleep and dreamed of the town. The carriage continued with its driver on their way without disturbance.

CHAPTER 10

The celebration in Herium was a happy one. Music in the town square played louder than normal. Food lined the left side of the square that seemed to stretch for miles. Elves were thrilled Gavid's reign of the town was done.

Ledric leaned back against his chair outside the square to observe. Linden and the rest of the family joined him. "So, what are you doing just outside of the square and not enjoying the party?"

Ledric glanced up to them as they sat down and handed him a plate of food. "I am watching this town being happy, but tomorrow is a wake-up call. There are goblins ready to attack and they are very unaware of it."

They all were in agreement there. The town seemed to be unaware of anything happening outside their borders and didn't seem to want to be bothered about it either.

Ledric looked toward his left in the darkness and noticed four snow elven men quietly looking at the square and whispering to themselves. He pointed straight at the four and Linden gave a slight sigh. "Where are the guards to protect this town? They seem to be wanting to do something that will not benefit this place."

He and his three brothers rose and walked toward them, Ledric watched as the three of them talked to the others.

Terian gave a soft comment, "They don't like what is going on around here. In fact, they hate that they were gone so long."

Ledric turned to her and regarded her for a moment then looked back at the group. "They didn't know it was this bad. I didn't even know it was this bad. I could have been here sooner."

He stood up as the three brothers got into a fight. Linden ducked and two were against him. He planted a blow on one that knocked the man off his feet, turned and swept the other with his leg and made him fall.

Davignon grabbed another's arms and wrestled him down to the ground while Jayidus took the fourth and tackled him.

They looked up at Ledric when was there in moments. Linden sighed and looked at the group of men on the ground. "They wanted to rob houses while people were out here celebrating."

Ledric nodded and said a word out loud. Soon there was a charcoal skinned elf with jet black hair and pine green eyes. "You called me, sire?"

Ledric smiled to the man and looked at the four on the ground. "Yes, Tedian. Please, take those four men away. I am sure you were watching the entire time."

The man gave a nod and then asked Linden, Davignon, and Jayidus to stand up. As they did, the four men vanished into the darkness. They all returned to their spot and Linden grumbled.

"There really is no protection. We'll have to do something about that soon."

The party slowly came to an end and people returned to bed. The morning would be an eye opener. They all returned to the inn for the night.

When morning arrived, people were slowly getting up, that was one problem of partying too much. Linden stood where the stage was in the town square. He looked around and yelled out at the people. "Men, women, and children alike, I need you at the town square as soon as possible! We have trouble just outside of town. Goblins will be attacking the city and we don't know when. We all need to be prepared for this."

Wives darted in to get their husbands and husbands gathered their families into the town square. Soon everyone was buzzing with the chance that, while it was short lived, the town would be overrun with goblins.

Linden spoke again once everyone in town arrived. "We need to get prepared! I need blacksmiths making armor and weapons. I need tailors making leather and clothes. I need bow makers creating staffs with a point on the end. I need anyone and everyone including the children."

Some mothers shook their heads and shouted out their displeasures. Linden spoke loud enough for everyone to hear, "I will not put your children in harm's way, but they will be of a benefit to our town. I promise you, Gavid might not have protected you, but I will!"

There were elves who were not happy the brothers were alive and that they didn't come into town, it was understandable. Davignon stood on the stage and spoke, "We were just as paralyzed as you were. We were told everything in town was okay. I realize now that was a lie. Just like the lie about the woman that was with Gavid was just a simple slave. We should all be ashamed of ourselves that we allowed even the thought of a slave in our town. She perished so that it would make us all aware as to what was really going on."

Ledric was amazed Davignon kept quiet about his sister being alive and well, but the town was hanging on every word as Davignon continued, "Now, let us get out and prepare the defenses of the town. We can and will help you. We can build walls to protect this town, but time is of the essence."

They got off the stage and people mumbled about what was going on. All those who had a craft went to them and asked to be assigned to help. Soon they were assigned and got to work.

Ledric spoke to Linden. "We need to find a sorcerer soon to help us determine what we're up against."

Linden agreed then turned to assign someone who could find the right person to do the job. They were now all hands on deck, busying themselves with tasking the town, finding everyone jobs they needed to do.

"I can't believe you were able to do that, Meranda. The casting is something else, but seeing head of you, I only knew of Esteem Elders knowing this."

Gervis looked at the young elf. "What are they teaching you in the training center? Surely you have learned weapon casting and other spells?"

Treidon stared in disbelief. "There is no such thing as weapon casting. There are only spells and swords. You can never cast spells through those weapons."

Meranda rolled her eyes, she put her elbow on the armrest and looked out the window. Treidon glanced over at her. "What was that for?"

Meranda turned her attention back to him. "I have learned that weapon casting is an important skill. You have learned that by now, of course?"

Treidon shook his head and sat in disbelief for a moment. "There is no way that weapon casting is even in use. The Esteem Elders are the only ones who know this. Gervis, who trained you?"

"Esteemed Elders Omahin and Nysyen trained myself and my wife before she left. They showed us the importance. I trained my daughter in the abilities too. Even in an unconscious state."

He sat in silence as the carriage arrived in Derlwood. They checked out a few rooms and headed up stairs. The night was very uneventful and they all got to bed early. Once Meranda shut her eyes for the night, Treidon closed his eyes slowly and concentrated on his father. Soon he heard a voice. "What is it, son? We're busy here."

He opened his eyes to see his father and several other Elders in the room. Treidon regarded two people. One was an elven man with dark clay colored skin, ruby red hair, and cobalt blue eyes. The other was a female with biscotti colored skin, coffee brown hair, and bronze colored eyes. They nodded at him and he looked at his father. "Cirian and Aislinn, I'm glad you are here to hear this. I have found her and we are on the way."

Cirian regarded Treidon and smiled. "So, does she have the talent?"

Treidon turned to the pair sitting in front of his father and smiled. "I have seen things that I have only seen Esteem Elders do, but I don't understand how it is possible to train while she was unconscious. I understand what we do is mostly repeated and unconscious, but can you really learn skills while in a mental state like you and I are in right now?"

The questions were well placed and Pagues leaned back, looking at the other Riftriders in the room. Aislinn gave him an answer, "Yes, most of our training is repeated until you know it as an unconscious skill, and yes, you can learn the skills while even in a coma."

He heard a soft groan in the background and looked at the room. "Also she has mentioned that there is someone trying to take over the snow elven region. Might there be someone trying to take over our kingdom?"

They caught the worry sound in his voice and Pagues let him know quickly. "There is nothing wrong here. Although there are a few we are fighting around us."

"Could the two be connected?" Treidon asked.

No one had thought of this before. Pagues spoke up. "You are bleeding, son. What's going on?"

Looking down at his arm he knew what was going on. "She is having nightmares, we will talk again soon."

He quickly waved the image away and opened his eyes to her. Gently he ran his fingers through her hair and talked to her in a calming voice. Treidon put his forehead on hers and continued to talk softly until she calmed down. He laid in the bed next to her for the rest of the night.

The next morning he woke before she did and got of the bed. He knew the rest of the trip would be one of warmer weather than she was acclimated to. He pulled a ring out of his pack and gently placed it on her picky finger. It shrunk down to fit her small finger.

Treidon freshened up and woke her gently. She opened her eyes then noticed the scratches on her arm and his arm were unhealed. He had forgotten, he reached into his pack and pulled out a healing potion. He drank it and they were both healed.

She got up and refreshed in the bathroom, walked out with the same clothes on the day before. It was then Treidon realized, there was a need for an entire wardrobe for her. He gently took her hand and opened the door.

Gervis looked at them and smiled. "I see you are ready to go."

They agreed and walked out. Gervis noticed the ring on her finger. "Where did you get this?"

Treidon spoke and took her hand. "It's from me. It's a climate ring. We're going further into the plains and forest, she is going to need it."

They checked out and soon were back in the carriage for the next city, Aldell. Treidon decided to pick up the conversation from the night before. "I talked to Father, Cirian, and Aislinn. They were telling me that it is possible to train without being aware."

Gervis gave a nod and stared at Treidon, while placing his hand on his own knee. "Well, did they talk about weapon casting?"

Treidon shook his head. "No, Meranda started to have another nightmare."

She looked down to the carriage. "Thankfully, Treidon was aware of what was going on. Those things are getting more dangerous."

"Where are the items your brother gave you?" Gervis questioned.

Meranda shrugged. "Still in my pack. They feel like shackles when I wear them."

Gervis nodded. "We'll have to find something else to go on those arms. It'll be okay. You have Treidon nearby, he is able to help you when you are in danger."

They all sat in silence for a while on the way to the next town.

CHAPTER 11

Walking up to the door of Ugex's office, Jael paused for a moment and then knocked loudly. He waited to hear the words to invite him in then he entered.

"Something has to be done about that evil man, Gavid," Jael said as he sat down. "I don't like the fact he left us down here to defend this place and he gets to reap all of the benefits."

Ugex sat and stared at him for a moment and then spoke, "Well, what do you plan to do about it? I mean, he still communicates with us through the mirrors. We can't just deny him the access, unless..." he paused, leaving Jael wondering what he was thinking.

"Unless what?!" Jael stood up as he shouted. The frustration in his body was apparent, his brows were knitted and his eyes showed a bit of anger.

Ugex leaned back, not worried, then spoke, "Unless, we can break the mirrors and do things for ourselves. We would not have to answer to Gavid and we could take him out, if he came here to kill us."

Jael relaxed, it hadn't occurred to him to do something like that, kill Gavid and take over the town, like he wanted to do in the first place.

Ugex looked at the change in body language and spoke again, "We need to check to see the progress of the town. I will send out two orcs to help me make a better plan of attack."

Jael snorted in laughter and shook his head. "Orcs are as about as quiet as a room full of swords on a windy day. There would be no way that your men, no offense, could creep up on a town. Let me send two of my own. I am sure they will be quiet and get back to us with a full report."

Ugex shook his head. "Your group would probably steal and just run back home to never return. Besides, you with your size, you could easily be mistaken for a rabbit by a coyote."

The casual remarks by Ugex upset Jael, he got up and jumped over the table, tackling Ugex to the ground with a dagger at his throat. The fire in his eyes told Ugex he had been down here too long and was ready to fight. Ugex remained calm as Jael spoke, "We would out-run your kind any day. Give me one reason, as well, not to kill you right here."

"Well for one, you wouldn't make it out of here alive either," Ugex said calmly. "My men would be here in a moment to take care of you. Then there would be an all-out war in the cave and only the fittest would make it out of here. That would not accomplish anything remotely close to what you want to do with Herium."

Jael grumbled, let him go, and walked back to the chair. "You are right. We shouldn't be fighting amongst ourselves. Gavid has us wanting to kill one another. If that's the case then he will want to take everything that we worked so hard for, to get it done."

Ugex gave a quick nod, stood up, and then casually replied, "Well then, perhaps we should send two goblins and two orcs. We need to know what is going on in town. We can't just let the unknown make us hesitate."

Jael agreed and began to walk out of the door. "That's fine, whatever you want to do. I'll send mine out tomorrow. Just don't trip over our feet as we go along."

Ugex simply gave a nod and watched as Jael left the room. He slumped in the chair and cursed under his breath having to work with such a vile beast.

"What do you want us to do, brother? We can have him and the others killed," said the voice behind him.

"Not yet, Quesep," Ugex said without looking. "I want to take care of that in town once we are there. We have a way to sabotage him easily now. Break the mirror, we will have no way of communicating with Gavid at all. That will be one less stressful thing to deal with. I need to go talk with the armor makers about skipping steps as well."

Derix walked from behind his brother. "I think the goblins need to be taken care of. Shouldn't we do something about that?"

"Not yet," Ugex spoke in a hushed tone while putting his hand up to silence his brother. They listened for a moment to hear goblins walking by them. Once the voices passed, Ugex continued, "I need the pair of you to check on Herium. There has been no word on what has been happening there. Father doesn't know what Gervis and the others are doing. We have not even heard from him or anyone else for that matter."

Derix gave a long exhale and took a deep breath. "That poor woman should not have suffered at the hands of Gavid. If I knew where he was, I would kill him right now."

"I have an idea of where he might be, but that's not the problem right now. The problem is those goblins are going to spy on Herium. We need to get there and get that problem solved before we leave this place. I am getting tired of it as I know everyone else is too," Ugex said as he stood up and turned to his brothers.

"What we need to do is get out there and follow the goblins, or alert the shadow elves or someone of the goblins plan," Quesep said. He had been sitting quietly for a while.

Ugex and Derix nodded as they turned to him. Ugex spoke, "I'll handle the shadow elves and those goblins going to track Herium. You go out and go to town then find out what you can."

The brothers walked out of the room, leaving Ugex along. He gently touched the shadows of the wall and spoke an archaic word.

A shadow elf appeared before him. "What do you need, my lord?"

He looked at the elf and smiled. "Weisgar, I need you to kill those pair of goblins that plan on going to town, coming back, and reporting what is going on. Do you know what is going on there?"

Weisgar gave a smile. "The brothers Linden, Davignon, and Jayidus have made it back into town. They are going to announce that there is an attack coming soon. Tonight there was a celebration, but tomorrow will be a rude awakening for the poor town."

Ugex smiled and gave a slight chuckle. "Can you please take care of those goblins? I'd hate for the word to get back to Jael that the town is aware Gavid is away and they know what is about to happen."

Weisgar gave a slight nod then vanished back into the shadows. Ugex sighed in a hushed breath and walked out of the room. He went down to the blacksmith area and noticed there were no goblins in the area. This made him smile.

The head blacksmith, was a dark green orcan man with bright green eyes. His hair showed a bit of white in the long black locks he had. The man was muscular from working on metal for long periods of time. He glanced up in time to see Ugex approaching. He took a glimpse around before he approached Ugex and shook his hand. Then leaned in and whispered, "How much longer do we have to keep this up? Those goblins disgust me, simply working with them repulses me. I will not allow my talents to go to benefit them. I would rather kill them with one of these swords than work with them any longer. The others are in agreement with me. They would rather be helping those poor people in Herium."

"Even if they hate our kind?" Ugex questioned. The man gave a quick nod as a goblin ran behind them carrying armor out of the room to the storage. Ugex understood and felt the same way. He clasped the blacksmith on the shoulder and gave a soft reply, "We will be heading to Herium soon. You can get some blood shed there. I want you and the other smiths to start skipping steps to make the armor weaker."

This delighted the blacksmith, he spoke in an archaic language to the other blacksmiths and they responded in kind back to him. The blacksmith gave a quick nod to Ugex and then turned back to working on the current piece of armor. Soon, the armor would be weaker and could easily help kill off the goblins. This was a good way of dealing with them without them being aware of it. Ugex went back to his room for the evening meal and a discussion with his father about plans to would get him out of the cave and into Herium.

The carriage stopped abruptly and announced they had arrived. Gavid woke at the start and stared out the window. He slowly got up out of the carriage and looked around the town of Beaumarion. It was a quaint town with a few desert elves and more plains elves. There were few shops that were scattered about the place, but most were in the center of town. Finding a quaint inn, he checked in. The room he got was perfect, it oversaw the entire small town. It also gave him a view of the castle in Rishmede.

He liked the town, no one knew who he was. The townspeople seemed to be miserable and poor. It reminded him of Herium and all the troubles they were having. It reminded him to contact the wives of the brothers. He grabbed the mirror and spell components and waved his hand, soon the images swirled, revealing nothing but fuzzy and broken sight.

Seeing that, he knew it as a sign the brothers were dead. He decided while he was contacting people, he would contact Ugex and Jael. When the image changed to Ugex's mirror it was oddly fuzzy as well. This was confusing, but didn't matter. He knew they could do the job he set out for them to do. Perhaps, they had gotten into a fight and broken the mirrors. He didn't know what was going on.

He walked down to get a meal and enjoy the entertainment. The inn seemed to be dreary and boring. They really didn't care much about happiness. Most of the entertainment was sitting in silence. He wondered if there was someone controlling this town, but he knew it was probably because of how close it was to Rishmede.

A forest elven woman gently placed a bowl in front of him and then his drink.

Glancing up he smiled. "Thank you for this."

The woman gave a shrug like it didn't matter and walked on.

He picked at the stew in front of him. It was a bit salty, so he picked up a piece of bread and dipped it in. It helped cut the salt and he was able to finish the meal. He took a deep breath and listened to the cheerless music. There seemed to be no hope for the town.

After his meal he went upstairs and sat out on the balcony. Siebrien's castle stood above the hills of the plains. He drifted into a thought of what it would be like living in the castle.

"Would you like some more, sir?" He opened his eyes to see a plains elven woman holding a pitcher of ale, waiting for her to give the go ahead. She was a dark tanned woman with soft green eyes and blonde hair. She smiled to him. "Is there something wrong, sir?"

He shook his head and gave a grin. "Not at all. Please give me some more. And can I have some more of the food please?"

She ran her finger down his arm and it tingled, she spoke in silken tones. "Anything you need, sir. I am here for you." He watched as he poured the ale in the glass and walked off. This was better than the life in Herium. He took a deep breath and looked around. The room was ornate and dark. Dark woods trimmed with gold and silver throughout.

There was a dagger nearby which was made of mithril and dark rubies. There was a sudden burst into the door and a man in dark clothes approached him. He waved his hand and froze the man in place quickly. He walked up and uncovered the face and he was chilled to the bone. The face before him was of the woman he enslaved.

Gasping for a moment, Gavid growled then touched her with the dagger. She fell in on the ground, lifeless. He walked to the mirror and waved his hands to see the town of Herium and how it was going.

The carnage was rampant, there were people crying and begging for help. There was nothing peaceful about the town. He smiled in delight as he saw a few demons roaming around, making things more miserable.

He dismissed the image and sat back at the desk. Soon a forest elven man walked in. "Sir, we have to get going. The people desire to hear you speak."

He rose up and walked to the balcony, he heard the crowd cheering his name. He raised a hand to calm them and spoke, "People of Rishmede, we are more prosperous than ever. We have riches that no other town in the realm can fathom. Hear me now, Rishmede. We will be the one town that others want to live in. We will be that one town that people flock to because they need what we have."

The crowd cheered loudly for him. What he didn't see was the shadow lurking behind him, pulling him deeply into the darkness.

He jumped up out of his chair and scanned his surroundings. He was still on the balcony in his chair. Gavid relaxed and smirked as he looked back at the castle.

Thoughts of everything going the right way made him extremely happy. He got up then pulled out his pipe and the packing. Returning, Gavid sat down and filled the pipe. Soon, he lit the cylinder and blew smoke rings in the sky. He relaxed once the realization of being awake and present hit him. What he didn't see were the shadows moving about him, observing him. He rose and leaned over the balcony. He took a deep draw on the pipe and closed his eyes, enjoying the savory flavor. It had a bite of cinnamon and a hint of wood.

He looked down at the town below him. There were people robbing others, while others were begging for money. It was a thing of beauty. He, again, imagined the town of Herium suffering the same fate.

There was a knock on the door. He was curious as no one really knew he was there. Walking to it, Gavid opened it up and glanced around. There was a small dark elven girl with dark blue eyes and black hair looking up to him with a cute smile. She spoke sweetly to him while giving him an adorable look. "My lord, can I bother you for a moment?"

He grumbled and gave her the indication to proceed. She stood up straighter and smiled. "My mom is dying and I need a little money for a healer. I will be an orphan if I can't get her well."

He grumbled at her and waved her off. "Find someone else to bother. I just used my last gold to pay for the room. I have none."

The little girl leaned, peering into the door. Gavid stepped in front of her gaze. She looked up to him and grumbled, "You are a heartless man." She stormed off and down the hall and into the shadows.

He shrugged, he didn't really care. He had the gold if he wanted to help, but he would rather people perish than survive. Walking back into the room, Gavid smiled. This room was comfortable for him. He did like the view and he wasn't in a rush to get to Rishmede. He decided it was bedtime, however. He picked out a change of clothes for the morning then took a relaxing bath. He changed into his night clothes and climbed into bed with his spell book. He turned on the light over the bed and began to study the spells he might need for the next day.

The girl vanished into the shadows and transformed into a taller, darker woman. She glanced at Gavid's door and gave a knowing grin, then vanished into the darkness, reappeared in the office of a dark elven man. "My lord, he is in Beaumarion. It seems, he is settled there for now. Apparently, he's in no rush to be in Rishmede. He seems to be happy and relaxed. It also means he is unaware of what is going on."

The elven man had dark brown hair, dark green eyes, and was dark skinned. He turned to her and grinned. "Good. We need to tell Hariton where he is and what the plan will be for him."

The woman nodded then looked around for a moment before meeting his eyes. "So what is the plan, Eston?"

The man turned her and gave a smirk. "For now, we will just keep an eye on Gavid until we are given the word."

The woman nodded then vanished into the shadows to watch Gavid as directed.

CHAPTER 12

Aldell was a quiet and pleasant plains elf town. The temperature was vastly different than that of the snow elven region. The carriage stopped and arrived at an inn. The driver waited until everyone was unloaded and entering the inn before he drove off. Gervis checked everyone in and they all went to dinner together. Their meal was a pleasant, roasted sausage and lentils. They ate it and enjoyed a bit of conversation.

"Father told me that it was possible that Meranda could train in the abilities of a Riftrider without being awake," Treidon spoke up.

Gervis nodded and poked at his food for a moment. "Most of the Riftrider training is mental, after all. Receptive, boring, and

Treidon. You don't know how to weapon cast. Why is that?"

Meranda turned her attention to Treidon now and he stared at his plate then back up. "Well, it's not important. We, as Riftriders, have to protect ourselves and not kill, if possible."

Gervis nodded in agreement before he spoke. "Yes, but what happens when you are out-numbered, like we were earlier? You can't rely on your weapons to help you. What if there is a spy and he is running away? There are spells out there than can stop him, but you have to find a way to touch him as he is running away and not within the reach of your spells."

"I think it's ridiculous that you don't know how to cast spells through your weapons," Meranda said. "It's important that we use these skills."

Treidon shrugged again and looked at her. His heart melted every time he stared into her lavender eyes. "It is one of those things that students and masters thought was not important and soon it was a nearly forgotten skill. The Elders and Esteemed Elders keep trying to show us how important it is. I still have my doubts."

The corners of Meranda's mouth turned downward in a frown and she looked at her father. "If they don't think this skill is important then how can you pass on to be an Elder or an Esteemed Elder?"

Gervis didn't know the answer and Treidon spoke, "There are a rare few that are now Esteemed Elders. Cirian and Aislinn are Elders and they both have tried to prove to me that we need weapon casting, but I fail to see its value."

Meranda gave a yawn and stood up. "Well, have a talk with Cirian and Aislinn about it. I am heading to bed. Tomorrow is another long day and we have a long trip ahead of us."

Treidon rose as did the others and watched as she headed to her room. Erissa looked at Ivadian and grinned. "Ready for bed, my sweets?"

He gave a loud chuckle and stood up and held out his elbow. "Whenever you are, my dear."

The pair excused themselves and Gervis looked at them. He missed his wife, wherever she was. He made it a point to contact her once he was in the room. Treidon looked at Gervis. "She knows a lot more than I do, doesn't she?"

"Indeed. I agree with Meranda, you need to have a talk with Cirian and Aislinn. They will give you more information on the importance of casting," Gervis replied as he stood up and left a tip on the table as well as the money to pay the bill for the evening.

This left Treidon alone for a moment. Before long, he rose and was walking to the room. He mentally contacted Aislinn as he walked and opened the door to see Meranda curled up on the bed sleeping. Not long after, there was a reply, he sat down and closed his eyes. He focused his thoughts on the Elder, soon he opened. Before him, sitting in a nice office, were Aislinn and Cirian.

She gave a soft grin and spoke. "So Meranda knows weapon casting, you say?"

Treidon confirmed it with a shake of the head and then spoke, "We had an altercation with bandits on the road, but I have not seen any weapon casting. So I am not sure. Although her father has said she does. He was trained by Omahin and Nysyen, but they have been retired for some time, right?"

Aislinn lean back and smiled. "If he was trained by them, then she was trained by Gervis in the way he knows, then she knows weapon casting."

Treidon shrugged and there was still doubt in his voice. "She seemed excited about the weapons that King Ledric brought her before we left."

Cirian who had been quiet for some time spoke up, "What did they look like?"

Treidon described them in detail, down to the darkness of the dagger. Cirian nodded as he listened to every detail. "You'll see soon enough. I hear you are still doubting, but believe me, you will understand it all soon. I can't wait to meet the woman, it seems she has stolen your heart."

Looking down at his hands he gave a long sign and then stared at them. Aislinn was smiling, "There is something more to it, isn't there?"

Treidon shook his head in agreement. "She is my bonded mate. The last time we talked, when I was bleeding, she attacked herself, in her nightmares." His face turned from contentment to worry. "She really has been troubled with those nightmares. Also, I have seen her in pain when there were demons around. I don't know what that is about, but I have not felt that pain. All other physical and mental pain I have felt. That I have not."

Treidon sensed Meranda's mental troubles starting up and excused himself. He opened his eyes and walked over to her. Gently sitting, Treidon placed his hands on her face and talked soothingly to her then connected his forehead to hers. Soon, she relaxed and fell into a deeper sleep.

He wondered how much was going on with Herium and how deep it went. There was something missing. He decided to contact his father for a moment and talk. Pagues replied and Treidon opened his eyes. "Only a moment, Father. Have you heard anything from Herium?"

Shaking his head no, Pagues sighed. "Afraid not, son. How is Meranda and where are you?"

"In Aldell, Father. We will be there in a few days. Meranda still has nightmares as well. I wish there was something more I could do for her, but I can't. I was telling Aislinn and Cirian about the weapon casting she said she knew, when I had to leave. I still have my doubts. There are only a few left that understand that skill."

Pagues nodded and glanced to him. "Son, perhaps she does know it. Just because you haven't seen it doesn't mean it's not true. Now relax and get some sleep. We will all see what she knows when you get here."

Dismissing his father, Treidon woke up and stared at Meranda. She was still sleeping peacefully. He crawled into the bed next to her and held her tightly until morning.

When he woke she wasn't in the bed, but he heard the door open and sat up to see her ready to go. He climbed out of bed and hugged her gently then got ready himself. Soon, the four of them were out again on the road to Rishmede.

Treidon glanced at Gervis. "I spoke with Aislinn and Cirian and they seem to think that since you know weapon casting that you would train Meranda in it as well. I still have my doubts. That skill has gone away with the Esteemed Elders."

Gervis leaned back against the padded cushion of the carriage and spoke casually. "I am sure Aislinn and Cirian are correct. I was trained by Esteemed Elders and I trained my daughter that way. You will see for yourself what she knows. Quit doubting the facts. Don't they teach you to see things for themselves? You have already seen Meranda do things that are not within your understanding. Why is it that you doubt she understands weapon casting?"

Treidon shrugged and looked at Meranda. Why did he doubt she knew it, just because he didn't? He put an arm around her and smiled. "I'm sorry. I shouldn't doubt that you have skills beyond my comprehension. It's just, I have never seen it in action, so I can't understand it."

Together, they road, talking about weapon casting, the skills she might know compared to the ones he had.

Derix and Quesep arrived in the forest outside of town and then walked to Herium casually. Elves were hustling and rushing about. He stopped a snow elven man who looked at him with slight disgust then he changed his facial expression. "What do you need?"

"I was out hunting and my wife came to me saying I needed to get back to town. Apparently there are goblins in the south?" questioned Derix.

The man relaxed realizing what was going on and nodded. "Ledric and the sons of Gervis have told us there are goblins in the cave near the desert area. He also said there are orcs there. According to Ledric, the news reached him in time. We are trying to prepare for the attack, although I don't think we have the resources."

"Who is in charge, sir?" Quesep asked casually.

The snow elven man looked around for a moment and then pointed in the direction of a white haired man with a few children. "That's Linden, Gervis' son. He will be able to tell you more."

The pair thanked the man and walked off, approaching Linden. He was kneeling, teaching a child how to throw a rock in a sling. Linden looked up to the pair and stood up. "How can I help you?"

In the back of Linden's mind there was something familiar about them, but he couldn't place it. He listened as the snow elven man before him spoke, "We wanted to know if you needed extra troops. I am Quesep and this is Derix."

Linden shook both men's hands and then spoke, "We could use all the extra troops we can get. There is so much going on. Poverty and disease, the goblins and the orcs south of here do not help matters. We are healing those who are sick and working those that can help as hard as possible, so yes, any extra hands you can give, we could use."

Derix listened for a moment and put his hand on his chin in thought then replied, "We are in the town east of here and the rumor came to us that this town will be under attack. My brother is the lord there and wanted to see what you needed from us."

Linden nodded in understanding and asked the kids to practice while he talked with the gentlemen. "I need blacksmiths, archers, anything or anyone to help us. I don't even know how many goblins and orcs are out there, but I have to trust my sister."

"The woman that was locked outside of the keep here? We tried to free her several times, but she somehow managed to get back here. That's your sister?!" Quesep acted surprised.

Linden glanced to them. "Yes, that woman. Why didn't you keep her in your town and keep her safe?"

Quesep shook his head. "She would be gone by the next morning. We don't know what would happen with her." That was a lie, but it would be a good excuse for now.

Linden gave an exasperated sigh and then noticed the children had gone off task. "If you will excuse me, it seems the children have decided that it is time to take turns on one another. Please, any help would be grateful."

He excused himself and Derix noticed the town in a rushed state. He turned to Quesep. "We need to get back here quickly. They are far from prepared for the battle. Even if it's only a few goblins, they will be overrun easily."

"I agree, let's go tell Ugex what is going on," whispered Quesep. Together the pair left town and made their way to the forest where Weisgar waited for them. They vanished into the shadows and reappeared in the shadows of the cave. Ugex was talking with some goblins and they decided to wait until they left.

While in the shadows, the pair changed their appearance and then walked out once the goblins were gone.

Ugex turned and regarded his brothers. "What is the news in town? How are they faring?"

Derix shook his head in disapproval. "It's not good, brother. The town is scurrying all over the place. They are totally unprepared for the attack. We must get there as soon as possible."

Ugex stood up for a moment and then looked at the door. "We'll give it a few days. There are some more things we need to do before we can leave. That town needs resources, we have plenty of them here. We need to get the shadow elves to help us take a bit here and there, when and where the goblins won't notice it."

Weisgar appeared out of the shadows and smiled. "We will be happy to help you there. Herium needs those resources to make armor and weapons. They are working on barely nothing as it is. Just a little, like a day's worth of mining. That way it seems small, but it's significant in Herium."

Ugex agreed with that and smiled. "Let Linden or King Ledric know there are more resources from my town. Just tell them I sent it to them for help."

The shadow elf gave a nod and then vanished into the darkness. Ugex sighed quietly. "That takes care of one problem, but we still have to find a way to slow down the goblins."

Derix gave it a thought and then spoke up. "We can always move the armor from one place to another. This would make them believe they have to start over and then the armor would be in a safe place."

Ugex shook his head. "That might work, but not all of it, just a few pieces. Make it seem that they have worked hard and they aren't that close to finishing. If we take all of it, then they will suspect something."

"Also, can we tell the blacksmiths to slow it down a bit? Perhaps, pretend to wait for ore that never arrives?" questioned

Quesep. "Maybe they can hide it somewhere as it arrives for the shadow elves to take?"

Ugex liked the idea and smiled. "Together, we can get the town some help and then we will get out there and help them protect it. Now, go and get what you need to get done."

Opening the door, Ugex and the brothers walked out and went in different directions. They spoke to other orcs about a few things then they got back together. By then, it was time for dinner and they sat down to eat happily.

Ugex watched his brothers and sighed. This was not how things were supposed to be for their race, however, that's what his father wanted for them currently. This was one way to protect the town without the snow elves being aware of what was actually happening.

They ate and were pleasantly full. Soon Derix and Quesep excused themselves and left Ugex alone with his thoughts. He sat down and turned his chair to the mirror and waved his hand. The white haired man with lavender eyes appeared and smiled. "What is it, Ugex? How is everything in Herium?"

Ugex leaned back and waved a hand to lock the door then spoke to his father. "Hariton, things aren't good in Herium. You need to get there and help them. I know you are busy with other things, but this is the town your son and grandchildren are trying to protect. They might turn on Gavid soon enough, but for now, they need a Dragon to be there to show that the goblins are not going to take over the town."

Hariton shook his head and replied softly, "The town will be all right. You have a plan in place and you will be there to help. I suggest you leave soon. Sabotaging or stalling the goblins will only give you days, at the most. They are resourceful creatures and will do everything in their power to accomplish what they need to. Get to town with the rest of the group and protect them. I know the situation there is dire, but when Gervis returns, with the boys there, there will be more determination in them."

Ugex rubbed his forehead. "Fine. We will get there as soon as possible, but I wish you were there to help too. They need you more than ever. I am sure that town would rather be happy instead of poor and sick. It's like the Dragons don't care."

"We care, you might not see it. Son, Siebrien has a plan and we are trying to figure out how best to get word to everyone. Pagues hates shadow elves, as do others, so it is up to us to find a way to prevent this. I wish we would have never listened to the demon woman that entrapped Gervis."

There was an angry knock on the door and Hariton vanished. Ugex sighed, he knew what it was about, but casually walked to the door and waited to open it. He changed his mind at the last minute and sat down gently, letting the small goblin wait until his anger cooled.

CHAPTER 13

Jael walked through the cave and decided it would be good to check on the progress of the orc blacksmiths. He walked into the cave area. He noticed as the smell of sulfur, smoke, and brimstone wafted through his nose and the sounds of sizzling metal in water along with clanking of hammers. He smiled at one orc and watched him for a moment.

The orc, not realizing he was there, skipped the step of putting it back in the water once it was hammered out. Outraged, he looked at the orc. "Just what do you think you're doing?"

The orc turned and looked down to him. "I accidently missed a step, I can fix it. I'm sorry, my lord."

He grumbled and stormed off. It wasn't an accidental mistake, he purposefully skipped the step. Jael finally found himself at Ugex's door and banged on it loudly. Waiting a moment, he knocked even louder. The unopened door angered him even more. "Ugex, open the door! We need to have a talk!"

As Ugex slowly opened the door, Jael burst through, knocking Ugex off his feet. He looked up at Jael who was furious and had his small dagger drawn. "We're done. You have told your orcs to skip steps in the armor!"

"I have no idea what you are saying, but sometimes it is necessary to skip steps to put the magical abilities that you wanted in them," Ugex said as he tried to get up.

Jael was on him in a moment with the dagger at his throat. "That's a lie as well!"

Ugex was calm and glanced up to Jael. "No it's not, but since we're done, I can leave here and go back home. Gavid has not been in contact with us in days. There really is no more reason to be here."

Within the split second of Jael being distracted, Ugex took his shirt and lifted the goblin off of him, putting him to one side as he stood up.

"Ever wonder why Gavid had just suddenly left us to fend for ourselves?" Ugex said putting doubt in Jael's head.

Jael shook his head and looked up. "I really don't care at this point. He has betrayed us and left us down here."

Ugex gave a slight nod. "I am tired of this. We are fighting with one another far too long. For what? The satisfaction of working for Gavid? I'd rather take what little I can bring back home. The riches down here are far greater than what my town will ever imagine. Even just a small bit of diamonds would suffice us for a long time."

Jael agreed and glared at the orc. "Fine, be on your way with whatever you want, but don't come back here. This is our cave now and we will be here for a long time. We will attack Herium and then we will have the cave and the town."

Walking to the door, Ugex gave a nod and motioned for Jael to leave. "If you will excuse me, now I must tell my orcs we're done. You can have this place. I don't plan on ever coming back. If I do, it'd be to kill the likes of you and your kind. I learned one thing, goblins are the greediest, nastiest beings in the realm."

This angered Jael again and he peered up at him. "I can say the same thing about your kind. I hope we do cross paths again, so I can take care of you and the like." He stormed out of the room and Ugex slammed the door behind him.

Jael walked back to his room, angry and flustered, he told his aid to go get his second in command. The aid, a small goblin with dark gray skin, balding head, and green eyes gave a nod and spoke in a raspy voice, "My lord, what is going on?"

"We are cutting ties with the orcs. Now do what I tell you," Jael said in a nasty tone.

The aid then bowed out of the room and left Jael alone. There was something else, Gavid hadn't contacted them in a while. They were truly on their own. He heard a knock on the door.

Jael gave the command to come in. A small muscular goblin came in. He was well groomed, for a goblin, and stood up right, compared to most, including Jael. The goblin sat down and glanced out the door. "Why are the orcs packing up and leaving?"

"Urdun, I'm tired of pretending we get along, you and I both know we don't. They have decided to go their own way and we have decided to stay here and attack the town."

Urdun gave a nod in understanding, "But why now? I mean, we have been down here for years together. Why the sudden change?"

"Because, Gavid is gone and it's time we got a move on. We have been sitting down here far too long with no action. Gavid promised us we could take over the town when the time came, but the time never came."

Urdun understood it. It had been some time, they did nothing but mine and send some of it to Gavid. They were peons to him.

"Good, now you understand. We have to come up with a plan of attack on those who plan to do us in," Jael said as he looked around the room.

"How many goblins do I have to work with?" asked Urdun.

Jael thought for a moment, but he didn't have the answer. "I will get back with you on that one. We have to plan it out. Since we're done with the orcs, they won't be helping us with armor any more. We will have to find goblins who can do it for us."

Urdun then stood up and glanced at Jael. "I will find them for you, relax, it'll be okay. We will take care of the orcs and Herium. We will be rid of all of those that hate us soon enough."

The goblin walked out, Jael sat back and took a deep breath, letting it out slowly. The caves were warm compared to the spring above them. He did, however, miss his home.

He rose, went to the door, and walked out of the room. Goblins were scurrying about the place, screaming and shouting at others in their own language. Most of the conversation was trying to find a blacksmith, however, there was some excitement about the attack on Herium and possibly the orcs. The goblins were ready to leave this place, they were ready for some action. They had gotten too compliant for far too long.

Jael walked into the dining hall for a bite to eat. Several goblins came up and asked him if it was true about the attack on Herium happening soon. He told them it would be. Jael liked this type of excitement. Several orcs walked by and grunted about the troubles they were getting into. He turned only to see an empty cave. Jael leaned back in his chair and watched the dinner time rush happen, there were only goblins coming in.

Wondering if the orcs already left, he got up and walked around the cave. There were a few packing, but there were less than there were before. Perhaps they left once the word got out. That didn't matter, they were gone. Soon the place would be theirs. It was a shame there was no bloodshed, but at least the cave would be a good place to set up camp.

He stood and left the make-shift dining hall, soon he was in the storage room. Several goblins stopped their work and turned toward him. He waved them off and told them to continue. The storage room had mounds and mounds of riches, soon it would all be his. He grinned then walked away from the storage area to the armory and sighed. There was plenty of armor, but knowing what he knew, he didn't know which pieces were good or which ones had a step skipped. It really didn't matter, the men going into combat wouldn't have to worry much about a fight. He turned around then walked back to his room to see who could fight and who could not. A lot was happening in such a short time. He covered the mirror in case Gavid tried to contact him and soon was drifting off to sleep with peaceful dreams of domination.

Linden watched as the two snow elven men who arrived to find out the situation, left the area. He turned back to notice there were a few elves who hadn't understood the method he taught them to build the wall. If they didn't do it right, they would have a weak wall. Showing them, he made sure everyone was watching. When they finally got it, he left them to do their work.

A woman ran to him with a sense of urgency. Her light green eyes showed worry and fear as she spoke to Linden, "Sir, there are people who are packing up to leave town! We have to stop them before they go into the forest where the dangers are worse!"

Linden whistled to his brothers and got their attention. They approached, glanced at the woman, and then their brother. Linden thanked the woman, staring at his brothers for a moment. "There are some packing to leave town. We need to convince them, they are safer here than they are traveling in the forest with the goblins."

They arrived at the part of town where people were packing wagons up to leave. Linden spoke to one snow elven woman, "Why are you leaving? You're safer here than you are out there."

She looked up at him, her blue eyes were full of sadness. "Sir, we won't stand a chance here when the town gets attacked by goblins and orcs. We aren't even ready for it and my husband has passed in the battle of Huyton. There is nothing here for us anymore. It's best to move on."

Linden took her hand gently. "We were there at that battle. I can tell you, your husband fought hard for your protection. We must not flee from this. Everyone who plans on leaving, would those that passed on in previous battles want you to leave?" He looked around the area before he continued on with the elven woman.

"I can tell you, they all fought hard. We just happened to make it back on one piece. They wanted to keep you all safe and leaving will only make what they did pointless. We will protect you."

Others gathered around and watched the scene. The families were still packing when they heard a voice in the crowd. "Please believe me, I will do my best to make this all better. I am as much responsible as Linden and his brothers are."

The crowd split as Ledric walked up to the center of the scene. "We should have been here sooner. I have heard reports of the hardships and I did not follow up on them. Please, stay, allow us to protect your families. We can not protect you while you are traveling away."

Soon those that were packing stopped and looked at him. Most where women with small children. The woman that spoke earlier turned to Ledric and nodded. "Fine, only if you tell me that those beasts will not reach our home."

Ledric gave a nod and took the woman's hand gently. "I promise, I will not allow them to get past the forest. We are working on a plan now and we need everyone's help to get this done. Now unpack when you have time and the children can go see the brothers. They will have things for them to do. Everyone find a way to be useful. We need all the skills we can get."

The families started unpacking the essentials and the young children followed Linden, Jayidus, and Davignon to where there were others. There were a few children that were uncertain about the new editions. Some even ridiculed them. The older boys were especially hard on the poorer of the children.

Ledric and Linden both pulled those boys aside. Linden spoke up to them. "If you think you're better than them, you're wrong. Those kids had families that stood up to Gavid. Your families did not. If you choose to stick with your choices, then by all means leave. We do not need those that bring others down here."

The snow elven boys turned and looked at one another. They wouldn't think of speaking up with the king present or the lord's sons speaking with them. Ledric could tell the doubt in their eyes. "Who are your parents?"

One boy spoke up, "They are Ahtareth and Mirie. They work at the blacksmith shop down the way here."

Ledric nodded and looked back to them. "Did your parents work with Gavid?"

The boys again looked at one another and then they both shook their heads. "No, our parents wouldn't work with him, he was a mage. Although he did come into our shop asking for their help. Our parents didn't want to, they also kept their noses out of trouble too. Unlike those kids' parents."

The boy lifted his head to the poorer kids who were having fun with the slingshots and were not bad at it. Linden gave a grumble. "Those kids' parents were looking after the town interest, not just to stay out of trouble. If you will excuse me, I have some things to do."

Linden walked off as Ledric looked at the boys. "If you choose to stay, then you're helping the town and trying to defeat Gavid's plan. If you go, you will be considered a helper of Gavid and you will be asked to leave. That's up to you."

He excused himself and watched as the boys started back to the others, helping those who were struggling with the slingshot. He sighed and wondered how many people in the town were poor and struggling.

Soon, nightfall came and a few people that had been working hard, came to the inn where the king, the brothers, and their families were all staying. The tavern of the inn was buzzing with excitement. A bard was playing a happy tune as people enjoyed their meal. The music stopped playing for a brief moment when suddenly there was shouting. "You filthy beast! Get your hands off of my food!"

Ledric and the others turned to see a large elven man with dark brown hair, white skin, and brown eyes holding a smaller pale skinned elven man with light green eyes and soft brown hair by the arm with a dagger drawn ready to attack.

Jumping, Ledric rushed to the smaller man's aid and asked what was going on.

The frail man looked at him. "Sire, we just want some food. My family is starving and most of this just goes to waste. He was finished. I was just going to take the scraps home to my family."

The larger man growled. "He wanted what I could give my dog is what it is."

Ledric stood in shock and others watched on. "Is this what we've become? Every man for himself? No one helping their fellow man, no matter the cost? You would rather this man and his family starve and give those last few bites to your dog?"

The man didn't like Ledric's tone and he stood up. He was a good head taller than Ledric, but he put his hand on the man's chest and pushed him down with a strong force.

"I don't need this here and now. This town suffers. I am sure you are one of those who aided Gavid in his attempts to run this town."

The man said no words, only looking into the fire like a scorned child.

Ledric growled and spoke in an angry tone, "You must have helped Gavid. You think you're better than those around you. I don't need you or anyone else who aided that man in ruining this beautiful town. If that is the case, I need you out of this town. You can face your own fate with the goblins he has waiting to attack us."

The man looked at him and shook his head. "We did not help the man, but we did not stop him either. We watched family and friends perish and where were you? We aren't the only reason this town is suffering."

Ledric gave a nod. "This is true, however, I'm here now and I'm making things better. What are you doing?"

He then turned to the feeble man and spoke, "Bring your family here and you can dine with me. I will put you in a room here and we can discuss what you can do to help us tomorrow."

By now, others turned their attention away from the conversation, but the other man was still angry. Soon his anger changed to sadness as he realized who the man was with. He quickly got up and hugged a small elven woman. Her dark brown hair, white skin, and dark eyes gave her the same appearance as the man who hugged her. Ledric stood in confusion for a moment, but then realized what was happening. The woman was his sister. He returned to his table and listened to them talk.

Soon, the evening was over and everyone went to bed. Ledric had to figure out a way to find out what was really going on. He made a mental note of going to the poorer parts of town soon.

CHAPTER 14

T he carriage was traveling at a good rate until they slowed down. "We have trouble!" the driver announced loudly as they stopped.

Gervis poked his head out of the window and noticed a tribe of gnomes coming down the road. He looked at Meranda and gave a knowing grin. "Now is a good time to show Treidon what you can do."

Together, they climbed out of the carriage and Meranda observed the gnomes charging, now, with swords raised high.

She pulled out her bow and a black arrow then mumbled a word. It glowed with excitement as she launched it in the air. Before Treidon could remind her it was not appropriate to kill beasts, the arrow landed in one gnome's chest and shocked four around him.

Gervis looked over at Treidon and spoke, "She knows what she's doing. She's been trained by me and I have taught her well."

Drawing his weapon, Gervis ran into the crowd of gnomes. Treidon followed suit, only to see other gnomes falling at his feet. Soon the gnomes died down in drastic numbers. Gervis was too far away as Treidon was outnumbered by gnomes. He could not defend himself against those who were licking their thin lips to attack him. He backed up only to see that he was surrounded. Adrenaline pumped through his veins as he drew his sword, ready to take down many.

There was a scream of attack, but there was a hint of a whistle in the background. He knew not to move and found an arrow landing in the ground before him. Soon, a gust of wind exploded through the arrow and knocked all of the gnomes down.

He quickly ran away, knowing what would happen next. As he looked back, he noticed at least six were shaking.

Turning to Meranda he spoke, "You know not to kill them."

"Did you plan on making yourself dinner? Because they had every intention of killing you," Meranda said starkly as she climbed into the carriage. "It's either kill or be killed. There are monsters out there who would rather see us all dead and take over the realm than keep us alive. We are one of the few races that would try our best to protect the way of the realm. I would rather you not die at the hand of those beasts."

She sat down and looked at her father. Treidon sighed then climbed in and sat with her. Gervis then spoke to Erissa, "Check him over. Make sure he didn't hit his head. He seems to have forgotten that a Riftrider must protect those around him, not the monsters that plan to kill us first."

Treidon started to speak up, but he knew Gervis was right. He hadn't remembered those gnomes were out to attack and kill them. There was no point of trying to save them. He took a deep breath as Meranda spoke up, "Just be glad I was there with my bow and weapon casting. Had I not been, you would not be here either."

He forgot that she was doing all of the attacks from range. "How could we be so dumb and blind not to see its importance?"

Meranda shrugged and smiled. "You are not dumb, it takes a lot of work to perfect weapon casting. Most don't care for it now because it is so tedious. It takes a lot of patient and concentration to do it."

Treidon gave a slight nod, but sighed. There was a lot wrong with training as a Riftrider and weapon casting was one of those things. He would have to make a point of bringing it up to his father once they got to Elmwick. They were only three days ride away and he was anxious to get home.

Soon they were in Rishmede and Mcranda climbed out of the carriage. The plains were a beautiful sight. Grass for miles around her. The smell of farmlands and flowers drifted through her nose. She enjoyed the moment as she walked around the area. Meranda was fine until she noticed a plains elven man at a fruit vendor talking. She gasped and quickly climbed back into the carriage.

Everyone noticed that she ran back, Treidon looked around and did not notice anything out of the ordinary. He walked back to her and the carriage, he noticed her fear. "What is wrong, my dear?"

She pointed toward the fruit vendor and spoke, "The man buying the apples, that's the man in charge of taking over the realm."

"The realm?" Treidon questioned loudly, getting the attention of the man, which made Meranda duck down in the carriage.

He turned back around and Treidon whispered, "You can't be serious, that is Lord Siebrien. He is ruler of this part of the world. Such a nice man."

"I know what I saw and I know what I know," Meranda said as she continued to hide in the carriage. "That man wants to control the realm, its resources, and everyone in it."

Treidon shook his head. "They won't get Elmwick, it's too strong."

He climbed in the carriage and sat pulled down the back window, the others noticed something and Meranda sat up. "They are going to choke out the larger cities. That's why Herium is so important. It is one of the trade cities to Yeverdin and others around."

Treidon looked at her, but her face said it all, the fear in her eyes, her body language was tense as well. He also could feel the fear physically. "We need to get going. If what you say is true, we need to tell my father and others about what is going on."

He climbed out of the carriage and on top with the driver, telling him to get a move on. The driver waited until the others were in the carriage and they were off. Treidon told the driver to pause only to let the horses get a break. The driver gave the nod, Treidon climbed up and balanced himself as they were moving down the bumpy road. He grabbed the rail of the carriage and flipped into the window. He let go of the rail and found himself in Meranda's lap.

She blushed and gave a knowing grin. "Happy for you to drop in, but believe me, I would not tell you this without just cause. But what's the rush? It's not like you are part of the royal family in Elmwick, are you?"

Gervis looked at Meranda. "My dear daughter, Treidon here, is the Prince of Elmwick. He is the oldest in line for the throne. Pagues is his father. This is very important to him. However, Treidon, what did you think she was talking about when we first went on this ride? It's not like she didn't include your city."

He slipped out of her lap and sighed. "I just thought she was talking about the smaller towns, not Elmwick itself."

Meranda shook her head and looked at Treidon. "No, Siebrien wants the entire realm. He wants to control everything and is using people like Gavid to make that possible."

She turned toward Gervis and Erissa. "Do you think we could get the shadow elves to spread the word to the other towns?"

Treidon shook his head. "Those vile beasts just want us dead."

Meranda sat in shock then looked at her father and waited for answer.

Gervis gave a reply, "We will see what happens and then get the shadow elves to help. I'm sure they are already aware in Herium and are probably spreading the knowledge to others. Treidon, those *vile beasts* saved my daughter's life and our lives too many times to count. I even remember a time when the shadow elves were working hand in hand with your father. What happened?"

The disgust on Treidon's face was evident. "They killed someone. One of them tried to deny it, but there was evidence that pointed to him. He had a knife in his hand and was standing over the body when we arrived."

"Sounds familiar, but just because someone stands over someone with a knife doesn't mean he did it. He could have been at the wrong place at the wrong time. Shadow elves as well as other races are always accused of something they didn't do."

Treidon leaned back and fumed for a moment. Meranda looked at her father. "Well, I hope the shadow elves have gone and spread the word, even if stubborn forest elves won't listen to reason. Perhaps there are a few that will."

Gervis shrugged and gave a knowing grin. "My dear, they have probably already been in contact with Pagues, there are several Treidon does know, but they haven't told him what they really are."

Treidon turned his attention back to Gervis. "You mean there are those who are friends with me who are shadow elves?"

Gervis nodded and smiled. "I won't tell you who they are though, because then you will judge them for what you have learned from your father and not what you know of them."

Treidon sat in silence trying to figure out who it was as they rode along in the forest toward Elmwick.

Ugex watched as Jael finally left. It was finally time to go help Herium. He called his brothers into the room. "Time to get our stuff and head out. Break the mirror so there is no contact with Gavid in any way. We have other ways to contact our father."

Quesep and Derix left to get the others ready to leave. He touched the shadow on the wall and a dark woman appeared before him. "Deandra, I need the help of the shadow elves so we can leave as quickly as possible."

The dark elven woman gave a grin, her dark blue eyes sparkled in delight as she touched his arm. "Let me know when you're ready, my lord. I'm sure they're all ready to get out of here. Are you heading home?"

He shook his head and grinned. "No, we're going to Herium to help them. We'll need your help there as well."

Soon, the room was packed up as best as possible and the shadow elves took Ugex's belongings back to his home as commanded. Slowly, one by one, the orcs stepped into the shadows of the cave and vanished. Quesep and Derix walked into Ugex's room and smiled. "They're all gone. Ready to head to Herium?"

The brothers nodded and took the hand of Deandra as she vanished into the shadows. In a moment, they reappeared in the forest not far from Herium. Quesep changed his appearance as did

Derix. Quesep looked at Ugex. "You might want to *not* look like your natural self. People might confuse you with someone else."

Ugex understood what his brother meant and quickly changed his appearance to a dark skinned man with light green eyes and white hair.

Derix gave a knowing nod then they walked into the city. He quickly turned to Deandra. "Tell the other shadow elves to take all the resources in the cave and bring them to the storage area here."

She gave a slight nod and vanished into the shadows again. Soon, the rest of the orcs that were in the cave were with him, transformed into some form of snow elf.

Ugex, with the others, walked into Herium and sought out Linden.

Linden was with the kids teaching them the sling shot again and looked up to see a group of snow elves approaching. He stood up, walked over to them, and clasped his arm in greeting. "What can we do for you?"

Ugex smiled and introduced himself and his brothers. "We're here to help you. Our city to the south heard of the dangers and we brought people to help you. Tell us where you want us and we will be there."

Linden looked at Davignon and Jayidus. "Can you take care of the kids? I need to put these folks in a place that would be most helpful. It seems they are more ready than most of us."

They gave a nod and Linden smiled at Ugex. "The pleasure is mine. Please, come with me. I think I have a great spot for you to set up."

They walked through town and others regarded them, but thought nothing of it, turning their attention back to their work.

Ugex spoke. "Those walls should slow the beasts. How many soldiers do you have?"

Linden shook his head. "Let's just say, there are a hundred times more of you than there are of us."

"It's a good thing we came to help," Ugex said as he observed the town. "No one is ready and it looks like no one really cares."

Linden gave a long frustrated sigh and continued on to an inn in a good spot where the goblins were likely to attack. This part of Herium was the poorest part of town. "The inn is empty. There is water and power in there. This is likely where the goblins and the orcs will attack. It's the poorest and weakest part of town. This is where everyone who didn't help Gavid resides."

Ugex took a glance around the inn. "This is the perfect place for us and I don't think you have to worry about the orcs. I don't know how that man, Gavid, could get those two species to work together anyways. They are always battling over supremacy of this part of the realm. Not to mention, the different tribes. Where are they located anyway? Perhaps we could flush them out sooner."

Linden liked the determination, but shook his head. "We could use the man power here. Please, get settled in. If you and your men would like to meet us for dinner later, you are welcome to."

Ugex clasped Linden's arm and thanked him. Linden slowly walked away mumbling something about looking familiar.

Relaxing for a moment, Quesep spoke up. "Thank goodness we got here in time. They're unprepared for any kind of attack. Sure, there is a wall being set up, but that's not going to slow down anyone."

"I'm sure they have other plans. Did you see those children practicing with the slingshot?" Derix questioned.

Ugex pointed toward the inn and the rest of the elves made their way inside. He turned to his brother. "I did. Children should be used when defending a town, but only if they know what they are doing."

They went into the inn, which was nice and surprisingly clean. He flipped the switch and the light came on, brightening the entire lobby. It was small, but he could easily house all of his troops in the building. He smiled and looked at his cooks. "I hope you found the kitchen. We will need to serve more than our men. The people outside are those who refused to help Gavid. We need to thank them. They are probably starving and in need of a place to sleep as well."

The cooks walked into the kitchen with bags and boxes to start setting up. Ugex looked around at the others. "Find some rooms on the lower floors. I'm sure there is more than enough room for us. Those elves out there will need a place to stay to remain safe. I am sure Ledric will do something as well. Unless, he doesn't know about them and if that's the case, we need to make him aware."

There was a voice behind him. "I am aware and I do plan on doing something about it soon."

Turning around, Ugex saw the king before him and quickly bowed. "Sire, it is good to see you."

"It is good to see you too, Ugex. Why did you come here? I'm sure your town is safe."

Ugex nodded and shook the king's hand. "It is, your majesty, but we can't leave our brothers and sisters to be taken over by someone like Gavid. Especially since this is such an important town. This is a trade city for us. It's close to the desert, which made it easy for someone like Gavid to come in and take over. What I don't get is, why we were not made aware sooner?"

"That's my fault," Ledric said shamefully. "I ignored the rumors that were coming from here. I chose not to listen to the pleas for help."

Ugex nodded and put his hand on Ledric's shoulder. "I'm sure you didn't mean for it to go this long. Mistakes happen. We have to move on and continue to do the best we can."

Ledric nodded and gave a weak smile. "Thank you, my friend. We will make sure everyone here in this part of town is taken care of. I was here to talk to them, then saw your clan coming into the inn and wanted to say thank you for your help. We could not have done it without you."

Ugex gave a smile. "I wouldn't have it any other way. As I said, we cannot leave our brothers and sisters here to defend themselves against those beasts. We will protect this part of town to the best of our ability and then some. We will not allow them to take this part of Herium."

Ledric smiled and shook the snow elven man's hand. "It was good to see you again, Ugex, although I don't know why you changed your appearance."

Ugex knew that Ledric had the ability to see things as they were and smiled. "To cause less confusion and less ridicule, sire. You know there are still people who hold resentment for those who are a bit different."

Ledric understood and shook his hand, excusing himself while Ugex set up the troops. He decided to sit down and make a plan to defend this part of town. He also sent out his brothers to bring many of the people in the poor part of Herium into the inn for protection.

CHAPTER 15

The orcs really had Jael upset as he paced the room. He began talking out loud to himself. "How could Ugex do that to us? Why would he think it would be okay to do something like that?"

"Do something like what, Jael?" the voice behind him questioned.

Jael slowly turned to see Gavid at the mirror with a curious look on his face. Jael gave a sigh and began to stumble over his own words. "My lord, Ugex left...gone...lost his mind as well."

Gavid gave a simple nod, his dark eyes showing no anger or any indication he was upset. "Then be done with him. You have your tribe, kill him. We can't have someone like that working for me. You're in charge now, please take care of him. When you're ready, you can attack Herium. Things are still on the right track. You need to have Herium cleared out when I return. That shouldn't be too much longer."

Jael nodded, this gave him the chance to take care of Ugex and keep everything else for himself. "Thank you, my lord. I will be right on it. Everything else is running smoothly. We should be ready soon."

Gavid seemed pleased, but there was something else. "Good. Just make sure you kill the orcs then attack the city. Leave no loose ends."

Jael gave a nod and Gavid dismissed the image. Jael relaxed. He shouted to his second in command. Urdun, who happened to be walking by, opened the office door. "You bellowed, your majesty?"

"We're going to kill the orcs and take the town of Herium when we're ready," Jael said with confidence.

A confused look on Urdun's face made Jael wonder what was going on. Urdun then cleared his throat. "The orcs are gone, all of them."

Jael shook his head. "That's not possible, they were just here. I had a fight with Ugex about skipping steps in the armor."

"Yes. Then the orcs left and took most everything they could get their hands on."

Jael ran passed his second in command and straight to the armory. As he was told, there was no armor or evidence there were any orcs in the cave. He turned and went to the storage room and relaxed a little, only to notice half of everything was gone.

The goblins gathering resources looked at him. "Sire, is there a problem?"

Jael looked at them and couldn't believe his ears. "Don't you notice that half of the resources are gone?"

A goblin shook his head. "We work hard, dump what we can, and then go back to work. We noticed the piles were smaller, but we figured that someone was out smelting the ores for armor. The diamond pile has been untouched at least."

Jael stared at the uncut piles of what could have easily been crystals. He shrugged. That wasn't the point, the armor was all gone.

Urdun approached him. "What do you need me to do, sire?"

"I need you to go and find me some goblin blacksmiths. They have a lot of work ahead of them if we are going to attack Herium."

Urdun looked at the ores. "There is enough here for at least three hundred goblins weapons and armor, but I realize you want more."

"I do, Urdun. We can work on that later. Right now, find me some blacksmiths here in the cave."

Urdun gave him a slight bow and walked away from him to do what was told. Jael walked out of the storage room and sighed quietly. There was so much left to do. With no weapons or armor they would be stalled a while.

He walked back into his office then sat and grumbled. "How could this happen? We had been prepared, but why did Gavid put the pair of us together? We could have done all of this on our own. Did he not trust the goblins or was there something more?"

Jael came to the realization of what Gavid was really planning and spoke out loud to know one in particular. "He knew we didn't get along. He knew we would kill each other eventually and then he would be left with the wealth of what was in the caves. He never intended for us to reach Herium."

Turning to the mirror, he slowly became enraged with Gavid. He picked up a small wooden chair and flung it at the mirror. The wooden chair only cracked the glass and Jael sighed. He walked over and picked it up off its hook. He walked out of his office and out of the cave slightly then threw the mirror onto some rocks nearby. It shattered into a thousand pieces, scattering them everywhere. He ducked from the flying pieces then walked back into his room. Gavid would no longer be in charge, if he were to return to Herium, he would be killed on sight.

Walking into the blacksmith area, he noticed twenty goblins working, smelting ores that were brought to the room. They worked diligently, getting ore smelted properly then hammering out the metal to shape it.

He walked away grinning. Returning to his office, his plans were slightly altered, but wouldn't keep him off course for long. Jael sat at his desk, realizing he was finally free of the commands of Gavid. He was also free of the orcs and their lumbering bodies that were constantly in the way. Now he could focus on the task at hand, getting prepared for the attacks on Herium. If nothing else, to send a few hundred men then go back home. He didn't know how prepared the town was and knew he needed someone to scout the area for him.

He called for his aid again. The door opened and the aid came in, sat down, and looked at him. "Sire, what do you need today?"

Jael smiled and asked the aid to sit for a moment. "We are no longer taking commands from Gavid. We're doing this alone. Gavid had the nerve to try to get us all killed by the orcs. The orcs are gone now and I need to know what Herium is aware of. I don't want to go in blindly. I need to know that they're unaware of us."

The aid nodded and looked at him. "How soon do you want someone to go out?"

Jael leaned back and though for a moment. "In a few days, we need to get re-established first and then we can get the word out. Those orcs really put us in a bind, they took over half of the supplies in storage."

The aid flipped a few pages in his book and shook his head. "They took more than half according to what I have here. There has been some slipping out on a daily basis. We've been losing resources every day, according to what I figure."

Slowly, Jael closed his eyes and counted down from ten then gave a relaxing breath. "You're saying the orcs were stealing from us long before they left?"

The aid gave a slight gulp and nodded. "According to the daily tracking. They had been taking a little more than what was mined. It was either the orcs or some of our own doing it. I don't think our own tribe would steal then just pack it away."

"Never think for a second, a goblin wouldn't hide a little away, but that would have to be several storing things away for themselves. Yet, we are goblins, it is in our nature to do something like that. Perhaps, it was one of our own taking the daily, but over half during the night? That is the work of the orcs. They took what they could. We will have to be ready, they might come back for the rest," Jael said.

The aid gave a nod. "Is there anything else, your majesty? I need to find a scout to go out there and tell us what is going on."

Jael waved him away. "Send more than one scout though, if it's one, they might not return. Send out ten, that way at least one will return and give me a report."

The aid stood up and excused himself, leaving Jael to continue to be frustrated with what happened. Armor, weapons, and resources were gone. He needed to pick up production. Ugex and his tribe probably planned this along. He rubbed his forehead in frustration then turned back to the empty space where the mirror was. He was free of Gavid and the orcs to do what he wanted to now. He got up and walked out of the room for a meal, it was time to start planning the attack on Herium.

The carriage slowly came to a halt, the driver announced the horses were tired. Meranda climbed out of the carriage, thanking the driver. The others climbed out as well. The forest where they stopped had a clearing perfect for setting up camp until the horses were ready to go.

Meranda sat on a log while Gervis, Treidon, and Ivadian found some wood. They set up the fire and Meranda mumbled a word, lighting the kindling underneath. Soon the area was warm.

Treidon looked at Gervis then at Meranda. "There's no way the shadow elves are helpful. I've seen things, unexplainable things. It could *only* be the shadow elves."

Meranda shook her head and looked at Treidon. "There are other ways, the realm is full of monsters and unseen creatures. You can't just put that on the shadow elves. They've protected me and helped me when I needed it. I don't believe that, for once, they would do something without the permission of the Dragons. After all, they are who the Dragons send when something or someone needs to be taken care of."

He shook his head in disbelief. "Father said the shadow elves killed my uncle."

Erissa, who had been quiet for most of the trip, spoke up. "Ever thought that your uncle was doing something that wasn't beneficial to the realm? Ever wonder if there was something more to it? Your father might not believe his own family would do something that would hinder the realm, but the shadow elves only follow the orders of the Dragons."

He folded his arms in defense and didn't believe anything they said. Gervis took a deep breath. "Look, your uncle, he was not the best person in the world. He worked with the blood elves. Together, they were going to take your father's place on the throne then kill all of you. Your uncle was working without the knowledge of your father. He seemed to be a nice person to the family, but I've seen it myself, he wanted you dead. I was on that case with

Anmylica and I discovered things about your uncle that we could not convince your father were true. The shadow elves, with the command of your mother and my father, took out those who intended harm against you and your family."

Treidon continued to refuse to believe it. Gervis took a long deep breath and turned to Meranda. "He won't budge, but his mother will set him straight eventually. We need to talk as well. I can understand what the shadow elves face."

Meranda didn't understand but Gervis didn't elaborate and changed the subject. "You might know some of those shadow elves. They're friends of yours. They protect you whether you know it or not."

Treidon growled, stood up, and stormed off to be alone. The fact that Gervis accused his mother of being a part of this was the final straw. He turned back to see Meranda looking concerned, but he knew she could feel his anger. He took a deep breath. There was still the fact that someone wanted to choke out the larger cities, including Elmwick. He slumped his shoulders and turned back around. As he approached the group, he noticed a pair of his friends were talking to Gervis, Erissa, Meranda, and Ivadian. "Oriana, Kavan, what are you doing here?"

The pair smiled to him. "Keeping your friends company. They're nice," Kavan spoke softly. "They have been telling me there is danger in Elmwick? Surely they are kidding."

Treidon sat down and put his arm around Meranda in a loving fashion. "They aren't kidding. Meranda here said she had witnessed Gavid and Lord Siebrein talking about taking over the realm. We were on our way to Elmwick to spread the word to other cities."

Kavan looked at Meranda. "You should have told us sooner, it wouldn't be so bad."

Meranda gave a shrug. "No one believed me. Every time Weisgar came to my aid, I would tell him, but fear made him send me back to Gavid. I was stupid to believe that Gavid would not torment me so."

She curled up in a tight ball and winced in pain. Glancing around, she looked at Kavan and whispered, "There is a demon nearby."

Kavan stood up and turned around to survey the place. "How do you know?"

Treidon, Ivadian, and Gervis grabbed their swords. Meranda winced again. "I can sense it."

Oriana gave a slight nod as she was sitting silently then vanished into the shadows.

Treidon stood in shock for a moment, but Meranda winced again in fear. Something in her heart told her danger was coming. The three men and Erissa stood around Meranda who was in pain.

Watching, Kavan gave Meranda a nod and gently took her hand then vanished.

Treidon, unaware, stood protective over his love until he heard the haunting screams of something deep in the forest. He turned to see Meranda was gone.

Gervis looked back to see Treidon in shock. "She's fine, she will be back with us shortly."

Treidon growled in anger. "Where is she?"

Erissa talked to him soothingly. "She's fine, trust me. Her father wouldn't allow her to be harmed in any way."

Treidon turned to her. The anger in his eyes were apparent as she continued, "What does your body say? Are you still connected?"

He gave a slow nod as she continued. "You know Kavan and Oriana. They've never harmed you yet. They won't harm her now. She's safe."

"Erissa's right, you know," Meranda said coming out of the shadows. "Kavan and Oriana were just making sure I was safe.

They don't know why the nightmares are haunting me, they think it has something to do with Siebrein."

He relaxed for a moment and noticed the couple walked out with her. "How could you keep this a secret from me? Why didn't I know you were one of them?" The word them had a distain in his voice.

"That very reason, Treidon," Oriana spoke. "You treat us like monsters, but we only looked out for you and your best interest the entire time. Your family is constantly in danger and we've set out to protect you."

Meranda sat back down at the fire. "There were several nightmares in the darkness. Kavan and Oriana took care of them."

She rubbed her shoulder and took a deep breath. "The pain has subsided too. I don't know why I feel pain when those things are around."

Kavan and Oriana quickly glanced at each another and started to ask a question when Erissa spoke up. "It doesn't matter, dear. They're gone now. They won't bother you any time soon. I'll continue to stay with you until I have to go back to my duties in Herium."

She glimpsed at the pair and they walked away with her. Meranda sighed and sat back down on the ground. "How soon will the horses be rested? We need to be going soon."

The driver spoke up, "Shouldn't be too much longer. We've been sitting here a while now. We should get going shortly. The sooner we're in the city the safer you will be."

He seemed to be concerned about her and Gervis nodded. "Indeed, I would feel better if we were in Elmwick right now. If someone wasn't so stubborn then we could be there by now." He glanced over at Treidon who was guarding Meranda protectively. Treidon shook his head.

"There's no way I'm going with them. They will kill us all. My uncle never returned and you're all telling me it was because he wanted us dead. I never noticed that plan, *ever*"

Meranda took a long irritated sigh. "You seriously can't believe that. I'm here with you again even after going with them. They aren't out to kill you. You apparently need to have a talk with the Dragon Counsel."

Erissa, Kavan, and Oriana returned and looked at Treidon. "She's right, you know. You must learn to let go of the enmity. We did nothing wrong to you or your family, in fact, we protected you. That, I guess, goes thankless any time."

Treidon shook his head and they decided to wait until the sun rose to finally get moving. Treidon was still not happy his friends were with the shadow elves.

They rode in silence for a long while, but Meranda wanted to get to Elmwick quicker. The shadow elven pair understood how she felt, but decided to wait it out. They rode in silence for the better part of the morning until Treidon finally drifted off to sleep.

CHAPTER 16

L edric walked around town and was impressed by the way everyone came together to prepare for the oncoming attack.

While there were a few who still wanted to pack and leave, most people were willing to defend the town. The elves of Dalyor came in to help with the battle. They were strong and were able to defend the weaker parts of town. He continued to walk around and heard a voice to his left.

"Sire, where do you need us to be?" the voice questioned.

He turned to see the chief of the knights standing before him. His eyes were lime green, his skin was the color of oats, and his hair was a soft walnut color.

"It's good to see you, Oron. Please, come with me and I'll show you where you need to set up."

They walked together to an area that seemed to need the most help. Oron nodded in understanding. "I will get the knights ready for the oncoming battle. Do you know when it will be?"

Ledric shook his head and gave a sigh. "Sadly, I don't. I just know it's coming."

Oron thanked the king then excused himself to help the rest of the knights set up a defensive barrier. Ledric longed for his wife and thought about her as he walked back to his room at the inn. It had been a month since he last saw her. He turned and looked out the window then smiled. Ledric hoped everything would be ending soon, so he could fix this town and get back to his home. He knew there were other places like this one preparing for battle. It was best she wasn't here, although it might have done the town some good to see her and his family together.

There was a soft knock on the door and he knew it was time for dinner. He walked to the door and opened it. The woman had her head down, but her ivory colored hair flowed down toward the small of her back. He turned to get some gold when movement caught his eye.

Turning, he looked and saw his sons before him. "What are you doing here?!" he said in surprise.

Cadhla, Maellan, and Keilan grinned and the porter looked up at him. "You think you get to have all of the fun? Besides, this town and others need us. There are rumors spreading that Lord Siebrien is trying to choke out the larger cities. We had to come tell you, but it seems you have your hands full, too."

He smiled at his beautiful wife, Rainah. She had long ivory colored hair, light sky blue eyes, and soft porcelain skin. Their children had her features, but looked identical to him. "I heard Gavid was trying to take over the town and I told you, I was coming here to investigate."

Rainah nodded and looked out the window. "Yes, but you didn't tell me the town was so bad. There are others like this one across the snow region. It seems there are other people out there just like Gavid. You need to be there for them too."

He nodded and a defeated look appeared on his face. "How did it get this bad? I thought I was aware of everything going on around my area. I am sure the other kings of the snow region aren't aware either."

She continued to look out the window. "So what makes this town different than the others?"

Ledric watched as his sons walked out of the room to find a room of their own and he spoke gently to her, "Because Gervis' daughter, Meranda was enslaved by that monstrous beast. Do other towns have this problem? Besides, look at this town. There are hundreds who've defied Gavid and are now starving and poor, for standing up to him. We can't just abandon them."

She turned to him and gave a beautiful smile. "This is true, the places aren't near as bad as it is here."

"Also, there are goblins and orcs who plan on attacking the town. There aren't any others who are in this dire need, are there?"

She shook her head and turned to him. "Not in the least. What can I do to help?"

He heard the door open to see his sons entering the room. Ledric spoke to all of them, "There is a lot of people in the really poor part of town that I need to convince to come here and stay. Perhaps you could go and bring them here? They would be safer here, as that's the weakest point of town and would be the easiest part to attack."

Cadhla looked at his father and spoke, "They're seriously in that much trouble? Why wouldn't we have heard about it any sooner?"

"Because Gavid kept things controlled and I was a fool to believe things were that normal. I'm hoping Meranda gets to Pagues in time. She was the one that informed us about what is going on," Ledric said as his eyes glazed in thought.

The queen touched his arm and snapped him out of thought. "We'll get things back to normal. We will make sure those people that refused to help Gavid will be rewarded. There are towns out there that fought back, but this one seems to have been caught by surprise and now there is nothing they can do about it. I will go out there tomorrow and convince them that it's okay to come into town."

Maellan nodded and looked out the window. "I'll go out there and help those farmers and archers with improving their aim. We can't let this town go. It's important to our region. Mother, have you forgotten, the others are so remote that they aren't as important? This one is, it's the trade town between Yeverdin and Quarden. This town helps both cities bring things from there to here. Gavid knew what he was doing."

Rainah stood, shocked for a moment, then realized what her son was saying was true. She glanced at Ledric. "I'm sorry. I had forgotten how significant this town was. Maellen, you are right, this town has more right to protection than anyone. We cannot allow them to take this town over."

Ledric smiled, his family certainly had a way about them, but there was no doubting their determination. "Just make sure those poor people can get here to the inn. I've checked out all of the rooms to help them. Also, Lord Ugex and his brothers are planning on helping them as well. Those people should be safe. We just have to persuade them to come here."

He held out his arm and smiled. "How about we actually go down and get something to eat in the tavern and invite those who can not afford a meal to come eat with us. Perhaps we can get them here that way."

She took his arm and smiled. "Ledric, I'm sure you will have no problems telling people to come to dinner."

Together they walked out and down to the poorest part of town. Rainah and their sons didn't like what they were seeing in the least. They invited everyone to dine with them tonight. Some where apprehensive, but others were willing to go. A free hot meal meant they wouldn't starve another night. Soon, they persuaded others to join them. That night no one went hungry and others were happy to join in, helping when the time came. Rainah couldn't believe the conditions of the once beautiful town.

As they headed to their room, Rainah looked at Ledric and spoke quietly, "Why weren't Gervis' sons involved in the town at all?"

Ledric patted her hand, opened the door to their room, and let her in. After they were inside, he closed the door and glanced her way. "The sons of Gervis were told that there was no reason to go into town by their wives. However, someone put temptresses into the bodies of the wives. They were assigned to kill them when Gavid gave the command. Thankfully, Meranda recognized it."

"Who is this Meranda?" she questioned as sat on the velvet cushioned chair and stared up at him."

Ledric sat across from her and leaned back in his own chair. "It's Anmylica and Gervis' daughter. They had her while the war of Terian was going on. Then, I guess, the Dragons sent Anmylica out and left Gervis to raise her."

"It still makes no sense as to how she became a slave to Gavid," she said confused. "Or how Gervis vanished to allow this to happen."

He sat and explained everything to her, from the fact that the demon Irisa set a plan in motion to how Meranda was tormented and enslaved.

Rainah was on the brink of tears when she spoke, "We have to do something for that poor child."

Ledric couldn't help but smile and spoke, "She will be taken care of. She is with King Pagues' son, Treidon. They are bonded."

This made her smile and they talked about the happiness of having a bonded mate, then set off to bed to prepare for the next day.

A knock on the door woke Jael up from a nice, wonderful sleep. Something he hadn't had in some time. He stood up slowly, put a shirt on, and walked to the door. The knock was slightly louder, but the noisemaker didn't seem to want to bother him either. He finally got to the door and opened it up.

Three small male goblins with charcoal skin and hair to match stood before him. They gave him a ceremonious bow and introduced themselves. Lugduf was the one that seemed to be in charge and spoke for the group, "What do you need us to do, sire? We are awaiting your orders."

Jael stood aside, let them in, offered a seat to them, and then walked behind a makeshift screen to change into some proper attire, he spoke to them from behind it, "I need you to see if Herium is aware of what's going on. I'm sure they probably aren't or we would be in a battle right now."

Lugduf stared at the other two who had puzzled looks on their faces, but Lugduf jerked his thumb toward the door. The two other goblins briefly glanced at him then they understood. They got up and walked out of the room. "We will be on our way shortly. What is our payment? If they do know of our presence then they will surely kill us."

Jael understood this and handed him a pouch of gold. "That should suffice. I will pay you the other half once you return."

The goblin weighed the gold and gave a satisfying nod and stood up. "We will be leaving in a few moments and return as soon as possible. Is there anything you request of us while we are gone?"

As Jael sat he shook his head in a slow motion. "Not that I can think of. We will be attacking as soon as the armor is ready."

"How much longer will that take? I've heard mumblings that there are some of us getting anxious to leave. They're talking about just walking out and heading home," Lugduf spoke with concern.

This concerned Jael also and he stood up, walking over to the goblin scout. "Perhaps we should allow those who are ready to go home to do so. They will not take part in the reward once we have Herium in our control."

Lugduf gave a nod in understanding and stood up. "That might be for the best, more for us." He shook Jael's hand then walked out of the door.

This news left a foul taste in Jael's mouth. He turned toward his desk and spoke out loud, "Why would those people be ready to go home instead of attacking Herium? I can understand it, I miss home, but we need to take this trade city over. It has vast riches."

He looked over the empty desk then turned back toward the door and decided only a small amount of goblins would attack Herium. He was almost certain there would be some who wanted the taste of blood, but the fact that they were down there alone meant it was pointless.

He walked out of the door and looked for Urdun. The goblin was standing over the blacksmiths who were hammering out a sword and showing them a better way to make it stronger.

"Urdun, I need your help," Jael said and looked around. The image was discouraging. Not enough armor and fewer swords meant the decision he made was the right one.

The second in command walked up to Jael and smiled. "What's up, commander? I was just showing how to strengthen the swords for better fighting."

"Yes, that's fine, thank you. I've decided that we'll make a small effort to attack Herium. I mean, if they aren't aware of us, the small effort should be enough to take over their town," Jael said, looking on as the goblins worked.

Urdun shook his head. "Why, sire? While there isn't as much ore for armor, this doesn't mean we can't make a large scale attack, given time."

Jael shook his head. "We've been in this cave far too long following a desert elf. Why? Why have we not stood up and attacked him and Herium? We could have easily taken him down and the town."

Urdun gave a nod then suddenly agreed. "Why didn't we kill him when we realized what he was doing to that poor girl? We could have killed him then. We just sat by and watched."

Jael made up his mind and patted his second in command on the back. "Get at least five hundred pieces of armor ready, we will make it look like an effort if we don't succeed. If Gavid comes back, then we're gone and he'll never find where we are."

Urdun then gave a nod. "I'll need to go find men who are willing to come with me to Herium as opposed to those who are going home."

Jael smiled as he watched as Urdun excused himself. He decided he needed to take care of the miners and make sure they were only getting ore for now. They would take the remainder of the resources home to split amongst the men who worked in the cave.

As he arrived, several miners and his aid bowed to him. Jael grinned before he walked into the storage area. "How does it go? Do we need to up the limits for the armor?"

The aid flipped through a few pages and shook his head. "According to this, we're doing well, sire. Please, step into the storage area and tell us what we need to do."

They walked through the room to notice most of the ores and gems were gone. The aid turned to the miners in anger and shouted, "Where is everything?!"

The miners came in and dropped the ore down then stared in awe at their king.

He cursed under his breath and turned to his aid who was shuffling quickly though his papers. "Sire, it was all here just a moment ago. We have enough ore to do what you request though."

Jael clinched his fist then spoke through his gritted teeth, "Do we have enough ore for five hundred goblins to attack Herium?"

More shuffling could be heard behind him as the aid shifted through pages, then looked around and spoke with a frustrated sigh, "Sire, we have enough for three hundred."

Jael then shouted to everyone in the storage room, "Only mine the iron for now! The other minerals we'll get back to when we have enough time. How could this have happened?"

He turned to his aid who was clueless, which angered him more. He stormed past the aid and cursed more under his breath. There was no way that many resources could vanish in a matter of moments. The aid was not at fault here, but someone was.

He walked to his room and flopped down in his chair. He stared at the map, he knew where Herium was. He decided to throw himself into his work to try and forget the fact that someone was stealing from him. Again, silently cursing, he could not believe the incompetence going on while handling the resources in the storage room. Not to mention the armor. He rubbed his forehead in frustration.

He spoke out loud to no one, "How could this get out of hand so quickly? How could we just allow this to happen without our knowledge?"

He sat in frustration. Perhaps the best thing to do was pull up and leave, without dealing with the armor. If those elves were not aware. What would be the harm in trying?

Leaning forward, Jael tried to sort out everything he could in his mind. There were more issues with not knowing. He leaned back again on his chair. The stress was getting to him, but he knew the reward would be great if he could get everyone on the same page.

He sat up and took a deep breath. In that moment, he decided to leave Urdun in charge and go with the others back home. There was no need for him personally to go take the town of Herium over. Once that was done, he would tell Urdun to be the lord of the town.

Walking out, Jael looked around informing everyone as he walked through the cave, if they still wanted to attack Herium, they could. They did have the option to go home though.

Jael walked toward the cooks and told them to prepare to go home soon as well. They rejoiced in this fact and soon the entire cave was buzzing with excitement.

CHAPTER 17

"I can't believe you want to go to Elmwick with *them*!" Treidon shouted. He stood in defiance of what was going on.

Erissa was tired of this and took Treidon by the arm. "Treidon, you have to trust them. They are your friends for one. And two, Meranda is in danger if we don't get to town."

Gerivs gave an apologetic look to Oriana. "I'm sorry you have to be treated so poorly by a friend. The truth stings only for a moment."

Kavan rubbed his forehead in frustration. "Treidon, we're friends and have been for a while. Let us get you home. Erissa's right, the longer we're out in the woods, the more you're all in danger of the monsters out here."

Kavan approached Treidon, who quickly pulled his sword out and leveled it at Kavan's heart. The dark elven man chuckled and vanished into the darkness. Oriana sighed as she watched Treidon eyes widen, he let out half of a scream and slipped into the darkness. He reappeared in Pagues' office. Together they were both shocked to see one another. Treidon was confused as to what happened. He still had his sword in his hand and Pagues wondered how he got there so quickly. Treidon sheathed his sword then ran and hugged his father tightly.

Pagues was still in shock. "How did you get here, son?"

Spinning around, Treidon didn't notice Meranda or the others when Pagues spoke again, "Treidon, how did you get here?"

Treidon turned back to his father. "I was holding my sword out toward Kavan when he laughed then vanished and something grabbed me by my ankles. Next thing I know, I'm here."

He suddenly paled. "Meranda and the people with her are out in the forest with those shadow elves."

There was a sudden knock on the door. Pagues sighed. "You are telling me, you were facing shadow elves in the woods and didn't head straight home? You know how dangerous they can be."

Pagues opened the door to see Oriana standing before him. Treidon quickly pulled his sword and stood ready to attack.

Turning, Pagues stood in disbelief, confusion appeared on his face as he glanced to Treidon. "Is this how you treat a friend?"

"It's okay, he's been through a lot already. Meranda and her family are safe, they're in the dining area. Do you need me to tell them to come upstairs?" Oriana spoke without entering the door way.

Pagues gave a nod and she excused herself to bring the others up. He turned to his son. "Have you lost your mind? Is that how you treat someone who's worked so hard for us in the past? She's helped you on many occasions protecting this town."

Treidon tried to speak, but he was still confused as to what happened. "Father, she's a shadow elf."

Pagues laughed loudly and studied his son. "Have you lost your mind? She's not a shadow elf. Yes, she is a bit darker than other forest elves, but she's not a shadow elf."

There was another soft knock on the door and Pagues opened it to see Oriana with Gervis and three others he didn't recognize.

Oriana spoke as she bowed and moved out of the way. "Your Majesty, this is Gervis, Erissa, Ivadian, and Meranda. They're here to tell you some important news and I must be on my way."

"Oriana, please wait. My son seems to think you're a shadow elf. Is he crazy?" Pagues stopped the dark elf before she left.

She glanced at Treidon who was confident in what he saw and then back to the king. "I'm not, sire. Treidon has been through a lot already and the fact that there were unseen things in the forest would make him see many things. When he vanished, I brought everyone here as quickly as I could."

"Okay, thank you, Oriana. That will be all."

Treidon stood as he watched her vanish behind Pagues back and he sat down and grumbled. Meranda stood before Pagues as did Gervis and the others.

Pagues regarded Gervis and hugged him tightly. "My dear friend, you should've told us sooner that your town was in dire straights. We could have helped. Sent someone."

Gerivs looked at Meranda and then back at the king. "Sire, I was taken in by someone who was pretending to be my wife. She suggested that we don't bring this up to anyone. I am constantly kicking myself over it, because my daughter suffered at the hands of a monster."

Pagues stared at the girl before him. She was stunningly beautiful. Her long curly hair flowed about her shoulders, but she had her head down.

Treidon cleared his throat, but Meranda didn't look up. Pagues could tell something was going on and gently lifted her chin. As he did, he felt something wet hit his fingers. He glanced at her closely and noticed tears falling down her face. Treidon was unsettled as well. He turned to look at his son, but didn't see the tears. He couldn't help but hug the elf before him tightly. She had such pain in her entire body, but the tears were something more than a release. He held her tightly as she took deep breaths and constantly apologized. Treidon knew it was something more. Mentally, she was fighting something deeper. He touched Pagues shoulder.

Pagues stared momentarily at his son, who spoke, "Let me handle this, father. She's having a waking nightmare."

He started to speak up then noticed she had the same scars on her arms as Treidon had on his. He watched as Treidon hugged her tightly and spoke soothingly to her. Pagues gave Gervis a quick glimpse, Gervis gave a nod and spoke quietly, "They're bonded, sire. He'll help her through those problems."

Pagues understood everything then. He hugged them both and spoke, "Treidon, I'm sure Gervis is aware of everything that's happening. Why don't you take her for a tour around town? You can show her the sights."

Meranda shook her head. "You need to be aware, sire, the cities outside of yours are being taken over by Siebrien. He plans on choking out the larger ones and taking over the entire realm."

Pagues stared in disbelief. "That's not possible."

"Sire," she said as she pulled away from Treidon. "I heard Siebrien talk about Taleah, Lewood, Blegrove, and Erbury all being in his control. He will soon have them attack your town if something isn't done soon."

Pagues sat down and invited everyone in the room to do so. "Are you sure?"

Meranda sat with him and nodded. "Gavid thought I was someone who didn't understand what was said, he treated me like I knew nothing."

"This is not good then. How many other towns does Siebrien plan on taking over?" he questioned her.

"All of them."

"No, he would spread himself too thin if it was all of them. It can't be possible," Pagues doubted.

Gervis spoke up. "Unless he has people who work with him. People that are willing to pay him a fee of some sort to get the right to own the towns."

Meranda nodded, glanced at her father then over at Pagues. "Sire, I would not dare tell you lies. You have to believe me, your kingdom as well as other kingdoms are in danger."

Pagues took her hand and patted it gently. He looked at Treidon. "Such a strong head on her shoulders. She will make a beautiful wife and a great queen. Please, take her out to see the sights and get her mind focused on something else before the nightmares return. Perhaps, take her to the training area. She will need to be tested soon."

Treidon smiled, but Meranda looked at Pagues. It felt as thought he was trying to get rid of her and continue not to believe what she was saying.

Treidon felt this and looked at Pagues. "Father, Meranda doubts that you believe her."

He gave a concerned grin. "My dear, I believe you, but I have doubts believing he'd do that."

She sighed and took a deep breath. "Perhaps you might believe it more if you check with your towns. King Ledric is trying his best to protect Herium because Gavid is a servant of Siebrien."

Sitting down next to him she stared in his eyes. "Search my memories, you will find out that it's true. There's no way I would come here, set up my bonded mate, and make things up. I have scars from that beast."

Pagues suddenly believed everything she had to say, the conviction in her voice and the determination in her eyes proved it to him. "I'm sorry, I just couldn't see how he could have done something like this without our knowledge."

She stood up and took Treidon by the arm. "Perhaps, you were knowledgeable about it, but you passed it off as rumor. King Ledric did the same and now he's paying for it. Ask the Dragon Counsel."

She walked out with Treidon and left Gervis, Erissa, and Ivadian alone with Pagues.

"She's headstrong, isn't she? I'm surprised this Gavid person did so many bad things to her."

Erissa stood up and took Ivadian by the arm. "Come on, dear. Let us find an inn for the night."

Pagues shook his head. "No, stay here in the castle. Keep an eye on Meranda if you can."

Together, they nodded and left the room for the evening, leaving Gervis to talk with Meranda's future in-law.

The poorer part of town was made up of make-shift shelters. They were scattered about and seemed to be grouped in certain ways. Rainah stood on the edge of this section of town when she heard a familiar deep voice behind her.

"Think you could convince them to come into a safer environment instead of out there?"

She turned and smiled at the tall elven man. "Ugex, when did you get into town? Ledric didn't tell me you were here."

Rainah hugged him and her three sons took turns shaking his hand as he replied to her question. "Just a day. We've been setting up in the inn here to take on those goblins that will come this way. This is the weakest part of town after all. Those poor snow elves will be causalities if we don't do something soon."

He nodded and looked around the area. "These people stood up to Gavid and he makes them suffer. We need to take care of that and make sure he actually pays."

There was something in the way he phrased his words that sounded like he was angry in some way. She let it go and simply nodded. "I'll go see what I can do. People can't say no to me."

Ugex gave a smile and walked away as she went further into the poorer part of town. People who saw her ran into their homes to hide in shame. Others came out and told her point blank, they weren't there from the beginning and they don't need their help now. Rainah frowned as she stared at the conditions. She turned to Maellan as he went deeper into Herium. One elven man came out and shook a stick at him. Maellan shook his head and explained how they should have come sooner. As the man defended his home, a small beautiful snow elven girl came and hugged his leg. Maellan looked at his mother, the family walked toward the man.

Rainah spoke to the man, "What did you do before you stood up to Gavid?"

He pulled his shoulders back and stood up right as he spoke. "My dear, I was a blacksmith, but I told the king what was going on. Gavid gave my shop to someone who was willing to work for him."

Cadhla looked at the little girl, knelt down, and spoke, "Would you like a hot meal, a nice bath, and some fresh clothes?"

The girl bit her lip and looked up at her father who was shaking his head by now. She frowned, Cadhla stood up and looked at the man. "Sir, we're trying to make things right. We'll give you money, we'll help you to establish yourself and your family."

"That doesn't matter," the strong man said, standing tall. "We will still be ridiculed by those who helped Gavid. As long as that fear is there, they will give us grief. I'd rather suffer than have my family live that way."

Keilan turned toward the town and wondered out loud, "Who would allow Gavid to do something like this to Herium?"

The man gave a soft frustrated sigh. "The same people who believed what he was doing was right, that it was best for the town, despite it not being."

Keilan turned to the man and gave a nod. "Then tell me who those people are and we shall make sure they pay for this. Our region is under attack and he's part of the reason for it."

The man gave a slight nod then spoke of several families. Although Keilan and the others didn't want to be rid of them currently, it would be taken care of after the attack.

Rainah spoke again. "Come with us, we could use your skills as we could use others. Gavid punished you, we will make it right. Get a hot meal, a fresh bath, and some clothes. Why not stay in the inn right here. The snow elves from Dalyor are willing to keep you safe."

The man looked at the inn where there were several snow elven soldiers walking around and setting up a defensive place.

He looked at his little girl. "It would be nice to feel safe until this blows over. I'm sure there would be others who would be willing to go there."

She smiled, she heard another voice behind her and smiled more. The man quickly bowed and Rainah turned to see Ledric.

He walked to the group. "How bad is it, my dear?"

149

"Worse than can be imagined. These people refused to help Gavid. According to this man, there are people in town who are well off for helping Gavid because they believed it was best of the town."

Ledric looked at the man and then back toward Herium. "Do you know who it is?"

Rainah knew Ledric was angry, but hiding it. "I do. When we get back to the inn I'll tell you so you can take care of them."

Maellan looked at the man. "Can you get as many people from town into the safety of the inn as possible? The safer they are, the less likely they are to be killed. Gavid is not going to return here for a while, he fled for a reason. I'm sure that if he knew we were here, he would never come back at all."

The man looked at his daughter then spoke about getting their family and others to come into town, he would take them to the inn closest to their homes.

Ledric liked this and was proud of his sons. He took Rainah by the arm and walked her away from the area speaking softly, "We have to give them jobs and get rid of the people who would rather help Gavid. I'm sure he gave those who favored him the shops of the ones who didn't."

Soon, the families who were living in huts in town were in the inn nearby. Ledric and his family joined them in a time of happiness and celebration. Ugex and his group were more than happy to have them and utilize their skills.

There were several discussions, the skilled elves were happy to help those who helped them in return. Plenty of armor and weapon crafters were glad to help.

Ledric told an aid to set up a blacksmith shop not far from there. There were several elves that said there were two shops empty. He decided that's where they should be. He informed people of the several empty buildings and Ugex told them they could have as much ore as they desired, he had plenty to help. He would pay for their services as well.

Soon, the poorer elves of the town were set up in Ugex's inn. They were buzzing about returning the favor of those who helped them. He sighed and leaned back. Soon Ledric was alone with Ugex, Ugex's family, and his own.

Ugex sat with his brothers and Ledric's family. "Sire, the situation is bad. How could those people think Gavid's plan was the best for this town?"

Maellan grumped and looked out the window. "It's those people who helped pull down this town. Where was the leadership in this?"

Ugex sat and looked at Maellan. "Gervis believed that it was safe to do this. He, as well as us, were tricked into thinking Gavid wasn't going to do what he did. We were told, by the Dragons, just to keep an eye on him until further notice. We didn't realize he was going to do something so evil."

He stared down into the glass he had in his hand. Ledric's family could tell there was something more in how he regarded this, but something told them to let it go.

Maellan was unsure, but spoke anyway, "So the Dragons allowed this to happen? But why?"

Ugex regarded Maellan and rubbed his forehead. "Because someone informed them it would be okay. Turns out, someone was tricking everyone and was actually working with Gavid. Gervis wouldn't have done half of what he did, had he not been charmed into believing she was his wife. We tried to tell him otherwise."

Maellan was confused and wanted to ask, but Rainah put her hand on his and patted it. "Maellan, there was a woman who claimed to be Gervis' wife, she told everyone it would be best if they faded from the scene and allowed Gavid to take over Herium until they returned. She said their lives depended on it. Turned out, it was just a trick."

Ugex was feeling remorse and didn't look up. He was hurting deeply, but he continued to keep it to himself. Sensing the awkward situation, Ledric told his sons and his wife it was time to check on their own inn and leave Ugex and his brothers alone. They agreed and left for the night.

Derix cleared his throat and stood up. "No need reflecting, brother. We have other things to do right now. When the time comes, we'll make this right."

Ugex gave a slight nod and then went to check on everyone. In the back of his mind he was still mourning over what happened.

CHAPTER 18

Lugduf wandered through the cave in the darkness with two other goblins. They were set to scout the town of Herium to see what was there. Slipping through the shadows, the goblins snuck around the trees skirting the town. Herium was much further than they believed it to be, but they managed to find it. The night covered their presence, but would not for long.

As they approached the town, Lugduf stopped and noticed there was a wall of stone before them. The elves walked around and didn't seem to care about the surroundings outside of it. The town was also prepping staves and covering them in the ground. Either they were aware of the oncoming attack or Gavid was not there and the town was simply protecting itself from his return.

The three goblins wrote down some notes, details about the town, soon they darted back into the shadows of the forest. The snow below their feet crunched softly, giving away their location if anyone else was paying attention nearby.

They were on the edge of the forest soon and the cave was in sight. Lugduf pointed at the opening and mumbled something about bringing information to Jael or going back home. They were close and it didn't like seem the town was aware of it. Jael paid them well enough to be happy and he would probably forget he sent them out. His memory had been fleeting a lot lately.

"What do you want to do, brothers?" Lugduf spoke softly. "Do you want to go home and be rid of Gavid and Jael or do we come back to Jael and report what's going on in Herium?"

The brothers didn't know how to reply, instead Lugduf gave a frustrating sigh and spoke for them. "Fine, we'll just go home. There's no need for Jael to know they're not aware of the goblins in the cave. He doesn't need us to get the information he needs anyway. I'm sure he could simply ask Gavid."

The brothers agreed with a shake of their heads. Lugduf and his brothers started to turn and make their way back home when they heard sounds behind them. They turned to see an elven ranger landing on the grass. He knelt down and the three goblins realized their position had been given away. They hadn't tasted the blood of an elf in a long time, without thinking of the mission, the turned to the elf with their daggers drawn.

The ranger swiftly drew his bow before the goblins could start their charge and was firing an arrow on Lugduf's left. The arrow landed square in the chest of one goblin, sending him flying into the darkness as the other two continued to charge. The elven ranger dropped his bow and drew his sword, waiting for the two goblins arrive. The ranger swung at the one on the right and was defensive with both of them. Soon Lugduf's brother fell and the darkness pulled him down. Lugduf, in a blind rage that his brothers were dead, went on the offense and found his swings being parried.

The ranger, calm and relaxed, parried every offensive attack Lugduf could think of and soon he was on the ground exhausted, but continuing to put up a fight. The ranger put his sword away then took Lugduf by the shoulders and lifted him up. He shoved him hard into the darkness. The shadows grabbed him and pulled him in. The last sounds of the goblin were screams of anguish. The ranger spoke out loud. "Why are they now deciding to leave?"

He climbed up the tree again and looked at the others who were scattered along the path, hearing his answer in the shadows. "Perhaps they were getting impatient, Sergar, and they're just ready to go out of the cave."

Sergar jumped and nearly fell off the limb that held him. The shadows grabbed his arm and pulled him back into the tree. Sergar grumbled at the shadows. "Weisgar, I wish you wouldn't do that."

The shadow elf came out of the darkness, his charcoal gray hair and ginger brown eyes were the only difference between being a shadow elf or a snow elf. Weisgar, sitting beside his friend, smiled. "So how many goblins have you seen?"

Sergar glanced to the cave and then back to his friend. "Those were the only ones we've seen. I'd like to know the numbers."

Weisgar slipped back into the shadows before replying. "Give me a moment and we can tell you what's going on in there."

Sergar shivered then sat in the limb and waited as Weisgar made his way into the cave. Sergar sat watching as did many others along the path line. He closed his eyes for a moment and relaxed. There were no other goblins coming and if there were, the shadows would have been alerted. There was a touch on his shoulder not long after and he opened his eyes to see another snow elven ranger, her hair was flowing and dark brown, perfect for blending in with the woods. Her green eyes seemed to sparkle with excitement.

Sergar spoke softly, "What is it, Celalwe? I haven't been here that long."

She sat with him on the limb and looked out at the cave, then back to him. "You've seen a bit of action. I just wanted to check on you to see if you were okay."

He glanced down at the blood on his shirt and nodded. "I'm fine. Some goblins came from town and I guess they were talking about what they were going to tell the leader."

She nodded. "The shadow elves mentioned to me that you had troubles and brought me here, but by the time I arrived to help, it was over."

He leaned back and smiled to her. She wore a dark green leather vest with a soft velvet brown shirt. "Well, I'm fine, okay," he said in a pretend grizzly tone.

"I see that and I just wanted to break the boredom. Watching that cave and sitting here doing nothing is boring as it is, but doing it for days is just insane."

He cut an eye to her and then leaned against the tree. Sergar couldn't help but smile at the vision he saw. They had been bonded for only a month and he knew she was to be with him forever. After being alone for sometime, it was going to take some getting use to.

Celalwe couldn't help but giggle and looked at the cave. "Still, when did the goblins leave?"

He turned his attention back to the cave and considered it for a moment then gave her a reply, "The shadow elves alerted us about an hour ago. Those were the only three, which is weird. Usually, if there was going to be an attack, they would have come out with more than just three goblins."

She sat and listened to him, placing her bow in her lap, looking at the cave again. "Perhaps they were seeing if Gavid left. I know they don't know the town is aware of them. I was informed they were unaware."

He grunted and turned back to the cave. "Still, something is off. I guess we'll have to wait for Weisgar to return and tell us what's going on and how many there are."

She stared distantly at the cave and shrugged. "Perhaps they're aware Gavid isn't in Herium and wanted to test the boundaries as to how far as they could go without getting caught."

He pondered the thought and just shook his head. "I don't think so. They would have sent more men to attack the town. I'm not sure why it was only three."

She kissed him softly and stood up carefully, turning to him for a moment. "Well, you can think on it more. I'm going to go back to my post. I hope to see some action as well."

Leaping off the limb, she blew him a kiss then landed on the ground. She walked as careful as possible back to her post.

Sergar looked at the cave again and continued to ponder the thought until Weisgar returned to him.

The ebon wood trees towered over Meranda and Treidon as they walked through the city.

"Do they still use the bark of the ebon wood in the swords and bows?" Meranda wondered out loudly.

Treidon glanced at the trees and shook his head. "No, they're sacred and we don't even think of using the trees in that fashion."

Meranda gave a long sigh then walked up to one of the ebon trees and touched it. She closed her eyes for a moment and mumbled a word. The tree lit up the night sky and everyone around came out to see what was going on.

Treidon watched in amazement as Meranda dismissed the spell and the tree faded back to normal. "You see, the Riftrider's weapons were made of ebon wood. I don't understand why they stopped making them with it. It's important for people to learn that again."

Rubbing his head, Treidon was still amazed and awestruck at the fact Meranda just cast a light spell through the tree.

He watched as she bent down and picked up a piece of the ebon bark and mumbled another spell and handed it to him. "Here. I still can't believe you don't use it in your weapons."

He took it and watched in amazement as she walked away from him. Suddenly, he looked down at the bark and it was ice cold in his hand. Catching up with her, he spoke gently, "Meranda, we can't just take the bark off of the trees."

She stopped walking as some of the townspeople were staring with fascination, she seemed to walk on air to them. "Why not? Who made them the most sacred things in the realm that we can't utilize the tree bark to help Riftriders protect the realm?" She was displeased at these facts.

He gave a shrug because he didn't know the answer. Aislinn stopped Meranda, noticing she seemed upset. "Treidon, might I ask who this fiery woman is?"

Meranda stopped and smiled. "I am Meranda, Gervis' daughter, and someone who apparently needs to show Treidon the value of the ebon bark."

Aislinn stood in amazement for a moment and glanced at Treidon who was flustered at her. "Tell her the trees are revered and we can't use them in our weapons."

Smiling, Aislinn looked at Meranda, gently took her arm and walked away with her. "I know that we use them in our weapons for their magical properties. However, someone a long time ago decided the trees needed to be preserved. We, as Riftriders, fought the news and we still sneak the bark off the ground to make some of our own weapons, but people like Treidon thought that weapon casting was crazy."

Meranda turned to Treidon who still didn't believe. "It *is* crazy and tedious. That entire concentration on the spell through the weapon is too much for me."

"You saw what I did out there. I couldn't have blown those gnomes away from you if I hadn't known how to weapon cast," Meranda said in a not so friendly tone.

Aislinn couldn't help but smile then pulled Meranda toward the trial arena. "Perhaps when the time comes for us to test you, you could show him how important it is. Once his father sees how important it is, perhaps he will allow us to use the bark again."

Treidon groaned and followed Meranda to the trial area. There was an elven man with long blond hair and dark skin looking down as the pair walked into the arena. She was immediately intimidated by the size of the place. It was painted with murals of Riftriders of the past who achieved things in battle which needed to be expressed. Slowly, she began to back away from the arena, but felt Treidon's hand grabbing onto her. She shook her head. "I can't, Treidon. I can't go in there."

"Not even for me?" He smiled with confidence then encouraged her to go in.

Against her will, she walked in and looked around. The building itself was beautiful with the stone work interlocking together. However, the inside was vastly different. The paintings towered all the way up to the top and chandeliers were hanging low burning brightly to help display the art to its best ability.

They finally arrived at one of the arenas and Treidon walked in with her, but she stood firm. The room was large. It had a wall that surrounded the dirt floor and benches above the wall leading toward the back of the room and angling up toward the ceiling. Some of the area seemed to be for important people with more comfortable seating.

Treidon walked in and looked back at Meranda. "This is where we hold some of the trials. It's not as big as others, but it does do a good job of showcasing a small group of Riftriders."

He held out his hand and she shook her head. Her body language changed from outside of the building to more child-like. Uncertain, lacking confidence, and hesitant, Meranda stood at the door way. She suddenly felt a pair of hands behind her shove her in. She winced in pain from her shoulder and the fall, she turned to see no one behind her. Continuing to bit her lip in pain, Treidon turned his attention to her and walked up to her. "Are you okay?"

She paled, then began crying and pulling away. Meranda tried to make her way to the door, she wanted to run, but it seemed she couldn't make her legs move.

The man at the door earlier walked through and noticed the pair. "Is she okay?"

Treidon shook his head. "Please close the door. I need her to realize she's fine."

The man closed the door and stood in the room with them, just in case he was needed.

Meranda fell to her knees and cried more. Soon she was starting to scrap her arms, making herself bleed. Treidon knew it was a nightmare trying to kill her. He went to her, knelt beside her, and touched her face. She growled and fought him, continuing to cry in fear. Ignoring the pain, he grabbed her arms and held her down as she fought.

"Is there anything I can do?" the voice of the man spoke up.

"Cirian, she's having a nightmare. I have to find a way to get her out of it. If not, she could kill herself. I've witnessed it many times, just stand there in case she uses her strength to get away," Treidon said, turning for only a second then looking back at her.

The tears flowed down his own face as he was both upset and from her tears. He closed his eyes and transferred gentle thoughts, helping her to fight the latest monster invading her mind.

Cirian watched in amazement as Meranda relaxed and Treidon opened his eyes.

Cirian spoke as he approached them, "What happened to such a brilliant mind? She would bring back the old ways of things if what you say is true about the weapon casting."

Treidon handed Cirian a piece of ebon bark. "She put a cold spell on it. She also cast daylight through one of the ebon trees."

"That was her?" he stared in surprise as he took the ebon bark. "She learned the ways from her father?"

Treidon sat beside Meranda as she slowly opened her eyes and looked at him, the man in the room then laid back on the dirt floor and groaned.

Treidon turned to Cirian and gave a simple nod. Cirian continued to stare at her. "So who did this to her? I'll make sure they pay for it."

Meranda sat slowly up, still feeling the pain in her shoulder, she turned to Treidon. Treidon glanced at Cirian. "We won't mention his name, but he *will* pay for this."

Cirian helped her up and smiled. "I'm sorry you're going through this, but we'll find a way to make things right."

Meranda rubbed her shoulder and gave a slight nod, Treidon gave a smile. "Well, if you will excuse us Cirian, it's nearly time for dinner. I'm sure my father has some things planned."

Cirian looked at Meranda and gave an encouraging smile. "It will be all right. I promise you, we'll make it right."

Meranda gave a slight nod, but was still mentally tired. She barely mustered the reply. "Thank you. I'm sorry you had to witness that."

Treidon took her arm and Cirian walked out with them. "Don't you think about it. We'll make this right and you won't have to worry about anything much longer apparently."

Meranda looked at Treidon who was grinning from ear to ear as they walked out of the arena.

Cirian watched as the pair walked toward the castle and he sighed. He walked back to the Riftrider building and looked at Quoin. "There has to be something we can do for her."

The mocha skinned colored man nodded. "We will. We've decided to do something unorthodox. Make sure she comes to the arena tonight after dinner."

Cirian gave a smile then walked out to take care of the request while Quion went to make sure things were prepared.

CHAPTER 19

U gex watched out the window as Ledric and his family slowly convinced the poorest townspeople to come into the inns. He looked at his brothers, telling them to prepare rooms for families and make sure they were taken care of. Derix and Quesep both walked out and Ugex went into the office of the inn. He walked up to the mirror and touched it after mumbling a short spell. Soon a white haired man almost identical to Ugex appeared in the mirror.

"Gervis told me they made it to Elmwick. I hope you're in Herium?"

Ugex gave a nod then looked around. "We are, father. It seems Jael was ready to be rid of us anyways, so we decided to come here and help Gervis' town while he's away. Gavid really did a bad number on this place. There are people who are struggling because they stood up for Gervis. Then there are those who conformed to Gavid and would rather not suffer the same fate."

Hariton gave a small frown and understood. "We'll send them funds to help get them back on their feet. I'm sure King Ledric would like the help as well. Just tell him, we'll be sending funds soon. So, what are you hearing about the attacks of the town?"

Ugex looked out the window and noticed Linden walking up then glanced back at his father. "We know they're planning to do so soon, although we did slow them down somewhat. There are plenty of ores and resources in the storage area. I'm sure we'll have people who weren't helping Gavid here and we'll be well supplied."

Hariton and Ugex both heard the door knock and Ugex turned to his father. "That's Linden. I'm sure he wants a report."

Hariton gave a nod then vanished. Ugex walked to the door and opened it up, seeing Linden before him. "Good to see you again, my lord. What can I do for you?"

Linden walked passed him and waited for Ugex to shut the door. "I'm just checking on the progress of the poor here on this side of town. Are they willing to come this far for protection?"

"King Ledric and Queen Rainah convinced them to at least come here or go to the inn where we are. We're slowing adding people in as they make their way to us," he said turning to the window.

Linden walked to the window as well and noticed at least thirty families in need and he gave a long sigh. "How could I not see this sooner? Why did I listen to my wife and not help them?"

Ugex gave the same sigh and replied, "Because we were duped into believing what we were doing was right."

Linden glanced with curiosity. "We? You're not part of this town. What were you duped into believing?"

Ugex sighed and tried to make an excuse. "*We* were duped into believing this town was okay. We had no idea that this town was in such shambles. Like you, we didn't know what was really going on."

Linden glanced at him and pondered for a moment. "You look familiar. Do I know you?"

Ugex shook his head no then gave a smile. "No, you don't know me, but we have been around this town doing some shopping in the past and trading, perhaps that's when you saw me."

Linden gave a nod and turned back to Ugex. "That's probably it. We're one of the only trading towns here in the snow region. I just came here to check on you and see what the plan was for your troops. They seem to have made themselves at home here in the inn."

Ugex couldn't help but grin and watched through the window as several of his own people helped those of the town make their way into the inn. He turned to Linden and spoke quietly, "They volunteered to come here. I didn't even have to ask them to do so."

"That's good to see, they actually want to help. I'm glad you were able to do so. Thank you for taking the time to talk to me. So, what's the plan to protect Herium?" Linden turned to the snow elf and waited for a reply.

Ugex gave a smile then spoke, "We plan on putting our troops outside of the make-shift part of town and wait until they come attack then counter-attack them. The shadow elves should help us too."

Linden gave a nod and stared at the elven man before him with kind and considerate eyes. "If you need anything, let me know."

Ugex gave a chuckle. "We have plenty. Your storage building is full of metals, gemstones, and the like anyways." Surprised, Linden didn't know how to reply. Ugex smiled again. "Think of it as a gift. The shadow elves told us about the mining in the cave where the goblins were. I made the suggestion to bring what they were mining here to your storage area."

"Well, we didn't think of that when we first saw the cave. Our first thought was defense and protecting this town. Thank you for thinking of us, but when did the shadow elves come to you?" Linden asked as he moved around the room and found himself a place to sit without seeming rude.

Ugex sat down on the couch across from Linden and glanced at him. "When the slave girl announced that Gavid had been doing what he was doing, the shadow elves brought the news to us. They knew you were going to need help."

Linden took a deep breath to cool his anger and turned to the elven man. "That slave girl is my sister. I know you didn't know that, but please don't call her that. Her name is Meranda."

Ugex mentally smiled, but gave a nod not to give it away. "I'm sorry. I just know that she was living with Gavid outside or I was told by the shadow elves. If she were your sister why didn't you save her?"

This question frustrated Linden, but not wanting to offend the elf before him, he stood up and turned away, walked to the window, and stared out of it. He watched the poorest elves of the town collecting a few things from their homes to make their way to the inn. Linden gave a soft sigh before he replied, "I was told she was fine."

Ugex noticed the turmoil and heartache in his face, walked up to him, put his hand on Linden's shoulder, and glanced out of the window with him. "Well, you found out otherwise and before it was too late. I hope she is safe now, but you can't beat yourself up over all of this."

Linden gave a quick nod, but didn't reply. Ugex could tell his heart was troubled by the way she was treated. He cursed inwardly that he could do nothing to help her before. Ugex could tell this troubled Linden and spoke, "Let's change the subject. There is more than plenty of ore out there to help everyone make armor and whatever else you need for the oncoming attack."

Linden turned to the man and shook his hand. "Indeed, it was a pleasure to meet you. I need to get back and get those ores to the smelters and whoever else can use it. Again, thank you for the help, in everything."

Ugex smiled which made Linden wonder again about how he knew this man, but he dropped it as Ugex gave a reply, "The honor was mine, my lord. Please, come back anytime. Until this thing is over we'll not be leaving."

Linden excused himself, Ugex walked to the window and watched him leave. Ugex sighed deeply, keeping his life a secret until the right time was painful and was causing more trouble than good, but to keep it from his own family was even more painful. He wondered how much longer he had to keep up the charade then decided to put it from his mind. He made his way outside to check on the troops, the town, and his brothers to make sure things were in order and the make-shift part of town's people gathered what they needed to make their way to the inn for protection.

Weisgar slipped away from the rangers and down into the forest. He asked several other shadow elves to follow him through the darkness to the cave to see what was going on. They split up and made their way deeper into the cave, using goblin shadows to find their way into the room of the goblin king. The shadows slipped around the room to see what the plan was. Weisgar knew he needed to inform those in command about it. He pulled the paper containing the plan from the top of the desk, waved his hand, and got an identical copy in his other hand. Smiling, he placed the paper back on the desk and wandered deeper into the cave. The goblins were clueless as to who was in the cave with them. They continued to mine and do their own work.

They soon hopped the shadows into the storage area. Weisgar turned to his friends and pointed to the resources. They all nodded and slipped under the resources, sending them by chain through the shadows all the way back to a storage area in Herium. This took the better part of the day, but they soon rid the goblins of most of their ore, gems, and other resources then slipped deeper into the cave to find the blacksmiths working on armor. Weisgar followed them into the shadows, soon he found where they were keeping the weapons and armor. Silently, while the blacksmiths' backs were turned, the shadow elves took the weapons and armor to the storage area in Herium for smelting and repurposing them for other things.

Weisgar looked at the other shadow elves and commanded them to take a count of everyone in the cave. They all separated into many of the cave's rooms and counted, giving a rough estimate of how many were in the each room. Once this was done they gathered outside and discussed what the possibilities were.

Weisgar pulled out the plan. "We have about three to five hundred goblins planning to attack Herium. How many do we figure we have in the cave now?"

The rest gave him an amount they saw in each of the rooms and he figured it to be around fifteen hundred total in the cave itself. He sat and figured out that over half of the goblins would be leaving for home, according to the plan.

He looked up at the group and decided they needed to report to the Dragons, letting them know what is going on. Then they needed to tell Ledric and the others know about it. The shadows faded away in the darkness and travelled to the forest elven town of Eimlar. The castle was guarded, but not from the shadow elves who slipped past them silently. They made their way into the dining hall where several of the Dragon Counsel members were eating. Weisgar knocked on the door, just to be polite, then waited to be asked to enter.

Hariton stood up and nodded at his friend. "How goes the snow region? What are you here to report?"

Weisgar noticed Morida then turned to Hariton. "Ledric and others in Herium are preparing for an attack from the goblins. The plan is, around five hundred goblins will be attacking the city. The others will be heading home. How is Meranda?"

He noticed Morida's mouth turn down and that was all he needed to continue with the question. "Is all okay with her?"

Hariton gave an exhausting sigh. "It seems that nightmare demons are trying to kill her, but we can't figure out why."

Weisgar gave a nod and then shrugged. "She was being attacked long before she was freed. Gavid was trying to kill her too. We have been able to stop some of those nightmares before. Now that she's in Elmwick, I'm sure she's safe."

"No, she had another nightmare demon attack her earlier and they continue to attack her. I need to do research to find out why or capture one and get it to tell me why," Morida said standing up.

A couple of plains elven men stood up and one spoke, "We've observed her birthmark, it glowed."

Morida nodded and regarded them. "We'll have to do research on that as well. Weisgar, can you find Kavan and Oriana and ask them to watch over her to make sure she's safe?"

Weisgar bowed and excused himself. He vanished into the darkness and made his way to the castle of Elmwick and appeared before Kavan. "Greetings, brother. How does it go?"

Kavan looked up from his desk and shook his head. "Treidon hates us, but I guess I should have known that was coming. What are you doing here?"

Weisgar sat across from him and smiled. "Always straight to business, eh? Word from the Dragon Counsel. You and Oriana need to keep a close eye on Meranda. Those nightmare demons have been trying to kill her and until the Dragons figure out why, you two are assigned to make sure she stays safe."

Kavan gave a nod. "At least she likes us. Treidon has anger for something we did when he was an infant to protect him and his family. I wish Morida would tell them what actually went on. Pagues really won't accept the fact that we saved his and his family's lives."

Weisgar paused for a moment and then looked at Kavan. "Perhaps Meranda and Gervis can help. They believe that we are there to help, not harm."

"Perhaps," Kavan said standing up and walked to his friend. "Perhaps Morida could tell Pagues the truth too. His own brother wanted to kill him."

Weisgar nodded in agreement and then looked around the room. "I have to get back to Herium. She's okay, right? Other than the nightmare demons? I'm sure her brothers would like to know as well as King Ledric."

Kavan smiled and reassured Weisgar. "Other than that, she's fine. She's been putting Treidon in his place. Although the nightmare demons pushed her into the arena area which made her drop her defenses then they attacked her. We killed one," he continued. "But the damage was done. Treidon saved her with the help of Cirian. Such a damaged soul. I hope the Dragons can find out why she's being tormented by the demons so much."

Weisgar stood up, shook his friend's hand, then turned to the door before turning back to his friend. "I'll let you know anything more I find out, but thank you for telling me about Meranda. As the counsel suggests, protect her. She might be more important than we can imagine."

He didn't wait for a reply, but left the room and faded back into the shadows, going back to Herium.

Kavan called Oriana to ask for an update. She appeared before him from the shadows and walked up to him. She wore a shirt and pants both made of black velvet. She sat on the desk in front of him and smiled. "Meranda is with Treidon right now. What do you need, my dear?"

He looked up at her in a serious mood. "The Dragon Counsel wants us to keep a protective eye on her. We do not have time to be with one another right now, she will need our undivided attention."

She frowned as she stared at him in a serious fashion. "Is she okay? I mean, I've seen those nightmare demons after her and we've stopped them, but there aren't any more are there?"

He stood up and glanced to her. "It seems, she's in more danger than we believed. We need to keep an eye on the child. She's faced enough adversity and I don't want her to face more."

Oriana gave a long and loving sigh. "When we have children, they will be loved and supported because you will not allow them to be unprotected. I love that about you."

Gently, she leaned in and kissed him softly then vanished back into the shadows.

He smiled, children would be a thing of the near future, not anytime soon. He stood up and walked to the shadows of the room, vanishing into the darkness to help his wife.

CHAPTER 20

As the darkness slowly came upon Herium, the town folks gathered into homes and inns around. A lot of the poorer people of the town found their way to the Hunted Fox Inn by invitation of King Ledric and his family.

The poorer elves did their best to dress nicer, but it was apparent who had money and who didn't. He welcomed the people who were more plainly dressed to eat at his table. Several of the richer elves poked and snickered at those around Ledric and his family. There were several remarks about how they shouldn't be allowed to sit at a prestigious table.

Ledric was frustrated at how everyone who was better off was treating those at his table. He stood up and addressed the entire room, "How are you better than these people at my table? In my eyes, those of you who're ridiculing them are worse off because you all agreed that it was better to go along with Gavid than to refuse what he was doing to the town. These people refused and they paid the price."

Several of the more well-off elves looked at their dinner plates in shame, but one snow elven man stood up and responded to the king, "Sire, we did what we believed was best for our families and we knew that it wasn't for the best. We needed to survive. We couldn't find ourselves like those people." He motioned to his table and several of the downtrodden elves did not even look up as he continued, "They chose this life. We didn't choose it for them."

Ledric clinched his fist and then felt his wife's hand on his arm. He took a deep breath. "You chose to help Gavid, but you could have also chosen to help those who were in need. We have to help each other or things will never improve. That's why things are like they are. No one seems to help anyone when they're down. It's not like they would simply kill you for what you have. Just help them."

The man shook his head and replied again, "Sire, Gavid had informed us that if we helped them, we would be in the same position. We couldn't have that."

Rainah had enough and stood up. "You should all be ashamed. Who cares that Gavid would take all that you had away from you just because you supported your friends. Some of you discovered that there were families in need, but you did nothing. Look at these elves! We all have to get along to survive! You could have reported to us! Why did you not do that in the first place? If you had, no one would be in this situation."

Ledric nodded and looked at the man who dared to stand up to the king. "Sir, what is your name and what do you do?" The man shook his head not wanting to tell him. Ledric grumbled. "Please, tell me your name and what do you do."

"The name is Finasaer, sire. I'm the chief blacksmith of the town. Gavid would hire me to do any metal working."

"Finasaer," Ledric said walking to the man as Rainah sat down. "I have met several poorer blacksmiths that do quality work."

Finasaer tried to back up, but he had no where to go. Ledric had his hands behind his back as he approached. "What did you do that is of quality that I might have seen?"

"Sire, I made the swords in which your guards carry," Finasaer replied with confidence.

A man jumped up and shouted from the king's table, "Those were my swords, Finasaer! You took them and showed them to Gavid! You were my apprentice until you saw an opportunity to take my shop from me!"

Ledric, without taking his hands from his back, turned to the man at his table. "You're telling me those swords the guards carry are yours?"

The man was now angrier than ever and just gave a firm nod.

Turning back, Ledric regarded Finasaer, "What is your reply?" Ledric asked in an even tone.

Finasaer shook his head. "That's a lie! I don't even know who that man is. I made those swords for your guards and sent them to you."

Ledric put his hand up before the man at his table could retort. "So, tell me, what are they made of?"

The man sat down and grumbled in frustration as others in the inn watched. Finasaer shifted his weight to his other foot, a show of nervousness, as he tried his best to reply. "Sire, they're iron. Crafted with bits of gold and copper intertwined into them."

Ledric gave a slight nod then something caught his attention. The man was shaking his head no. He called a guard to his side, who was willing to hand him his sword to show him the quality of work. He felt the blade, it was colder than a normal iron sword and he turned to the man at the table. "What is your name, sir?"

"Legimli, sire. That sword is not made of iron like Finasaer has said. It's made with a natural snow elven metal, Celomion, it has a slight green tint to it if you hold it to the light a certain way. The metal, when heated will turn a beautiful purple."

Finasaer shook his head in protest but Ledric sharply turned to him and the man stopped. He started to observe the sword, twisting it in the light in different ways. He walked to the candle on the middle of the table and put the tip in. The crowd watched as the tip turned purple instead of red. He carefully put it in a glass of water nearby to cool it off then Ledric gently handed it back to the guard. Smiling, he looked at Legimli, "Beautiful work. Please, I would like to pay you to do one for my entire army. That would be a thousand swords and sets of armor. What would be the price to do it in the same metal that you did that one in?"

Finasaer started to speak up again in protest, this was *his* money that *he* should be earning. He stood up and charged at the king. The guards were on the move to stop him when Ledric turned and held out a small dagger made with the same metal. Finasaer stopped within inches of the blade and looked at the king. "That is my work, I *swear* to you."

Ledric put the dagger away then looked at his guards. "Take him away for trying to attack the king. Put him in the depths of the dungeons here. Legimli, you can take your shop back then make those pieces, once things settle down here."

The guards grabbed Finasaer by the arms and took him away. He continued to protest that he made the swords.

Ledric looked at the rest of the crowd. "Anyone else care to tell me why they didn't help these people? Or just keep ridiculing them for trying to save their town?"

No one else in the inn responded, they feared the king. He finally took a deep breath, sighed and sat back down to regard those at his table. "I will commission everyone here to do something for my family and me. I will help you get back on your feet once the attack from the goblins is over. Please, this meal is on me and any others in the future. I'm sorry that I didn't come to your aid sooner. Please, accept my apology."

Several from the richer area of the inn came to Ledric's table and spoke to those sitting. Some were offered jobs, while others offered help. The lesson had been put out there. To help those in need help, not to take advantage of people in dire straits.

Soon, the inn emptied, leaving Ledric and his family alone. Maellan looked at his father. "I can't believe there are people out there who would take pride in someone else's work when they could do their own."

He gave a slight nod then turned to the door. Rainah looked at their sons. "As you can see, this town is more about who helped Gavid and who didn't. Those that didn't were on the bad end of this and that's not how it should be. Find out who helped. Although there were several here that did, I want to know about the ones who didn't."

Their sons gave a nod and excused themselves as Ledric turned back to Rainah. "That will be hard to do now, we've made a point and it will spread. We'll have to move swiftly before people are less likely to admit it."

Rainah smiled in agreement, taking his arm leading him to their room for a nightcap and bedtime.

After Meranda and Treidon left, Gervis sat down to talk with Pagues. "I'm sorry, we hadn't contacted you or anyone else about the situation. I was tricked into believing it was for the best. A demon in the form of a woman came and convinced me that it was."

Pagues leaned back and looked at Gervis. "We could have helped had we known what was going on. This news that Meranda has shared with us is grave indeed. However, I understand why you were doing what you were doing, but can you answer a question? What is going on between my son and your daughter?"

Gervis grinned and stared at Pagues. "They're bonded. Compare the scars, because they share the same ones. Treidon knew it was true the moment he saw her life fleeting before him. She's a great Riftrider and will put your students to shame when her time comes for a trial."

Pagues couldn't help but grin with him, then gave a long sigh. "I've heard you were brought here by the shadow elves, so you work with them. You know I don't like the shadow elves. They killed my brother."

Gervis face showed no shock, but he glanced at Pagues. "You know your brother wanted you dead, despite you not hearing a word of it. It's just like the towns around you, there are dangers you were not aware of, but they're there. They were assigned by your wife and the Dragon Counsel to take care of him. He wanted to kill you."

Angry, Pagues raised his voice. "My brother would never do something that severe to us. He loved me and my family and would rather die for us then to kill us."

Gervis grumbled and sat forward in the chair. "The shadow elves only carry out commands from the Dragon Counsel and protect those who need it. You needed it, your family needed it, and your kingdom needed it."

Pagues held onto his anger as he noticed how calm Gervis was. "You know nothing about those *monsters!*" he shouted at Gervis. "They killed my brother and I will not have that lingering on me. I do not believe for one second, my brother wanted to kill me or my family."

Gervis shook his head and stood up. "Your majesty, Kavan and Oriana are your protectors, they are sent by the Dragon Counsel, because of who you are. Talk to Morida, your wife will know the truth. You cannot know everything that goes on around you. Look at those towns being taken over, there's a plot to choke you out of your own kingdom. Now that the Dragon Counsel and the shadow elves are aware, things will be back to normal soon." Pagues fought the anger from his friend and turned away as Gervis stared in amazement. "Your denial will only hurt you. I would rather you and your family were safe for my daughter, than dead at the hands of someone who was greedy. Think about it. Did your brother do things that were questionable? Did he do things that would give you pause because it was something out of the ordinary and he would change when you caught on?"

Pagues was thrown off by this question and as he thought about it the more his anger subsided. Soon, he realized his brother was doing things he couldn't explain. "But why did he do those things? He didn't want to kill me or my family. I know it. He wasn't *that* heartless."

Soon a knock on the door made the pair turn, they both stood up and Pagues walked to the door, opening it to see Oriana and Kavan before him.

The anger came back full force as they walked into the room. He pulled a dagger that was at his side, quickly drawing it on Oriana.

She gave a long sigh and shook her head. "Pagues, do you really think you can kill me like that?" She pushed the dagger aside and walked further into the room. She felt the shadows moving and faded into the chair as Pagues tried to stab her in the back.

Kavan moved in rapid fashion and grabbed Pagues as he was off balance, took his dagger and helped him steady himself.

Oriana reappeared before him, sat down in a chair, and looked at him. "Sire, your brother was evil. He had a home not far from here, he was concocting some poisons to kill all of you while you ate."

Kavan gently let go of Pagues who was still in disbelief and shook his head. "While there were few things that would make me question what he did, he wouldn't kill his family. He simply wouldn't."

Kavan sat beside Gervis and his wife who looked at the king. "I know you doubt it, but it's true. That man was part of something evil. We think it was connected to this."

Infuriated, Pagues picked up a paperweight from his desk and tossed it at Gervis. He watched as Oriana grabbed the paperweight before it could hit Gervis, who was unmoved. She stood up slowly, walked to his desk, and put the paperweight down. "How long have we been friends before you found out this truth? It's been centuries and yet you're still holding a grudge about something that we did to protect your family. In those many years, we have yet to harm anyone else in your family. Have you ever wondered why that is?"

Pagues looked at her full of anger, but he never thought of why the shadow elves never took anyone else in his family.

Oriana started to take Pagues' hand and he jerked it back. She glanced at him. "Take my hand, I will not do anything that will harm you in any way."

Reluctantly, he took her hand and she sent him a wave of images of his brother grinding poisons, plotting his family's deaths, plans on how to make the kingdom the best without the Riftriders, and many other images that showed his brother in his true light. He jerked the hand away and fell backward. Kavan stood up quickly and caught him, gently sitting him in the chair.

Gervis watched the entire thing in silence. He watched as Pagues start crying. "How could I have been so stupid to believe my brother was innocent in any way?"

Oriana walked over to Pagues and knelt down to face the king. "Sire, we knew he was dangerous, you simply saw your family. You didn't want to suspect him of such evil, but anyone is capable of such things."

"That's the thing about family, no one expects them to do such evil deeds to their own," Kavan said. "You must teach your children the truth or they will continue to hate us for a long time."

He sighed and gave a long nod. "I'll have a talk with them. They need to know the truth. I am sorry for such hate for years. I realize that you and my wife kept trying to inform me, but I refused to listen. Can you forgive me?"

Oriana patted his leg and then stood up. "Think nothing of it, sire. We have already. Protecting you and your family is our top priority, although the Dragon Counsel has requested that we also watch Meranda closely."

This interested Gervis and he stood up. "Why would they want to watch Meranda closer than normal?"

Oriana turned and regarded Gervis. "The Dragon Counsel seems to think there are demons trying to kill her. We've seen several, as have you, out there. We recently stopped another one while Meranda was in the trial arena."

Gervis started at the pair of them for a moment. "Is she okay?"

The pair gave a slight nod and then looked at Pagues who stopped crying and looked more concerned about Meranda than what happened in the past.

He finally took a deep breath. "Perhaps having her tested might not be a good idea. Especially if her life is being threatened."

The shadow elves turned to him and Gervis replied, "Sire, she is ready for the trials, the demons will always be threatening. As I said, I had a demon of a woman who told me all would be okay. We don't know why they want her dead."

Pagues gave a slight nod and then stood up. "Very well. I have a dinner planned tonight, please join us before you head home to Herium."

Gervis grinned and gave a slight nod. "It would be my honor. Now, if you'll excuse me, I must freshen up."

The shadow elves excused themselves too, everyone left Pagues to his own thoughts of the past.

CHAPTER 21

S itting and staring at the map, Jael wondered how long it would take the goblins to get to town and report back to him. Urdun knocked on the door and waited to be let in.

"Sire, we have a problem," he said as he walked in.

Jael turned to him and waited for him to continue. Urdun paused, not knowing how to state the problem. Finally, frustrated, Jael spoke up, "Well, what is it?"

Urdun noticed the frustration and decided to continue. "Sire, there are several pieces of armor, weapons, and resources gone. It's like someone came while we weren't in the storage area and took nearly everything."

Jael gave a simple nod then turned back to his map. His anger boiled inside as Urdun spoke again.

"Sire, what do you wish me to do?"

He turned back around to his second in command and calmly spoke, "How much armor and weapons are remaining? In other words, how many goblins can we suit up for this battle to make it look worthwhile?"

Urdun paused in thought for only a moment and then replied with confidence. "Sire, we have enough armor and weapons to outfit three hundred goblins."

Jael gave a nod and then asked his second in command. "How many days until we can get things ready for at least two hundred more?"

Urdun was confused, but replied, "It shouldn't take us that long if we constantly work on the mining and blacksmithing around the clock."

"Then we'll do that, thank you." Jael said turning back to the map.

"Sire?" Urdun questioned.

"What?"

"Why are you not angry about the missing ore and armor?"

Jael turned back to Urdun and grumbled. "I *am* angry. Those scouts I sent to get a report on Herium must have stolen almost everything I had. They've gone while we weren't watching and taken everything. I *am* angry, but they're gone and there's nothing I can do but fix the situation and repair the damage that's done."

Urdun understood, it made sense to him that the missing scouts and missing items were connected. He stood up and bowed to Jael. "Okay, that makes sense. I'll get on those pieces for you and we'll work around the clock to get them filled."

Jael smiled apologetically and stood up. "I'll come with you. We can at least work on a plan on how we might go about attacking the kingdom."

They walked out and several goblins stared for a moment and wondered what was going on. Urdun glanced at Jael. "So what's the plan? I know we have more than five hundred goblins in the cave. What do you want to do?"

Jael gave a knowing smile. "What I want to do is leave this cave, have you attack Herium, then we come back and build the town just above the cave. That way we don't have to worry any more about it."

Urdun gave a satisfying nod and looked around. "So we'll just send a small wave of troops that should take over Herium then take over their mine too? I love that idea! We just need to work out how the town would look on the outside."

Jael liked that idea and gave Urdun a noticeable smile. "That would be a great idea. I was thinking of putting the town on top of the mine."

Urdun shook his head and frowned in disapproval. "Sire," he said watching several goblins mining. "The best way to do it is to—"

Before Urdun could finish his sentence, goblins came screaming from the blacksmith area, yelling about a fire. That wouldn't be good if they couldn't contain it. The pair rushed back with the goblin to a blazing inferno as others rushed to find water. Soon, Jael screamed about finding some magic users that might be able to do it. A few people knew a couple and rushed out to find them. Urdun and Jael got out as many as they could to save them, in no time, everyone was accounted for. Not long after, a couple of mages showed up and doused the fire. The goblins went back to work and fixed those pieces that were useless by smelting them.

Jael looked at Urdun and spoke to him. "How long is this going to set us back?"

Urdun gave a shrug and watched the goblins working hard to get back on track then stared back at Jael. "Sire, I will assess the damage and report to you in a short while, once we figure it all out.

I think your idea has been a good one. We need to leave, allow those who wish to volunteer to do so, and then come back to build. We need to regroup and bring more of our people here."

Jael gave an acknowledging nod and replied to him, "That's good, we need to get back on track as soon as possible."

He left Urdun to tend to everyone and get them back on schedule. Walking back to his room, he noticed several goblins who were anxious to get into battle. They asked him how long would it be and he smiled. "Soon. We'll attack within the week. Be prepared."

They left him with the thought of who would he put in charge and before he realized, he was back at his office. He walked by his aid and smiled. "I need you to find six good leaders for six groups of fifty soldiers."

The aid grabbed his pad then stood up and walked out of the room, leaving Jael to himself. He sighed and wondered if this was all worth it. Was it worth coming back to mine the caves or just leave it alone?

Knowing the elves didn't know made him realize the caves weren't that important. Sure, there were resources here, but once they took over Herium, they could always come back to the cave to get what they needed.

He heard a sound in the shadows and turned around, not seeing anything. Turning back to his desk, he soon decided the cave wasn't worth keeping and would send out three hundred soldiers to attack the city and go home.

He went back to work on how to get everyone out as the shadows moved about him. Jael was unaware as they observed what he was planning then faded into the darkness.

There was a knock on the door and Jael looked up, telling them to come in.

Urdun walked in and sat down. "Well, it wasn't as much damage as I thought. The blacksmiths said the fire started in one of coal pits. Something fell in and caught fire."

Jael grunted then stared back down at his work and Urdun was curious. "What's going on?"

Sighing, Jael turned to him. "I am thinking of just calling the entire cave thing off and even make a bare attempt at Herium. I'm thinking that even if we were to win the city, there would be a constant attack from the elves and lots of loss of life. What good would it be?"

Urdun looked confused for a moment and then agreed. "It would be best if we just headed home, sent what we can in an attempt, but the loss of life would be more important than taking the city. I say we only send three hundred, not five hundred to attack the city."

Jael gave a slight inaudible breath and nodded. "I was just thinking of attacking the city with even one hundred."

Urdun shook his head and disagreement. "Sire, three hundred would be the right amount and I think we have enough goblins willing to go. There are more here that want to taste blood of elves than not."

"Then I will leave you in charge of that," Jael spoke softly. "That way if we win, you will have the glory of it."

Urdun liked the sound of that, stood up and walked to the door. Before he left the room, he turned and spoke. "We'll make you proud, sire. Then we'll keep the city too."

Jael stood up and bowed to the man in respect. "Make it happen and I'll give you the city. It will be yours to maintain."

Urdun gave a slight chuckle and walked out of the room. As he did Jael's aid entered. "Sire, I found six good, strong leaders. Would you like to meet them?"

Jael shook his head no and then looked toward the direction of Urdun. "Urdun just left, go talk with him."

The aid bowed, excused himself, and left Jael to broil over plans to leave the cave and go home.

The trip back to the castle was uneventful. The sun was setting, making the forest look as if it were catching on fire. Treidon looked at Meranda and sighed happily. "Are you ready to be a princess?"

She stopped and stared at him in disbelief. "What do you mean...princess?"

He gave a chuckle, gently took her arm, and entered the castle. "I am a prince, so once we're wed you will be a princess. *My* princess."

She gave a long sigh and glanced down to the marble floor of the castle. "If my nightmares keep continuing, I won't be worth anything to anyone."

He gave her a confident smile once he lifted her chin and gazed deeply into her eyes. "We'll defeat those demons and find out why they're constantly attacking you. I'll make sure you're strong and up to facing challenges that come your way. You won't be alone in this. I have sisters and my father will help you as well."

She sighed and didn't respond. The pair walked to their room and she noticed a beautiful blue dress on the bed. It had white in the middle and there was gold trim around it.

Meranda glanced up at Treidon, he shrugged. "I have no idea what my father has planned, but we need to get dressed and find out."

She picked up the dress and walked off to the bathroom to change clothes, Treidon did the same. Soon, she came back into the room and stared at him in amazement. He stood, awestruck at her beauty then walked to her and kissed her lightly on the lips.

Her body lit up with excitement as he pulled away and stared into her eyes. "Come on, let's see what my father has planned."

He held out his elbow and she gently took it. Together they walked down to the dining area and she froze when she noticed all of the people.

Feeling the tension in her, Treidon gently patted her hand and glanced to her. "You can't do this now, we need to eat."

Everyone in the room noticed they arrived and most of the guests stood up in proper fashion. Meranda started to shrink away and Treidon glanced at her. "We have to go in. I'll be at your side, always."

He could feel the anxiety and the tears flowing down his own face as he blocked the view of the crowd in the room from his eyes and hers. "Look, my dear," he said lovingly. "Father wants to thank you and show you off. You're going to have to get use to this. I promise, meals like this one don't happen very often unless it's special."

He searched her lavender eyes as hers were shifty. "Meranda, believe me, no one here is out to harm you. In fact, no one knows what happened in your past. These are all the people loyal to this family. Meaning they are loyal to you too. That means, no one would harm you."

"Can I help?" a voice said behind them. Treidon turned to see Cirian looking concerned. Meranda looked down to hide the fear as Treidon spoke. "She's scared of the crowd like with the arena."

Cirian touched Meranda's chin and lifted it. By now the other elves in the room sat down and continued their conversation as Pagues commanded them to go about their business.

"We'll make this all right, but Treidon's right. You're his bride, everyone sees how you two are bonded, even though it's not apparent at first glance. Let's go get something to eat and then I have to ask you to come with me later," Cirian said softly.

She gave an inaudible sigh, straightened herself up, wiped her tears away then proceeded into the room, around the tables as to not disturb those eating.

Treidon started to pull the chair out near her father when Pagues spoke up. "I need her by me, son. I would like to have a talk with her."

He nodded then pulled out a chair and Meranda sat. The elven people murmured about how beautiful she was and they wondered what she went through to act like she had been.

"This is for show," said Pagues. "We want Siebrien to think that we're not aware of anything going on. This meal was planned long before you got here as I wanted to just catch up on the rumors and the gossip going around town without eavesdropping."

Meranda gave a nod and looked away from him and the others. Heirana spoke up as she poked at her food. "So, Meranda, what were you before you met my brother?" Pagues gave his oldest daughter a dirty look and she replied, "Father, I just want to know what kind of woman has stolen my brother's heart. After all, there have been many and he leaves us for months only to return with her."

Her tone was not a pleasant one and this made Treidon furious, but Meranda replied, "Well, before I met your brother, I was a slave in the forest of Herium. I was tormented and tortured by a man who wanted to kill me. I've had demons trying to kill me as well. While you were here living this cushy lifestyle, I was freezing nearly to death in the winter snow of Herium. Your brother is my bonded mate. I'm sure you've seen him in pain and have seen the unexplainable scars on him. We share the same scars."

Pagues watched in amazement as Heirana didn't know how to respond, instead she looked at her sisters who where giggling and she kicked both of them under the table.

Pagues glared at Heirana. "I'm sure your mother wouldn't like to hear you treating anyone like you're treating Meranda or your sisters. I'm displeased, myself. You need to learn to treat others with kindness. So what if you don't know who she is? I've noticed the same scars on Meranda as Treidon and I trust they're bonded. Now, apologize to her and to your sisters or I'll be forced to do something you won't like."

Heirana took a deep breath, rolled her eyes, and finally apologized after Pagues threatened to take the training away she so dearly loved. "Meranda, I'm sorry. There have been many woman in the past who've tried to win my brother's heart and he's turned all of them away. I don't understand why he suddenly arrives with a woman and expects us to believe it's real."

Pagues glared at his daughter. Treidon stood up and walked over between Heirana and Meranda. He looked at her and she gave a nod. He placed his right arm next to Meranda's and lifted her sleeve and his.

"Look," he said to his sister. "Look at the scars. I said no to those woman in the past, because I knew there was someone out there with the same scars and pain as I have. I finally found her and I expect you to be nicer to her."

Rasi and Lysiara glance at their arms and then to Heirana who still didn't believe her eyes. Rasi stood up and looked at her sister. "How could you not see it? That *is* Treidon's bonded mate. Just because she's someone you don't want, doesn't mean she's not."

Cirian finally came to the table and spoke to Meranda. "Come with me, please."

Treidon stood up and Meranda pushed her chair back, gladly leaving the room.

Pagues wondered what was going on, but he knew he would have to settle this with Heirana.

"Your sister's right," he said. "She's his bonded mate and it's just someone you didn't choose it to be. Just because you're displeased doesn't mean you should make her life miserable. She has had it hard enough as it is."

Treidon sat in Meranda's chair and turned to his sister. "Those scars are from evil tools, she was chained up outside, she's still having nightmares from it. You need to change this attitude, get over yourself, and accept that she's the one for me. Not someone you wanted."

Gervis was sitting at one of the tables, he noticed how uncomfortable the sisters were to have Meranda and watched as she and Cirian left.

He excused himself and chased down Cirian. "What's going on?"

Cirian laughed and looked at Gerivs. "Nothing to fear. She's safe and will be safe as long as I am watching. You'll find out in the morning, if I'm right."

Gervis gave a slight sigh and they continued down corridor and out of sight, he returned to see Heirana still displeased but more accepting now than before.

Soon, the meal was over and everyone retreated to their own rooms to go to bed. Treidon noticed Meranda hadn't returned, but it was not a bad thing. He knew she was safe. He slowly drifted off to sleep with peaceful thoughts.

CHAPTER 22

L edric walked out of the Hunted Fox Inn and watched as his family followed, coming to help the town deal with the issues of the day.

Rainah walked toward to the elves who were making stone walls and they bowed to her. She told them to get to work, but they continued to bow. Sighing, he watched as Rainah grabbed a nearby water bucket and tossed it on them. They all stood around in disbelief and shock that the queen would do something like that to them. He grinned as he watched her begin to help them do the work they needed to. They began to work on the fencing together.

Ledric turned his attention to his boys who were helping kids understand the sling shot. The kids loved his sons and flocked to them when they arrived. Each son took turns showing the kids how to use the slingshot and helped them aim.

"Your family has a way with people," a voice spoke.

He turned to see Linden and smiled. "They do. They want to help, but it seems they're so high on a pedestal, no one knows how to react when they *do* help."

"Your wife certainly knows how to intermingle with others," Linden said with a smile as he watched Rainah helping the other elves form the wall.

Ledric gave a nod and laughed. "Well, she's always had a way with men."

Linden started to speak when a young elven man came running up to them. "Your majesty! My lord, it's urgent! There are a few people that are packing to leave."

They both turned to the young man then Linden spoke, "Where are they? It's not safe for anyone to be leaving town right now."

Ledric agreed and the young man took the pair to a part of town. There were wagons in front of several homes, people carried items out of their hourse and placed them in inside.

Linden walked up the group. "Where are you moving too?"

One elven lady with chocolate colored hair and light green eyes stared in disbelief. "My lord, we're moving out of this town, it's not safe for me nor my daughters."

Linden looked at her with caring eyes. "Where's your husband?"

She stared at the ground and gave a long side before she looked up. "My husband, Minaeli died in the war of Teniquen. It's just myself and my girls. I will not have them subjected to the hands of those goblins." The woman was passionate as she pointed to the horizon and glanced to Linden.

He gave a nod and looked at others. "Are all of your spouses gone because of a previous war and you're afraid we cannot protect you from the oncoming attack?"

There were murmurs and nods, Linden spoke to the woman that was in front of him, "I served with Minaeli and he was a brave fighter. However, I don't think he nor any of the men who have died in the past would like that you don't trust me, King Ledric, or anyone else trying their best to protect you. Fleeing is not the answer to this problem."

The woman looked at him. "It's not that I don't trust you or the king. I fear for my daughters. We can't allow those goblins to enter and kill everyone here. My husband fought because he believed it would protect us."

Linden stood up on the tongue of a wagon and spoke loud enough that everyone could hear him, "Listen to me, everyone." He paused long enough to make sure he had everyone's attention in the area. "It is not going to be easy, but believe me, if you flee now, you won't be safe. There are more dangers outside of this town than there are if you stay. This battle is bigger than what's on the surface. There is a lord in the plains that wants to take over the entire realm. He has probably taken over most of the cities that are within a day's ride of here. If you flee, you might be walking into a situation like before we arrived. I know you don't want that," he paused and noticed there was more fear in the crowd's eyes. "I want you to know that King Ledric and I are doing our best to keep Gavid and others out of the cities," he continued and used his hands to gesture toward the rest of Herium. "But we need all of the help we can get. Leaving will not solve that problem. Your spouses would not want you to flee. They would want you to help."

He got down and the crowd was silent for a moment. Soon they all agreed with him and started to unpack things, then work toward helping the rest of the town with the defenses.

Linden got off the wagon tongue and walked back to Ledric. He was smiling and was impressed at the speech. "That was a well-spoken speech. I'm proud of you. Thank you so much for speaking your mind on this. Many forget the past."

Linden dusted his hands and turned to Ledric. "Many do forget the past, others, like these, remember it too well and take it further than need be. We have to remember and continue to protect each other. I'm not letting this city go without a fight and I know there are others than think the same way."

They walked together and watched as the town continued to prepare for the attack and Ledric glanced at Linden. "Will this town be ready for the battle? I've done what I can with the rangers out in the city."

Linden gave a nod and glanced at the bustling city. "I think we'll be ready. If we could know what's going on in that cave, I would be sure of it. As for now, however, I think we have it."

They approached the Hunted Fox Inn and Linden turned to Ledric. "So how are people in the poorest part of town doing?"

Ledric stared around at the crowd and gave a nod. "They're doing well. Some were taken in by Ugex and his brothers. They're helping by putting them to work for some money. Have you heard from your father recently? How is Meranda?"

Linden nodded in satisfaction at the sound of the news then gave a puzzled look. "I haven't heard anything from them recently. I'm guessing she's okay. I hope to hear something soon. Then again, we've been too busy to stop and ask anyone for anything."

Ledric gave a nod and then watched as Rainah approached them. He smiled brightly and gave her a hug. She looked at Linden. "Is everything okay?"

Linden gave only a slight bow and nodded. "We had a few people wanting to leave town because they thought it might be safer. I think I convinced them otherwise."

Rainah nodded and looked back to the group she worked with. "They're hard working elves, but didn't understand why I would want to help them. They believed the queen shouldn't get her hands dirty. I believe that if I don't work just as hard as they do, then I'm slacking."

Both men couldn't help but smile. Soon, the bell rang nearby, indicating the sun was setting. The elven workers stopped to clean up and get ready for a meal. A few of the knights that arrived to help Ledric went out to patrol the city for any wrong-doing while people were eating their dinner or asleep.

The day would soon come that the people of Herium would be on the defense against an attack of the goblins. He gave a sigh and retreated to the Hunted Fox Inn with a few of the elves from the poorest part of town. They seemed a bit happier now than they did when they first arrived.

The meal went off quietly, soon everyone was back in their rooms, enjoying the time being in a safer place than before. The town was quiet and settled into a peaceful state. He walked up to his room with his family, who turned in early. He walked out to the balcony and focused on his family and Herium. There were so many other towns facing the same thing. He would have to figure out a way to make things better for his part of the region. He was certain there were other kings in the snow region facing the same thing. Ledric knew he would have to meet with them soon. As the town slowly shut down, Ledric, watched over it quietly.

Gervis and Pagues walked back to his office after the evening's meal. They were both happy Heirana finally let go of her prejudice against Meranda. As Pagues opened the door, they both noticed his wife standing there before him. By looking at her, one could tell where Treidon got his looks from. He was identical to her. Bright red hair, light green eyes, and tan skin made her stand out amongst forest elves. Pagues smiled and walked up to her. He took her in his arms and hugged her tightly. "What are you doing here, my beautiful wife?"

She willingly hugged him back and looked at Gervis then turned back to her husband. "I'm here to talk about the recent events with Meranda. I'm thankful she's safe now. Had I known who she was—"

Gervis took a deep breath and tried to refrain from anger. "Had you known? Her life was in danger, as was mine and now the entire continent. Just because you're now aware of who she is, doesn't mean we should have ignored the situation."

Pagues turned to Gervis, he didn't like the fact that his voice was raised and his tone was disrespectful, but Morida put his hand on Pagues' arm. "Dear, it's all right. Gervis is right. We were duped by the same woman. Meranda was her focus, she wanted her dead. It wasn't about Lord Siebrien, whom we're going to take care of soon. It was about Meranda the entire time."

Pagues glanced down at Morida. "But why would someone want to torment a girl so badly? I'm sure Treidon could take care of himself, but seeing how he was so tormented with her scars, I hate to see what she was facing on her own."

Gervis sat, his anger was still there, but he was confused and wanted to know the same answers.

"We don't know. Hariton has a few people looking into it," she said as she sat in one of the chairs closest to Gervis.

Gervis gave a nod and looked at Pagues. "I should not have trusted a woman pretending to be my wife, changing her name, and telling me that it was more than okay to send her to that evil, wretched man."

Morida gently patted his arm and gave him a reassuring smile. "My dear, we all have perfect vision after the facts have come to light. What we do with it now, is we find out why and help Meranda."

Gervis gave a deep sigh and stared at the floor. Pagues was more confused and sat down beside the pair. "So, Meranda is something so important that someone is willing to kill her?"

Morida nodded and turned to her husband. "We don't know who, but all of the torments that she received from Gavid were orders from someone else. This whole thing was someone's idea of a sick game with Meranda being dead at the end. I'm thankful Treidon found her in time."

Gervis didn't want to argue, instead he decided to change the subject. "The shadow elves finally convince Pagues they had a very good reason to kill his brother."

Morida turned to her husband. "You were blaming the shadow elves for his death? They were just acting as our guards. He wanted my family dead and I wasn't about to have it."

He gave a look of sadness. "I had no idea he was trying to kill us. For years, I believed the shadow elves were murders, out to kill for the joy of it. I did not know that they were working with the Dragon Counsel."

Morida shook her head. "My dear, they wouldn't kill anyone unless it was well placed. We should have taken care of Gavid and Siebrien when we noticed something was out of place. That is in the past though," she said as Gervis started to speak up. "We can't let that stop us from making it right now," she finished.

There was a knock on the door and Pagues announced for whoever it was to come in. Oriana and Kavan walked in and looked at everyone in the room.

Pagues invited them to sit and then continued, "I have to show our kids they aren't evil. I taught them so much that was wrong. Treidon won't be that hard, but our daughter, Heirana, she's stubborn, like me."

Oriana glanced at Morida. "We need to have a conversation when you're done here."

She looks to Gervis and Pagues and then back to Oriana. "We can talk here, you know, they are aware of everything."

Kavan gave a slight nod and then replied, "Morida, Hariton and the others of the Dragon Counsel want us to take out Siebrien, but they wanted you to be aware. They want your advice on what to do with Gavid."

She turned her eyes to Gervis whose knuckles were white from clinching the arm of the chair tightly. She knew his anger was well placed and she turned to the pair. "I think there's something we can do with him. Can you bring him to the prison here?"

They gave a slight bow then vanished into the darkness. Pagues shivered for a moment and Morida placed a hand on his knee. "Don't worry, I'll never get use to it either."

Gervis gave a grin and excused himself. "If you will excuse me, tomorrow is a big day for Meranda and I want to be ready to support her."

The pair nodded and watched as he walked out of the room.

Morida smiled. "Where is that beautiful bride right now?"

Pagues gave an unknowing shrug and replied, "Cirian asked for her to come with him after dinner. I have no idea what's going on there. Treidon told us a few days back that she knew the old ways of the Riftrider. I noticed she was a bit timid when she entered the dining area full of people."

Morida gave an inaudible sound as she nodded. He turned and regarded her. "What is it?"

"As Gervis said, there have been demons attacking Meranda. We have to figure out why so we can keep an eye on her and keep her safe. We think she's important to the realm, but we aren't sure why yet," she said looked at him with compassion.

Pagues sat in his chair shocked. "So she's more important than just being the future queen of my kingdom?"

Morida nodded and looked at him. "There is a rune symbol on her shoulder we're looking into now. We've watched her agonize in pain when there are demons about her. It's going to take some time to figure out, so make sure Treidon keeps her safe. We've sent Oriana and Kavan to make sure she's safe too."

"What would demons want with Meranda? Sure, she's a Riftrider or will be soon enough, that shouldn't scare demons enough to want her dead though. We can combat them, but never send them back or kill them outright. There has to be something more to it," Pagues said with concern.

Morida stood up and walked to the window. She looked in the direction of the Riftrider arena and gave a long sigh. "I don't know, my love. I will let you know what I find out when the time comes. For now, just protect her as you would your own daughters. Gervis will be leaving soon for Herium to boost the moral there. There are goblins planning an attack. I need to go take care of the Siebrien and Gavid business as well."

He gave a slight nod and walked up to her and put his arms around her tightly. "Be safe. I will miss you so much."

She leaned back into his chest and sighed happily. "I will return once I find out more about that rune on Meranda's shoulder. I will miss you too, but there is still a lot of work to be done."

Morida turned to face him and put her lips gently on his, kissing him passionately. He placed his hands on her face and returned the kiss. Not wanting to pull away, Morida gave a long lasting sigh before letting go.

For a moment the pair stared into each others eyes and Morida walked towards the door. "Once this is all over, I will be back, I promise."

Grinning Pagues moved to a chair in front of a fireplace and looked at her. "You best make it quickly, I do miss you."

She blew him a kiss then walked out of the room, leaving him to his thoughts of the day. A lot happened, but soon the day was over and he could turn in.

CHAPTER 23

The cave full of goblins were gathering in the dining area for one last meal before they left later that night to raid Herium. Soon the cooks were packing up their stuff to go home. Jael watched as goblins ate happily, wondering how their king managed to get the entire group into this one area. He stood up and raised his hand, the crowd of goblins quieted.

"Tomorrow," he said, glancing around to make sure he had everyone's attention. "Five hundred of you will attack Herium." There was a loud cheer as the goblins celebrated leaving the cave. Jael put his hand up and the crowd calmed down. "The rest will go home to their families. Once we've taken over the town of Herium, we will return and continue to mine. Urdun will oversee those of you who are willing to attack. Be advised that we only have enough armor and weapons for five hundred goblins. After that, if you're still willing to attack, then you're on your own." There were a few murmurs and he raised his hand once again. "Now, once you're done eating, please go see Urdun and be assigned to a group. Enjoy your meal and may the best be beside you."

Jael sat and finished his meal, the crowd got excited because they were finally able to leave the cave in one way or another. He watched as the large group of goblins slowly left him in the dining hall alone to think. Soon, he got up and walked to his room. Along the way, goblins talked to him about how excited they were. As he opened the door, he stared at the mirror and wondered how it was back in working order. Before him, waiting, was Gavid.

Jael stood shocked for a moment then walked up to the mirror. "Evening, my lord. I hope you are well?"

Gavid simply nodded and spoke, "I want a status report. I want to be able to tell Siebrien what we're up to when I meet up with him."

Jael swallowed hard and then spoke up. "My lord, Ugex and the other orcs have left the cave, taking with them the resources we were using. We haven't heard from them or seen them in a few days. We don't know where they've gone."

Gavid gave a nod then smiled. "When I find Ugex and his clan, he will be taken care of. So what's the plan?"

"Well," Jael said in an unsure tone, "We are attacking Herium tomorrow."

Gavid paused for a moment, showed no reaction then smiled. "That is wonderful news, proceed. I want everyone out of town when I return. Then I can take over and have the resources for myself."

Jael relaxed, Gavid wasn't mad at all, in fact, he appeared to be happy with his news. "Very well, my lord. Is there anything else you need me to do?"

Gavid thought for a moment then said, "Make sure you attack Herium quickly. There's no telling what's going on there. I've lost contact with the wives of the elves in charge of the town now. I'm assuming they're dead, so the town is in mourning and at a loss. Do it soon. I'll be back in Herium in a few weeks. I want it to be ready for me when I return. Now, be on your way and I'll contact you later."

The image faded and Jael cursed him loudly. There was no way he could possibly find the ruby. He was also really losing interest in working for Gavid in general. He sighed deeply as he sat at the desk and looked over his plan to take over Herium. He had to make an effort or at least make it look like he tried. There was a sudden knock on the door and he told them to come in. Urdun entered and looked at him. "Sire, we have a little bit over the amount of men you wanted to attack Herium. What do you want us to do?"

Jael smiled at the news and gave a slight nod. "That's good. Just send them with the groups. Try to make a good even amount out of them. I'm sure they're anxious to get out and enjoy some bloodshed."

"Even if it's over a hundred more? What about armor and weapons?" Urdun questioned him, while placing a paper with a list of names on his desk.

Jael was surprised about how many goblins were willing to go attack the town and not return home given the option. He smiled and nodded. "Yes, even over a hundred more. We can do something with them. I'm sure armor and weapons won't be a problem, as the town is unaware of our presence. Gavid has said the lords of the town are dead, so they're in mourning. Herium should be easily taken over."

Urdun gave a slight nod then sat down in front of Jael. He leaned forward with his hands in front of him and he glanced at the king. "So sire, what will the plan be once we take over Herium?

We can't just abandon it and we both know Gavid will return. When he does return, he'll want to take over the town and us. We shouldn't give him that right."

"Of course not," Jael said staring at him for am moment and then at his paper work. "Those scouts never returned to me, so I don't know what Herium is doing right now, but Gavid told me what is going on as far as he knows. We'll set up our defenses, because you know those elves won't let it go without a fight. Then we have to have them ready for Gavid too. Between Herium and Gavid, we're going to need a lot of defenses."

Urdun pondered for a moment then nodded. "We need to bring some of the resources that are here to Herium to help. An armed goblin is a good goblin, I always say. We need to have food and drink there as well. Elves will be coming for trade, until the rumor gets out about the town being taken. So we'll need scouts out there taking those elves' wares as well."

Jael was surprised again with how much knowledge Urdun had. Then again, that was why he was his second in command. "I'll leave that to you. You're in charge of the town. Remember to set up the defenses first, then work on the other things. Spread the scouts out to keep them aware of things. You'll be paid richly for your help. Thank you for your service and may you be successful in the raid."

Urdun stood up and gave a simple nod then walked out of the room. Jael was left to ponder what to do about the extra hundred goblins that wanted to attack Herium. It didn't matter, they could go out there and attack the town with no guidance, but it always helped to have someone who could control them.

He drummed his fingers on the desk while he thought. Nothing was coming to mind at the moment and it frustrated him. They only had ten men for fifty goblins, he needed two more leaders that would help take control of the town. He wondered if there were two such men in the new volunteers. Looking over the list that Urdun left, he recognized a few names and checked off a couple. He wrote a note on the bottom of the page leaving those two in charge of the new goblins that wanted to taste blood.

This was going to be a successful raid, he thought. There was something nagging at him in the back of his mind, but he brushed it off. Soon, he relaxed and decided the bed was calling his name. Tomorrow would be a busy day for everyone, his rest would be important. He knew, however, there were some goblins doing too much celebrating about leaving the cave soon. Taking a deep breath, he got up and decided it was time to go to bed. It didn't matter that there would be a few people who would have issues tomorrow, they would be victorious. He climbed into the bed and slowly drifted off to sleep.

Leaning forward on the balcony railing, Ledric watched as the town hustled about below him. It was going to be a rough one once the goblins attacked. There was so much wrong with Herium.

People were untrusting of one another and didn't like the way others had been treated. The poor were worse off than anyone. This town was once thriving, now it was every man for themselves. He had to help put the place back together. With Linden, Davignon, and Jayidus around, that would help some, but he knew the town needed more.

He wondered how Gervis and Meranda were doing then took a deep sigh when he heard a voice behind him speak. "You know the town will be under attack soon?"

Startled he turned around to see Weisgar and nodded. "I do. We have been in discussions about this. How did you know?"

Weisgar walked and leaned over the balcony then turned to face his friend. "Sire, we were made aware of this by the Dragons. Here's a copy of their plan to attack Herium."

He handed Ledric the pages filled with the battle plans then turned back to the city. "Five hundred goblins, if not more," he said casually.

"This is not good at all," Ledric said as he read through the pages. He moved to a desk in the room and sat down. "We need to be prepared. Do you know when the attack will happen?"

Weisgar glanced down at the people below him and watched for a moment as they rushed into the inn to keep warm. "The others said it will be tomorrow."

"Tomorrow!" Ledric said loudly. "We won't be ready by tomorrow."

He turned to Ledric and moved gracefully to the chair in front of the desk and sat down. "We have to be ready. What do you need us to do to help you?"

Ledric scratched his forehead for a moment then looked over the plans again and nodded. "Can you and some of the shadow elves pull the goblins into the darkness? Can you also tell the rangers to shoot some of them in the back of the group as they head our direction? That might possibly slow things down and help us."

He focused on the pages again and noticed there was a note about a group going in a different direction. Ledric put his finger on it and looked at Weisgar. "What are they doing here?"

Weisgar stood up, moved to the desk, then stared at the plans and nodded. "That's the group leaving, according to the leader of the goblins. It seems he was tired of Gavid and is just sending a small force to attack Herium. That way if Gavid were to return it would look like they tried. However, they believe the small group should be successful in attacking the town, sire."

Ledric gave a thoughtful nod then looked up. "So, they're just sending a small force? Can you help us and kill some while in the shadows? I mean, if we can get it down to a hundred goblins we might stand a fighting chance."

Weisgar gave a grin and that was all Ledric needed. Shadow elves loved to take anyone endangering the towns they have sworn to protect into dark places never to be seen again.

Ledric stood up and pushed the pages back at him. "Good. Talk with the others and make sure they're aware of the area and what's going on. They need to see these plans as well."

Taking the pages filled with strategies, Weisgar placed them in his pocket and stood up. "Will there be anything else, sire? I need to get these to Queen Iriel. She would like to know where we are and what we'll need to do, promptly."

Ledric thought for a second. "Have you heard from Meranda, Gervis, and the group that left here a while back?"

Weisgar gave a slight nod. "Not directly, but they've arrived in Elmwick. Meranda told everything she knew to the king and his family. That's why I was sent. Meranda was able to relate everything."

Ledric smiled satisfied that she was safe. "What about Gavid?"

"The shadow elves have been asked to take him to the prison in Elmwick. For what purpose, I have no idea," Weisgar spoke in hushed tones.

Ledric gave a nod. "But he'll be punished?"

Weisgar gave a nod then looked around the room for a moment. "I'm not sure. I was just told that we need to bring him to Elmwick."

Thinking for a moment, Ledric stared at Weisgar. "Can you make him go crazy? He's already headed for death. I might know how. Losing his mind might be the best way to get him. I mean, he did treat this town poorly and deserves to be tormented some himself. Don't you think?"

Weisgar thought for a moment and gave a slight nod. "Indeed, sire. We will do our best to put that man into an insane state. It would be the best for everyone. Meranda didn't deserve what she went through, nor did the town. However, the town treated her just as badly."

"I know," Ledric said as he looked out of the window. "But once they realized who she was and what happened to her, they punished themselves. Don't worry about them, just take care of Gavid. He'll wish for death once he's sent to prison."

Weisgar stared at him for a moment and Ledric could see he was confused. He smiled and then explained, "Meranda will soon be the princess of Elmwick. The man she left Herium with is Prince Treidon. They're bonded soul mates. Things are going to be different for her. People will respect her more. She'll also be a Riftrider officially, soon enough."

Weisgar stood in amazement for a moment and shook his head. "She was already those things. We just needed to get her out of that bad situation. I'm glad she is."

Ledric gave a satisfying nod and then smiled. "I'm glad she's fine too." Regarding the king, Weisgar shook his head. "Had you come sooner, perhaps she would not have found her bonded mate and be on her way to becoming a real Riftrider. We need to focus on what is happening to Herium right now. Goblins plan on attacking the town soon and we need to get all of our townsfolk ready. I'll do what I can to Gavid. He *will* be punished for *everything* he did."

Ledric gave a nod and Weisgar said goodbye and vanished into the darkness. The door opened and Rainah walked in after the evening meal. "There you are, my dear. We missed you at dinner. Why are you up here?"

He smiled as he turned to her and walked up to her for a hug. "I was discussing business with Weisgar. Gervis and the others have arrived in Elmwick and the shadow elves have been commanded to take Gavid to Elmwick as well."

She hugged him back and then looked. "That's insane! The man who tormented that poor woman has been sent to Elmwick? Why would they do that?"

Stepping around the desk and back to the balcony to listen to the silent wind blowing for a moment. Ledric didn't answer her right away. She then asked again. "Why would the shadow elves do something like that?"

"The Dragons asked the shadow elves to find him and bring him to Elmwick. I don't know why, but I've asked the shadow elves to make him go insane. That will be my punishment for the way he treated this town. There are other people in other towns who will feel my punishment soon enough," Ledric said as he turned to regard Rainah.

Rainah looked at him and grinned. "Meranda will be on her way to successful life and we'll monitor everything more closely so it doesn't happen again."

He smiled and loved her more every time she opened her mouth. "Rainah, you're right. We're going to have to work harder and follow leads that come in more often. Not just ignore the facts, like we did with this city."

She gently took his arm. "Come on, let's go get some rest. Tomorrow is going to be an eventful day. Then we have to get this place back on its feet."

He gently patted her and stared into her eyes. "This town will be well taken care off. Ugex and his brothers will make sure of it."

Together, they walked to their room for a night cap then went to bed.

CHAPTER 24

G avid watched out of the balcony as the sun set. His time spent in Beaumarion was a great one. Good food, good company, and he'd forgotten the reason he was actually there. Although, with the constant reminder of Siebrien's castle in the background, Gavid put his plans off until later. There was a magical allure in Beaumarion. The people were friendly and he liked the way they treated their servants. The plains elves always bought their servants like slaves. There were black markets all over town that sold captives from other parts of the region.

He looked toward Siebrien's castle and decided he over-stayed his welcome in Beaumarion. Knowing he needed to get back into action, he decided this would be the day to get back on track. Not contacting the wives in a while, Gavid decided he would see what's going on with them. He picked up a few herbs and a mirror then cast the spell. The mirror came back with fuzzy images, indicating it had been broken. He smiled in satisfaction and put everything back up. He got up and decided he would get his meal, eat in the pub one last time before he left Beaumarion.

The tavern in the inn was a joyful sort. The people were talking, servants were waiting tables, music was playing, and laughter was in the air. He sat in a less conspicuous booth in the back and watched the townspeople relaxing and enjoying themselves.

An elven woman who had an ebony complexion and emerald green eyes with jet black hair approached him and smiled. Something about her smile made him uncomfortable, but her voice was soothing and made him relax. "My lord, can I take your order?"

He gave a slight nod and put in his order for the special of the night with a bottle of wine. She left, giving him a sly wink. That uncomfortable feeling rose once again, but the other people in the tavern didn't seem to notice it, so he tried his best to relax. No one in the snow region knew where he was and no one in this town knew *who* he was.

The music got louder and someone else brought his meal once it was finished. Staring at the patrons, he didn't notice the servant, but she must have worked there because his food arrived. It was mouthwatering and savory, the smell of the veal hit his nose. Picking up a knife and fork, he was soon cutting up his meat, dining on the veal and sides. The meal was memorable, certainly he would have to remember to hire the cook for his own personal meals once he controlled the realm.

Soon, he got up and left, paid for his meal with a little extra for the cook, then walked back up to his room and gathered his stuff. Some things were out of place and the furniture seemed to be rearranged. Gavid shook his head and walked out of the room after collecting his belongings.

He walked down to the carriage station and spoke to the clerk. "I need a carriage ride to Rishmede, please."

She stared at him for a moment and then smiled. "It will be sometime, but it'll be two gold. I will let you know when it arrives."

He gently slid two pieces of gold out of his pocket then he looked around for a quiet place to sit.

Finding one in a dark corner, he sat quietly and slowly pulled out his spell book. He needed to know a few spells once he arrived in Rishmede so he could subdue the guards and take over the castle.

"What are you doing?" a little girl's voice said behind him. He thought this was weird, because he was in a corner with a wall. He stood up and walked away from the corner then to a more lit area of the room.

A sultry voice behind him spoke, "Looks like someone's preparing for an all out attack. What's going on?"

Turning, Gavid noticed a beautiful young elven woman with mocha colored skin and emerald green eyes smiling, but concern was in her eyes.

He gave her a reassuring smile. "Nothing to concern yourself with. Once I go to Rishmede it will be taken care of. Go about your day and you'll see it will be all right."

She gave a sigh and then nodded. "That is good. We are on our way to Elmwick. The royal family has invited us to watch the Riftriders doing their training. They say there's someone special, a snow elf."

"We?" Gavid questioned, he hadn't seen anyone with her, and the mention of the snow elf didn't send any alarms into his mind.

The elf nodded. "Yes, we. My daughter, my husband, and myself are on the way to Elmwick. They say this girl has a special talent, but she has so much wrong with her that she might not be able to do the trial. Poor girl. Who would torment her so much?"

Gavid gave a shrug and just let the woman reflect on her own thoughts. He again heard the small child's voice on the other side of him. "Mother, why is he reading those funny words?"

He turned to see another beautiful girl, with the same mocha skin, but she had the most brilliant cobalt blue eyes, smiling at him.

"He's just studying, leave the man alone, dear. Come sit with me and we can talk about the trip to Elmwick," her mom said softly.

Not liking kids, Gavid got up and moved away from them. He sat in another area with the wall to his back. He heard giggling around him, he looked about the room and noticed nothing. Why was he suddenly starting to hear things? There was no stress in his life and he hadn't had any bad reports. In fact, the brothers were dead, the goblins were attacking, and he was on his way to stop Siebrien. Things couldn't have been better, yet he was starting to hear things. He felt something crawling across his foot, he looked down and moved it, but he didn't see anything there. Strange whisperings in the shadows spoke of Meranda being alive. He knew that was impossible, he saw her die, the bloody sheets, everything. She was dead in the best sense word. He shook his head and went back to studying the spells he needed. His imagination was not going to get the best of him.

He continued to focus, when he heard another voice whispering about Meranda marrying Treidon, prince of Elmwick. He looked up to see the couple seated behind his previous position had left. He wondered if that was who she was talking about. Shrugging, he looked back down to his book. There was no way Meranda was alive, much less becoming a Riftrider or marrying the Prince of Elmwick.

Gavid finally stood up and walked to the attendant. He asked, "Excuse me, how long until the carriage to Rishmede gets here? I need to get there as soon as possible."

Just then, an ebony skinned man walked out and gave the woman a nod. She looked and gave a simple nod back and then glanced up at Gavid. "The driver just indicated he's here." She pointed out to the doorway then started again at Gavid. "What are you waiting on?"

He walked over to the carriage and the driver helped him in. "Rishmede isn't a long drive, but you could get a bit of a nap in before we arrive," the driver said quietly.

Gavid looked at him curious, but the elven man touched his shoulder and smiled. "Just relax, we'll get to Rishmede in time."

Climbing into the carriage, Gavid suddenly felt like it was time for a nap and sat down on the bench seat. He was considerably tired and refused to fight his heavy eyelids. With a jerk, the carriage was on its way, but Gavid gently pulled down the shades on his side of the carriage and drifted off to sleep, peacefully.

The driver whispered into the darkness, "Tell King Pagues we have the package and it will be several days before we arrive."

A woman came from the shadows of the carriage and smiled. She was the same one from the station earlier. She kissed his cheek and then whispered, "I'll be on my way, if you need me just call and I'll be here as soon as I can. There are others in the darkness, working to make sure he doesn't awake, nor does he know that the path he was taking isn't the one he is on."

She vanished and he was left with a smile. He realized he needed to go faster and encouraged the horses speed up their pace.

Siebrien sat enjoying his meal in the quiet, the plan hadn't gone as expected. Other elves across the realm weren't able to obtain the kingdoms or townships Gavid had. Only Gavid had done what was asked of him. It was Gavid who would be rewarded greatly once Siebrien was emperor of the realm. Finally, after months of yelling and screaming, the others were on the same page as Gavid and in accordance. Soon, the towns would be his and he could choke out the kingdoms of the realm to claim every one of them for himself. He grumbled and shook his head. This shouldn't have taken this long, but it did. However, he was still under the radar of the Dragon Counsel and others who would put him to death if they knew.

He sat and poured himself a glass of wine then slowly sipped it. Gavid would soon have Herium under his full control. Those snow elves would be gone and Gavid would control the resources he needed. Smiling, he knew he needed to burn the evidence of his plans just in case the Dragon Counsel caught on. He hadn't thought of how to destroy or capture them, but he needed to figure it out quickly. Soon, Siebrien got up and made his way to his desk. He failed to notice the shadows of the room moving about and surrounding him.

He picked up a few pages and tossed them in the fire then sat and enjoyed its warmth. The crackling embers tantalized his senses making him feel peaceful. The spring breeze blew through the castle, giving him a chill. Getting up, he stoked the fire a little then went back to sit in his chair. As he sat down, he found himself falling instead. He landed on the floor and looked up to see his chair was slightly moved out of the way. He got up, dusted himself off, and walked around the chair then decided to sit again. This time he was successful, he relaxed and drank another sip of his wine, enjoying more of the moment. Things couldn't be going better. He began to feel slightly dizzy, he got up and laid on the long couch which was near the fireplace then pulled a soft blanket over himself. Slowly, he drifted off to sleep.

As he slept the shadow elves appeared and began to rearrange the room then picked up a few papers that were important before he burned them. They left the room as a woman gently coaxed him awake and vanished.

Sitting up, Siebrien looked around the room. With it being rearranged, he believed it was a dream. He placed his feet on the floor and looked down to see pitch black. He turned to the fire and noticed it was still burning. He rubbed his face, then started to stand up and walk, but found his feet were glued to the floor. He fought and fought, but the darkness started slowly pulling him in. Quickly, he sat back on the couch and kicked at the darkness, which seemed to screech at him and let go. He put his feet on the couch and looked down at the ground. Soon, he realized it was a nightmare, not a dream. He laid back down after his heart rate slowed down. Siebrien kept his eyes open and looked around the room in fear for his life. Slowly, however, he drifted back to sleep. While he slumbered, the shadow elves rearranged the room and allowed him to sleep for a bit longer until his body was relaxed.

A male shadow elf leaned in close to his ear then screamed loudly and vanished. Siebrien jumped straight up and looked around the room. Things were back to normal and the floor didn't appear to be black. He gently placed his feet on the floor, stood up, and walked to the fire, poking the flames again to make it burn brightly.

The wine was still on the table by his chair, he gently picked it up and walked back to the fire then tossed the wine in. The wine brightened the fire and made the room lighter, which revealed three shadow elves in the room. Startled, still thinking it was a nightmare, he laughed it off then walked passed them.

The three elves looked at one another then back to Siebrien, who was looking over the paperwork sitting on his desk. He picked up the pages and started back toward the fire. Before he could get there, one of the elves grabbed his wrist and threw him back in the chair. He stared at them with the papers tight in his hand. If this was another of his nightmares, it certainly was real, then again, the other one felt real too.

His heart raced as the lead male shadow elf put his hands on his chair and leaned forward. "Cancel all plans to take over the realm. Your life depends on it."

Siebrien let out a nervous laugh and shook his head. "This is a nightmare. There's no way, if I were awake, I would do this, even for you."

The elf leaned closer into his face and sneered. "Do it, this is no nightmare. If you don't, the Dragon Counsel will punish you far more than we will. In fact, with us, you're getting off easier."

Siebrien could feel his icy breath on his face, he shuddered and reluctantly nodded. "Fine, I'll do it."

He thought all along he was in some nightmare as the shadow elf lifted him and his chair then turned, slamming the chair down in front of the large mirror. "DO IT!"

Siebrien waved his hand and one by one the images of the people who planned to help him take over the realm agreed, although puzzled, to cease.

Soon everyone didn't question why and agreed to stop with the oncoming raid. He turned to them, thinking still it was a dream. "There, I'm done. The only person I couldn't get a hold of was Gavid."

"There are things in place for him. We plan on making sure he never hurts the girl ever again or anyone else," the burly elf stated then walked toward a female who had a two glasses of wine in her hand.

Curiosity struck Siebrien as he spoke, "What girl? I know of no one in Gavid's life, but Gavid himself."

The three shadow elves looked at one another and then back at Siebrien. The burly elf spoke in a curious tone. "You mean to tell me, you didn't know he had a girl he was tormenting? A snow elven girl, Gervis and Anmylica's daughter?"

Siebrien shook his head. "How did Gavid get control of Herium anyways? I never knew and just assumed it was an empty town that had no security or guards. I just wanted the resources."

"Do you know he tried to kill their daughter? He took over the town of Herium, was ruthless and evil," the burly elf stated.

Siebrien looked at him and stood up. "That's impossible. Gavid wouldn't do that to any child."

The woman snorted behind them and then spoke, "Just like you aren't trying to take over the realm?"

The burly elven man shoved Siebrien back to his chair and he shook violently for a moment then fainted.

The three shadow elves looked at one another, then backed up as Siebrien glowed red for a moment and a demon appeared before them. He laughed at the three and looked around. "She's alive isn't she? I have to go kill her now."

Before they could attempt to stop the demon, he vanished into the darkness. The female shadow elf and the other male vanished into the darkness quickly, leaving the burly male with Siebrien.

Not long after, Siebrien awoke and looked at the shadow elf. He stared in confusion and stood up. "What's going on? I've been having the weirdest nightmare that seemed to be never ending. Do you know where my wife and daughter are?"

The tone of his voice changed to a deeper baritone and his demeanor seemed to change. The shadow elf shook his head. "What do you remember last?"

Siebrien took the elf to his own room then explained about his wife being kidnapped by dark figures while they were sleeping. A demon told him he had to cooperate if he wanted them to stay alive. The burly elf gently took him by his arm and told him they would go to the Dragon Counsel and speak about this. He agreed and together they vanished into the darkness.

CHAPTER 25

C irian patted Meranda's arm as she held tight to his elbow. "It's going to be okay," he said, reassuring. "We'll make sure you will not have those nightmares nor be attacked while doing this. It will be safe. I promise."

She sighed as they walked up the stairs of the arena. "You know you don't have to do this," he said, looking at her with concern. "I'm sure the others would understand. They're waiting on us now, to get in there and show what you can do. I heard amazing things from Treidon, but I do understand, too."

Shaking her head, Meranda looked at Cirian with a smile. "I have to do this. How else would there be a witness to what I can do? I'm not going to do the trial in a large arena, maybe a smaller one will be less intimidating."

A door opened and a young forest elf appeared. Cirian smiled and regarded the boy. "Drenl, are they ready?"

The boy shook his yellow hair then moved out of the way. Cirian walked in with Meranda and they went into the center of the smaller arena.

She looked around for a moment, it was certainly less intimidating and stressful. Cirian waved his hand and the lights came on. The Elders and Esteemed Elders were sitting around the arena, in box seats, to watch what she could do.

She smiled to Cirian. "Certainly glad to know I have more than one pair of eyes watching me."

"You'll do fine. Just do what you do best and show us your talents," he said as he walked off to sit in one of the chairs in the arena.

Another spell was cast and a blue light encased the room. She stood ready, unsure about what would come at her. A small gnome with beady green eyes, balding head, and grayish skin came from a portal and looked around for a moment. Meranda stared up and around then gave a shrug. The gnome charged at her. She casually pulled out her bow and mumbled a word then let the arrow fly until it landed in front of the gnome. Confused, he paused for a second, staring at the arrow. He realized he made a mistake by stopping. He was frozen to the ground and stood as solid as an ice statue. Slowly Meranda walked over to the creature and pushed it over, it shattered into a thousand pieces.

She heard the murmurs and watched as the portal opened up to allow two large sentient spiders to crawl out. The pair turned and regarded one another then turned to her and charged. Shivering, she hated spiders, especially ones as large and intelligent as these. She didn't seem to make a move, but several Elders noticed her hands were glowing with soft blue light. They surrounded her and began to spew webs from their bodies. She leapt up and avoided the sticky threads, the spiders trapped each other. As she landed, she stabbed one in the back of the neck and heard him scream for a moment then die. That only left one spider who freed himself from the web. He charged at Meranda, she darted back and forth from the spider who was more nimble than she was and finally he pinned her down. There was no fear in her eyes as the spider leaned in to tangle her in his bindings. When she shoved her dagger into its mouth, the spider shrieked, reeled back, and tried to shake it off. Meranda rolled away from the spider who collapsed and dissolved into ash.

There was a pause for a moment then four ogres came from the portal. She dusted herself off and peered up as best as she could at Cirian with a look of confidence. The ogres all pointed as they noticed Meranda and started to charge her. She swiftly pulled her bow, began to cast several spells through the arrows, and launched them. One connected with an ogre as the others flew by and fizzled away. The ogre with the arrow in him began to flail about and dance until he finally vanished into a puff of smoke. This gave Meranda a chance to launch another volley of arrows. Once again, one landed and the others passed by them. The one that landed turned the next ogre into stone, which angered the others. They pulled out their large maces and approached the small woman before them. Both swung and she darted between them with nimble movements. They both growled in frustration then watched as she stood, paused for a moment, staring at them.

She mumbled something and those close enough noticed her daggers lighting up. The ogres tried their best to charge her, but she leapt up and danced around them, slashing and cutting at blinding speed. They were slow and useless against her, however, one managed to catch her in his large hand. She squirmed only for a moment and he chuckled, but she stabbed him in the hand and he let her go immediately. She growled at the pair of beasts. She mumbled again as she placed the dagger in one ogre's foot. She danced around as the ogres tried to grab for her. The problem was, as they were grabbing for her, they managed to touch each other and spread the spell that turned them both into stone.

She turned to the portal as it started to dissipate and she heard clapping in the room. Relaxing, she leaned back and heaved heavy breaths, it was over and she managed not to have a nightmare. At least she believed she didn't.

Suddenly, she knelt down and began to cry uncontrollably. The nightmare came at her full force. A new portal opened and a demon climbed through, staring at her. Meranda was helpless as he came charging at her. He lifted her up and began to choke her, struggling for her.

The Elders and Esteemed Elders all rushed down to try and help her, but they found they were unable to get down to her.

Meranda looked down at the demon who was happy he was able to achieve the unthinkable. He turned to look around as she struggled and clawed at his hand. Soon, a soothing voice popped into her head that she didn't recognize. "Fight him! Don't let him defeat you! We will get you through this, child! Now, fight him!"

She looked around the room, her nightmare was still clawing at her mind while her body was fighting off being killed. Battling through thoughts of the punishment she went through, she put her hands on the demon's arms and said something that sent a shock through his body. He let go, she fell to the ground and coughed for a moment. The demon growled at her and started to charge her when she put her hand up and froze him in position.

She stared at the demon, who couldn't move, fear showed in his eyes. She had new life in her body. Waving a hand, she lifted him up. The Elders watched as she made a fist with her hand and he began to choke. She approached him then mumbled another word, the demon began to shake and scream then he caught on fire and vanished.

She collapsed on the ground again, choking and coughing. Cirian came running up to her. "I'm sorry, I thought we had everything secure. It seems someone else had other plans."

Meranda looked at him with a weak smile. The other Elders rushed to her and smiled. Xerina glanced over at Cirian then at Meranda. "We had a discussion and it seems you've reached Esteemed Elder status. We'll have to put the tattoo on you, if that's okay?"

She nodded, Xerina touched her shoulder and she winced. Xerina turned to her shoulder and stared in disbelief at the glow, then she glanced back at Cirian. "We need to talk after she's gone to bed."

All of the Elders and Esteemed Elders gathered around and mumbled, her arm glowed for a moment. A tattoo appeared on her arm, it was a black bow with three silver roses surrounding it.

Cirian gave her a soft smile then hugged her. "You did well, now you can train those who don't understand how important weapon casting is. I can't believe we allowed people to forget that important skill. Thank you for letting us see that it's not totally forgotten."

Xerina glanced at Cirian then spoke to Meranda, "Go get some sleep. Tomorrow will be a very important day for all of us."

Cirian spoke and soon a forest elven man approached them. "Yaver, can you get her to bed? I'm sure Treidon's worried about her."

The blond haired, dark skinned elf grinned, he gently picked Meranda up and took her to her room where quietly placed her in the bed across from Treidon. She curled up in the bed and slowly went to sleep.

The crowd of goblins stood talking with one another, ready to be done with things in the cave. Soon, Jael stood on a rock above all of them; more than five hundred goblins were ready for the attack, anxious to get out and invade Herium. This made him smile, but he knew it wouldn't happen without a few losses. He raised his hand to quiet the crowd. They turned their attention to him and grew silent. "We'll be attacking Herium soon. We still have a few things to prepare, but we'll be able to go into battle. The time to attack is now. We've been stuck in this cave for far too long and it's time to claim what's rightfully ours." There were a few cheers amongst the crowd as Jael continued. "We cannot allow those snow elves to continue to live in a town that was chosen to be ours. We must take it back and take this cave for our own as well. You, my trusted volunteers, must take the city and kill everyone in it. Don't stop until the city is ours. Take no prisoners."

There were a few shouts in the background. "When do we attack?"

Jael squinted to see who asked the question, but it didn't matter. "We attack in the morning. That way the elves will not be fully aware of what's going on."

"Are there enough weapons?" someone else shouted.

Smiling, Jael responded, "There are enough weapons and armor for everyone who's going."

"Why do we have to wait if there's enough armor and weapons?" another shouted.

He took a deep breath. "Because we want the elves to be caught off guard. You'll go in groups of a hundred until everyone's gone."

There were chants in the crowd of "Attack now!" and "Let's go now!" soon building into a frenzy. About fifty goblins, in a fully crazed state, ran out of the cave to attack Herium.

Before Jael could stop them they were gone, he shouted to the others who were nearing the same point. "Don't go! We have to go together as a group! We cannot go as a few! Together we will go and fight the elves. If we go unorganized then we'll be easily defeated, once the elves start in. The elves won't give up the town without a fight."

Others watched then turned back to Jael who had a look of frustration on his face. "Now," he continued. "There are some of you who wish to go home. If that's the case, then we must pack up and go, to prepare for a return to Herium with our families. I'll dismiss those of you who wish to return home now."

Several goblins left the cave to go pack and he turned to everyone who remained. "Good. Now, let those of you who remain, prepare of the attack tomorrow. Be ready first thing."

He dismissed his people and they left. He turned to see his second in command, Urdun. Urdun spoke as they walked away from the meeting hall. "Sire, we have enough armor for everyone and almost enough weapons. Thank you for telling them, in the morning we should be ready for them."

"Good to hear, Urdun. I'm sure you'll lead them to victory and bring back the good news to our town," Jael said with a smile.

He patted Urdun on the back as they walked through the cave. They arrived at his room and Jael looked at Urdun. "I need to get packing so I can lead the others back to our village safely."

Urdun gave him a smile and excused himself. Jael opened his door and looked around. The torches still burned brightly, but there were always places that seemed to be darker than he liked.

He began picking things up and gently placing them in a large pack. Looking around the room, Jael sighed. He would leave the furniture, but he would take a few small things. He wondered how they got these things in here without any elves noticing. Finishing his packing, he turned and heard voices in the darkness. "Think you'll be ready?"

He glanced up and stared around the room. Thinking he heard it in his mind he spoke out loud. "Well, I'm ready to get out of here. Those goblins, not so much. However, the elves are unaware of us down here, it should be an easy task."

There was a whisper in the dark, about things not appearing as it seemed. He shuddered and glanced around the room. Nothing seemed unmoved, the torches still danced in the darkness and the room seemed untouched.

An aid came into the room and handed him a few papers, Urdun came behind him. "Sire, the troops are getting anxious, they're ready to go attack Herium. What do you think I should do?"

Jael smiled, he loved the anxiousness of his goblins, but knew it would be best. "Tell them they must wait for the morning. I don't want anyone to leave without my permission. Everyone who left earlier won't be rewarded after the battle."

Urdun walked out of the room after bowing and leaving Jael to go to sleep. He sighed heavily as he went back to the area where the others were waiting on word to leave. "He says wait. If we were to leave, we won't be rewarded."

The anxious goblins groaned in anticipation. Urdun noticed the sadness in their faces and spoke, "You'll be the first ones to head out. I'll send you out before Jael gives the word, be prepared to leave as soon as I do. He won't be here much longer. He witnessed those fifty leaving, but he won't notice you gone. He's already gone to bed. I promise you, it won't be long."

They looked defeated, but they understood and walked off. Urdun shook his head. He loved the goblins who wanted to attack, but that was the entire goblin race. It took a lot of restraint to *not* go out and murder everyone in the realm. Urdun knew their tribe kept their collective cool until it was closing in on time to kill. He knew they would need to be out there soon, they spent too much time being calm, not shedding blood. It was time to let out their rage.

Urdun walked up to the blacksmith and spoke with him, "How are things looking?"

The blacksmith glanced up from his work, nodded then turned back to it. "We won't be ready to send everyone out with weapons unless they wait."

He chuckled and looked around. "Do you think these goblins *could* wait long enough for weapons?"

The blacksmith continued to hammer and shook his head. "Nope, but they're going to have to."

Urdun liked the blacksmith and laughed as he watched him hammer. "Do you need any help?"

"I've got this. I'll be done in the morning, if you leave me alone," the blacksmith said, staring at Urdun as if he was disturbing him.

Urdun took the hint and walked out of the room. He turned down toward the kitchen, there would be no meal in the morning because the cooks would be leaving before the battle. He walked in and smiled as they were packing up their cooking items and turned to him.

"My lord, it's going smoothly. We have yet to run into any problems and we shouldn't either. Although, there have been a few people asking for food. We gave them what we could because it would go to waste otherwise," stated one cook.

"Good." Urdun looked around, noticing a few goblins grabbing pieces of food and leaving the room. "I'm sure they're happy there's some food left behind for them to eat in the morning. The taste of blood will also be thrilling for them."

They gave a nod and continued to pack up. He appeared happy that things were ready around the cave. Tomorrow the attack would be going on and they would claim Herium.

He finally walked into his room and collapsed in his bed. He felt like victory was at hand and knew it would be best to get a good night's sleep.

He was unaware of the shadows that surrounded him and took things from the room. They also went to the armory and took a few things. *An unarmed goblin was as good as a dead goblin.* The shadows melted away into the natural dark crevices of the cave's dark corners.

CHAPTER 26

edric watched as the town began preparing for their battle with the goblins. He knew, from the reports and the maps, it would be soon. He also knew the poorest part of town would be attacked first. He was thankful Ugex and his tribe were there to protect them. Although Ugex gave him a reason to be there to help, he wondered if there was more to it. He got lost in his thoughts and was brought out of them with a knock on the door. He walked over and opened the door to see his wife smiling back at him. "I knocked, not wanting to disturb you," she said with a smile.

Ledric smiled at his wife and sons. "So what's on your mind?"

Cadhla looked over at his brothers then at his father. "We want to see where Meranda was held captive. Her brothers want to go with us as well."

"That's fine," he said. "The people here are doing all they can to get ready."

He walked out of the room and down to the lobby to see Linden, Davignon, and Jayidus waiting on him. He grinned and shook each brother's hand. "Let's go to the keep where she was."

Several guards knew they had escort everyone despite feeling it was unnecessary. It took several minutes to arrive, but they got there with no problems. The guards spread out and patrolled the area while the families looked about the dooryard of the keep.

Ledric took them to the back of the land where the chain was still visible. Ledric led them to that area and spoke, "Here's where Meranda was chained to the tree and suffered the most."

Rainah gasped and glanced around sadly. "How far does that chain go and what were those tools used for?"

Ledric gently took the chain and dragged it toward the keep and stopped short. Linden shook his head. "Certainly not a way to keep her safe from the weather. Why did he do this?"

Ledric looked at Jayidus, then turned and regarded his brother. "I don't know why he did it, I just know he did."

Maellan walked over to the tools and picked one up. "What were these used for? Certainly no reason to have them outside."

Ledric turned to Davignon, who was silently fuming and sighed as he turned again to his son. "She was tormented with those tools. Once you meet her, you will see her scars. She, sadly, has nightmares and is haunted by those."

Davignon began to stare out into the horizon and shook his head. "Jayidus, how many times did we hear a woman screaming at night thinking it was a panther even though panthers are not in this region? We never once came to investigate."

Linden stood where the chain ended and looked up at the ruined building in the keep. "She surely would have died from a cold during the snow and winter season. What kept her from dying?"

"The shadow elves mostly and there are a few others out there that kept her alive," Ledric said as he continued to the shack nearby.

"What others?" Davignon glanced up and questioned as he walked with him.

Ledric arrived at the shack and turned to the family. "There was another tribe of snow elves that helped her out when she needed it. I still wished either that tribe or the shadow elves would have kept her from returning to Gavid."

He walked in and there were more questions. Jayidus followed up with one. "What kept them from keeping her safe? Why didn't anyone do anything?"

Ledric spoke kindly, but the words hurt at the same time. "She didn't want Gavid to be angry. It was your business to investigate, however, not a panther."

Before Jayidus responded they arrived at the bottom of the stairs and Ledric flipped on the light switch. There before them was the bed full of blood, bookshelves full of books, and more tools used for torture.

Everyone walked in and stared in shock. Jayidus was fuming with anger now as he walked to the bed full of dried blood. "I bet none of this was Gavid's."

Ledric took a deep breath and shook his head. "No, this is all hers. She's safe now and will not be punished like this any more."

Jayidus had pent up anger and began to pace the small shack, the others watched while Rainah sat at the desk and looked at the writing in Gavid's books. "He wrote about how she would respond to different tools and how her body would heal without anyone being around. He was puzzled by this and wanted to know more."

Ledric gave a slight nod. "That's because she was bonded to Treidon, who had access to healing while she didn't. If it weren't for that, there might not have been a Meranda at all. I mean, the shadow elves did all they could, there were others who tried to help too, but..."

Linden had been silent for a while taking it all in and then spoke. "Why didn't we come sooner? *Why* did we listen to our wives when they said it was nothing?"

Jayidus finally had enough and smashed a chair against a wall. Davignon walked over to him and put his hand on his shoulder then he knelt down and cried. The tears fell down each of the three brothers' faces. They knew their sister went through a hell they could never imagine.

Ledric turned to his own sons who were equally angry at all of this. "We can't allow this to happen again. None of this. Every time there's a rumor or something of the like, we must investigate it. I turned a deaf ear on the rumors constantly, because there was no actual evidence. I'm to blame just as much as anyone else."

Maellan glanced at his father. "How did it get this far out of hand? I mean, shouldn't the second or third report have been investigated?"

Linden glanced up and took a deep breath. "We should have listened as well. We were told that everything was taken care of by our wives. Again, we should not have listened to anyone and just came to see it ourselves."

Folding his arms, Ledric listened to everyone and then spoke softly. "The thing is, we all thought it was taken care of by someone else. We didn't realize it had gotten this bad. We won't let it happen again."

They all stood up and walked back to city limits of Herium. Linden, Davignon, and Jayidus went back to their own families. King Ledric and his family went to the inn.

When Ledric opened his door, he noticed Weisgar standing at the window. "What's going on?" Ledric questioned.

Weisgar turned to him, the shadow elf nearly blending in with his surroundings, he walked into the light so Ledric could see him. "Sire, the goblins are attacking in the morning. What do you need us to do?"

Ledric gave a moment's thought then spoke, "Go spread word to the others, then go to out to the rangers and ask them to pick them off as they come into town. Can you do anything to help as well?"

"I can. I will go tell the rangers then we'll pull the ones on the end of the line into the shadows and kill them. There'll be less than a hundred when we get through with them," Weisgar said with a bit of malice.

Ledric nodded. "Good. Let's get this started so we can be ready to counterattack them when they get here."

Weisgar vanished in the shadows. Rainah and Ledric's sons walked in from the tavern below. Rainah glanced at her husband. "I thought you would come down to join us for dinner. What happened?"

Ledric turned to his family and sighed. "The goblins are attacking in the morning. I have sent Weisgar and the other shadow elves to let the townspeople know and the rangers. We can't be unprepared for this."

Maellan walked to the window and noticed the town was starting to be more rushed than before. "I want to go down there and help if I can. I'm sure my brothers would like to go too."

Cadhla gave a slight nod to his brothers and Ledric smiled. "Go. Show them we're here to help them, not stand around and watch."

The three sons walked out of the room leaving Rainah and Ledric alone. "So we should be helping in some way."

"We will. Let's go find Ugex and the others residing in the inns and inform them as well." Ledric said. Together, the king and his queen walked out of the inn to help spread the word.

Sergar continued to watch the cave down the hill and behind several trees, but from this vantage point he could see what he wanted to see.

There hadn't been much action lately, which was confusing because he hadn't seen any orcs either. He wondered if Meranda had mistaken the orcs for more goblins. It didn't matter, his job was to protect Herium.

"They're still there, don't fret," a deep booming voice whispered behind him.

Jumping, Sergar turned and relaxed. "Don't do that, Weisgar! You scared the life out of me."

Weisgar smiled and looked out at the cave. "They're attacking in the morning. King Ledric wants us to pick off the ones on the end. They're sending their men out in groups of fifty. If we can take out a few before they get to town they'll be easy to overpower."

Sergar gave a slight nod and then turned to the cave. "So, not much longer before all of this is done?"

Weisgar shook his head. "Not in the least."

Sergar smiled then focused on the cave again. "Can you tell us what's going on in there?"

Glancing back at the cave, he agreed they needed to know. He slowly slipped back into the shadows and then, with a few others, slipped into the cave.

The shadow elves followed several goblins to a room full of them. They noticed their king stood in front of them, they were hanging on his words as he spoke them.

The goblins began chanting and screaming. Soon the elves began to shout questions out at the king, who replied to them. The elves again threw a barrage of questions, which several goblins agreed with and it brought them into a near fury. Several goblins in the back reached a frenzy and ran out without weapons, armor, or anything, screaming obscenities and madness as they went. The king yelled at everyone who remained to stay, they all turned and looked at him.

The shadow elves slipped out of the cave and back to the rangers. Sergar finished slaying a goblin when Weisgar cleared his throat, trying not to scare him.

"Well, you certainly know how to draw a few out," Sergar said without turning.

Weisgar watched a few other goblins fleeing and sighed. "We were trying to get them all to run out, but at least we're down a few more."

Sergar sighed. "Wish there were more. I'm getting bored up here watching this cave with nothing to do. At least it'll be over soon. The morning isn't far away."

"Not in the least be a little more patient. It will be soon enough."

Sergar turned to the shadow elf and smiled. "I've been ready since the day we arrived."

Weisgar nodded, leaving Sergar to his devices and plans, making it back to Herium to report to the king. Slipping through the shadows, Weisgar watched carefully to see if there were any goblins that slipped past the rangers. He suddenly stopped when he noticed a female shadow elf coming his way. The shadows held another world in them as they swayed, the darkness held it in secret.

"Juliane, what's wrong?" Weisgar stopped as she approached him.

She stopped and stared for a moment then continued with a quick pace. As she walked she spoke, "The child was attacked by another demon. I have to go find Macala and tell her to come to the Dragon Counsel."

He turned and walked up to her. "But isn't Macala a—"

"Yes," Juliane replied. "She is. I need to find her so that she can be caught up on what's going on."

He walked along side her. "But what *is* going on?"

Juliane stopped and turned to him. "The woman was doing her trial and finished it when a demon attacked her. Her shoulder glowed blue. Several shadow elves noticed it and reported it to Hariton. He wishes to speak with Macala now."

"But why did her shoulder—" Weisgar started to ask, but then paused and realized the significance. "Do you need me to come with you?"

She shook her head and continued on, "No, you have your own business. I need to get to mine before she's attacked again."

He watched as she hurried through the shadows, he knew he needed to get to the king to report what he learned of the day. The news that the girl was something more than they all believed was important, but how could they not notice the glowing mark on her shoulder? Pondering more, he finally arrived at the inn where Ledric and his family were staying. He walked in then up the stairs and knocked on the door. Not typical of a shadow elf, but his thoughts were focused elsewhere. The door opened and Ledric stood there, confused. "Why are you knocking on the door? What's wrong?"

Weisgar turned and looked around to see if anyone was behind him then walked in and shut the door. "Sire, I just ran into another shadow elf on her way to see Macala."

Ledric turned to him, concern appearing on his face. "Why would someone look for such an expert in *those* arts?"

Weisgar glanced into the shadows for a moment to observe the room. "According to Juliane, the girl had a glowing mark on her shoulder and a demon attacked her during her trials."

Ledric's eyes widen as he listened. He couldn't believe what he heard and sat down. "So, they're seeking Macala to go meet with the Dragon Counsel?"

Weisgar nodded then sighed. "The goblins are on their way tomorrow, however. Let's focus on that. We can see how the woman is doing later. She'll need us for support as well and a town to return home to."

Ledric nodded and sat as if he was told horrible news. "Yes, we have to focus on the issues at hand. I'm sure the Dragon Counsel has the other issues taken care of."

Weisgar agreed with his friend. "Ledric, we have a plan to take out the goblins before they get here. Only a few of them will come here to attack the town. Other goblins will be returning home to make plans to come back. We'll discourage them in their return, but we must keep that cave from falling into the wrong hands."

"Of course. What do you have in mind?" Ledric paused and glanced around for a moment. "Not too many people are willing to live out there."

Weisgar stood and looked out the window. He noticed Ugex and the others working to keep the poorest part of town safe. "What about them? I'm sure they would like to be close to family. Not to mention, help protect it."

Ledric was curious and walked to the window. He noticed Ugex and the others helping the elves get into the inn and ready for a night of rest. "I'll have to ask, but it's an excellent idea. They would be out of town, but close enough if we need them. Plus, they know that cave."

Weisgar gave a knowing smile and then started to slip into the shadows. "By the morning, this will be all over with. We'll be finished and the threat will be over."

Ledric nodded and stopped Weisgar. "What about Gavid? Have you found him yet?"

"Indeed we have," he said with a sneer. "He'll be taken care of soon. This will be over with before too long and then we can celebrate properly. Now, I have to go talk Ugex and see what he thinks of this idea. If you will excuse me."

Ledric shuddered but gave a knowing smile. "Go, talk with Ugex and let him know of the plan. Also, thank you for letting me know about Meranda."

Weisgar shrugged and vanished into the darkness.

As Ledric sat in his chair to process the news of Meranda, he heard the door open and watched as his wife and sons entered. She looked at his face and knew he received some news. "What is it, my dear?" Rainah asked as she sat beside him.

"The goblins are attacking in the morning and the Dragon Counsel has sent for Macala."

"Well, the Dragon Counsel always deals with the hunters. What has you looking like you've seen a ghost?"

He gave a smile. "Just thinking. The hunters are about to receive a bit of information that will shake them to their core. I'll tell you later, dear. Right now, we need to focus on the attack tomorrow. Let's go and see if they're ready."

Gently taking her arm, he walked out of the room and out of the inn; outside he wanted to encourage the people and help get everything ready before nightfall.

CHAPTER 27

Yaver snuck in and gently, placing Meranda in her bed, watching as she slept for a moment then he covered her up gently. He turned to look at Treidon and smiled. They certainly were bonded together. Quietly, he left the room, shutting the door behind himself, to leave them peacefully sleeping until the morning.

As the sun peeked through the window, Meranda woke to Treidon speaking with her. "Wake up. You need to get ready to go. It's trial day for you."

She shook her head, pulled her arm deeper under her pillow and spoke softly. "Not going. I was told, I don't have to do the trials."

He stared at her with confusion. "Dear, you have to. There are no exceptions, even from the Elders."

Meranda opened her eyes and stared at him for a moment then pulled the covers over her face. "There *are* exceptions."

Before he could protest, there was a knock on the door. He grumbled, stood up, and walked to it. "You're wrong," he said to her.

She didn't make a move and Treidon opened the door. Before him, Pagues walked past Treidon. "Where is that beautiful elf that will be soon my daughter-in-law?"

Treidon pointed to her bed. "She said she's not going to trial."

Pagues walked to her bed and sat beside her. He leaned in and whispered so Treidon wouldn't hear. "I think you should keep playing this up. He's clueless, you outranked him."

Meranda stirred and whispered, "I know he is and I'll keep doing it, if you help me."

"You're right, she's stubborn, Treidon. What can I do? I can't force her," Pagues said standing up.

Treidon's jaw dropped only for a second as Meranda rolled over and looked at him. "That's right, no one can force me to do something I don't want to. What if I have another attack? That wouldn't look good out there would it?" she questioned to him.

He folded his arms, he really didn't want her to give up on this. "But we couldn't get married if you don't pass this. That's the rules."

Pagues couldn't help but smile as Treidon was starting to whine. "Treidon, trust the Elders to know what they are doing. They have said she doesn't have to, then she doesn't have to. Meranda, at least join us today?"

She pulled down her sleeves and sat up and looked at the pair. "Of course, I have been invited to sit with the Elders."

"That's preposterous!" Treidon exclaimed. "How do they allow someone who hasn't passed to even think about joining them?"

Pagues stood up and walked away from Treidon to hide a chuckle. Then turned back to Meranda. "The horn will sound soon, I best get ready to go. I just wanted to come in and see how you were feeling."

She stood up and nodded. "I'm feeling fine. Thank you, sire."

Giving the simple nod of approval, Pagues walked out of the door, giving Meranda the chance to slip into the bathroom to change into a purple shirt with a brown leather corset.

She walked out and stared at Treidon who was still pouting. "Come with me. I know you're only a master, but I'm sure they'll allow you in. After all, you're a prince."

He sighed and walked away from her. She couldn't help but grin at his disappointment, after a bit he came out dressed and ready. "I don't see how they could allow you in the booth. What happened last night anyways?"

She sighed and looked down, she drew a circle in the floor with her boot. "Just a few things. The Elders noticed that I wasn't ready and decided to give me a pass. Cirian saw my nightmares. He spoke up for me."

Treidon gave a long sigh. He hadn't thought much about the nightmares, but it did seem to hinder her from excelling. He felt helpless when it came to helping her with those. He glanced at her with a smile and gently took her hand. "Come on, let's see what will happen today."

She squeezed his hand and glanced in his eyes. He could feel her excitement, but Treidon didn't know why. Together they walked to the trial arena. She wasn't intimidated in the least compared to the last time she was there. They walked passed other elves of different races. They greeted Treidon and asked who Meranda was. Treidon smiled and said a friend, but the others could see more. They arrived at the Elders' door and a guard stood before them. He was a sienna-skinned man, with long amber colored hair andeyes like the blue sky after rain. He looked at Treidon. "Can I help you, sire?"

Meranda spoke up. "Can you tell Cirian that I'm here with Treidon?"

The guard looked confused for a second and Treidon replied, "See, I told you, he wouldn't let us in. Even with who I am, the Elders always have their rules. No one's allowed in that hasn't passed the testing."

Meranda nodded and turned back to the guard. "Can you, please?"

The guard started to reply that Treidon was correct when the door opened. Cirian stood at it and looked at the guard. "Let them in. They're allowed to come in this time."

This confused the guard, but Meranda smiled and walked passed him. Treidon shrugged. He didn't know what was going on and walked in with them.

As they walked up the stairs to the box, Meranda sent a message to Cirian that Treidon was unaware of the events last night.

Cirian smiled and turned to Treidon. "There are some good trainees that are about to become your students, you need to keep an eye on them. We understand Meranda's situation and just want her to see what it's all about."

Treidon nodded and sat down with a pout. They watched as others went through the trials then there was an announcement.

Cirian stood at the top of the box and spoke loudly. "We have had a wonderful event today! Thank you all for coming. Those of you who have passed, congratulations! Those of you who haven't, please continue to train. We had the privilege of seeing someone amazing last night. She reached the rank of Elder while most of you were sleeping. Please, let me introduce you to Meranda. She has learned the ways of the ancient ones and weapon casting. She is truly a remarkable woman!"

Treidon stood shocked as he stood up and hugged her tightly. "Why didn't you tell me?"

She laughed as she returned the hug. "Because I wanted you to be surprised as well."

The crowd cheered her on and she felt the energy from them. "Can I show them?"

Cirian waved his hand and a set of stairs appeared from the elder's box to the stairs. "We will give you the last challenge. The three orcs. Show us something new."

She nodded and ran down the stairs. When she got down them, the stairs vanished and she stood prepared for the attack. A blue portal grew from the ground as the audience stood in stunned silence. Soon, three large orcs came from it. She gave a sly grin and sent a mental message to Cirian. *"I'm going to switch it up a bit."*

She whistled for her pet who appeared in a shimmer of green light. She pointed to an orc then commanded it to attack. It vanished. She drew her bow and an arrow then pulled it back. The orcs finally noticed her and were charging. She let the arrow fly and it landed at their feet as Soli appeared to attack the orc in the back.

Pulling out two daggers, she watched as the orcs jumped around because the ground was hot. She charged at them and jumped in the air. She mumbled a spell, the audience watched as the daggers glowed blue.

She swung with speed and grace, finally slaying one. While the other was still dancing around to cool off his feet. Once he did, he grabbed Meranda by the collar and pulled her toward him. She mumbled another spell and flipped the daggers behind her, which landed in the orc's hand. He tried to hold on to her, but was powerless and in pain, so he let her go. By now, Soli had attacked and killed the other orc, which left one to defeat.

She whistled for Soli to vanish. She stood alone against the last orc who was angrier now than before. He, with one good hand, attempted to grab her. She dodged with grace and spun around behind him. She said another spell and the daggers lit up again, she stabbed him in the back. The orc screamed in pain and turned to her, beginning to chase her. She stood in position and the orc's movements began to slow down. Soon, he was slower and finally, he was turned to stone. The audience could not believe their eyes as Meranda pushed the orc over. The statue fell and shattered into a thousand pieces.

Everyone, including Cirian stood in awe until Gervis, who was in the Elder's stand, started to applaud. The rest of the crowd slowly began to realize what happened and started clapping too. Meranda gave a quick bow and Cirian waved his hand for the stairs. She bounded up them and jumped into Treidon's arms. He kissed her deeply and she returned the kiss. The crowd erupted then the trial was announced to be over.

Gervis walked up to Meranda with a smile. "I need to get going, Erissa and Ivadian have already left. Goblins attack Herium in the morning and I need to be there for moral support. You have your family here, and after that display, your classes will be full."

Meranda frowned as Treidon pulled her close. "She'll be fine."

Gervis nodded and hugged her tightly then called for Oriana. She appeared and looked at Meranda who was tearful. "He'll be safe, dear."

Meranda shook her head. "I know, but I just got him back."

Gervis hugged her again and then they were on their away.

Treidon smiled. "Come on, we have a small party to get ready for to celebrate everyone who's passed and talk to those who didn't. I'm sure the ones that didn't would love to hear from you."

The audience was dispersing and went on their way to other things, including the party. Meranda and Treidon were soon on their way as well.

Gavid knew the trip to Rishmede would be a long one. He leaned back against the cushion of the couch and relaxed. The rhythm of the carriage slowly rocked him to sleep. Once he was asleep, he began to dream of a beautiful desert elf humming to him. Meanwhile, the carriage was driven by a shadow elf and the others around him were preparing him for the trip to Elmwick. They slowly pulled down the shades around him and the driver whispered into the darkness, "Go tell the Dragon Counsel we have the package. It will take us a few days, but we'll arrive in Elmwick soon for his sentencing."

The shadows danced around him and a woman appeared next to him. Her dark ebony hair flowed about her as her fossil-colored skin sparkled. "What do you need me to do, my lord?" she whispered softly.

The driver turned and smiled. "Go relax the passenger, keep him comfortable. I don't want him feeling any bumps along the way."

She nodded then vanished back into the carriage.

The horses galloped most of the night toward Elmwick without ceasing, until they reached a blood elf ambush stationed in the woods. The bright fair-skinned blood elves usually stood out amongst the dark woods and were easily spotted. A shadow elf appeared behind them and spoke, "Don't even think about it. There isn't any gold or prizes on that carriage. Just a desert elf going to be sentenced for a crime."

The three elves turned to the shadow elf and began to speak, but both the elf and the carriage vanished into the darkness in a gust of wind.

The driver looked back to see the blood elves slightly confused, but knew they had been tricked. A voice spoke up behind him, "King Thien, the Dragon Counsel says they'll meet us in Pagues' home in Elmwick. They want his punishment to be a swift one, but they need to speak to the girl about it."

He turned to see a beautiful shadow elf with dark skin and blue eyes. "Twilia, can you help Amelina with her task? Keep Gavid comfortable, I need him not to wake even once during this time. Keep him unaware of all that's going on around him."

She smiled curtly and vanished into the darkness as well. Thien continued in the darkness toward their destination.

The female shadow elves kept him comforted, singing quietly to him as they arrived and would vanish with him into the castle. They would keep him company until the time was right.

King Thien stopped the carriage in front of the castle and ran quickly passed the guards who didn't stop him, directly to the Dragon Counsel. He opened the door and they all turned to him.

Hariton stood up, gave a quick smile, and walked to him. "Has the package arrived?"

Thien shook the Dragon's hand and gave a swift nod. "It has. It's in a safe place and highly guarded."

He sat down and looked at the other elves in the room. The ten Dragons stared back at him and he spoke up, "So what's the plan for him? He did some wicked things to that girl. We need to make sure he's punished, rightly so."

An elven man with silver blue hair and dark gray eyes nodded and spoke in a hushed tone, "I have yet to see what he did to her. Can someone explain to me how we could let it happen? Why were we not aware of it?"

"Qaden, Meranda was tormented by Gavid. He, with the help of a demon, would constantly shred the skin from her body, cut her, torture her, and have tried to kill her several times. He also did some terrible things to the town of Herium. Those that didn't follow him were constantly ridiculed and had their homes and businesses taken away from them," Morida spoke up.

Shaking his head, Qaden was outraged. "We allowed these things to happen! We wanted the best for our realm and this is what happened! Who convinced us this was all right?"

King Thein didn't know the answer to this and spoke up with uncertainty, "Was there someone who said things were happening for the right reasons? I mean, this had to have started decades ago, when the woman was a baby."

Morida turned to Hariton who was shaking his head. She spoke for him as he seemed to be too upset over it all. "We were duped into believing it would be okay. Now, we're learning otherwise. Things were not as they seemed. Demons were working to take over this realm and we've been blinded to the facts. I've called for Macala to help us with this."

"That's good. We need her to tell us what the demons know and where they're trying to focus their energy right now," a raven-haired woman with soft mocha skin spoke up.

Thien nodded. "Noelaine's right. We don't know how much the demons know about anything, but it certainly is troubling for sure."

Noelaine gave a nod and continued, "During the girl's trial, a demon came from the portal and went straight at her, like he knew exactly what he was looking for."

Hariton got up and started chewing on a nail, pacing as he listened to her.

She continued on, "I sent a message to fight. She drew up the courage and defeated him. We'll have to keep an eye on the girl and talk to Macala to be certain. The demons want her dead for a reason."

Stopping and turning to the group, Hariton responded, "We were blinded, but we won't be again. Those demons weren't expecting Treidon to save Meranda, or for him to protect her from

Gavid's attacks. Nor were they expecting Ledric to come into Herium to see about the rumors. They were trying to keep him and his family out of the city."

All of the Dragons agreed. Thien stood and walked to the door. "If you will all excuse me, I need to see if Gavid is comfortable and if they need any help keeping him relaxed." He grinned wickedly and they knew he meant relaxing in the not-so-gentle way.

As he left, Morida glanced as Hariton as he sat down. "We cannot allow the past to beat us up. Yes, Meranda's been scarred. Yes, she's been tormented. However, with a bit of guidance, Treidon found her in time. She was going to die if he hadn't."

Hariton looked the other Dragons and grumbled. "We cannot let anything like this happen ever again. We must keep vigilant watch at all times. We got careless and in that careless attitude, demons have taken free reign of the realm. We must call the demon hunters and put them on notice, their jobs are about to get busier."

He put his hand on Morida's shoulder. "We need to keep an extra watch on Meranda. Stay here, but unnoticed. Make sure she's safe."

"You can't keep kicking yourself, Hariton. We both know you did your best, we were all blinded by this," Noelaine spoke up.

Morida turned to her as did Qaden and he spoke before she could. "Noelaine's right, we can't reflect on 'what if' or what *has* happened. No matter how much you want to. You have to reflect on what's happening now. She's going to be strong and powerful. Soon, that child will be a force of her own. We just have to let it happen and watch. Don't let those demons put doubts and regrets in your mind."

Hariton leaned back and rubbed his forehead. Morida touched his hand and gave him a reassuring smile. "Qaden is right, we can't focus on the past. Yes, Gavid was an evil man who did evil things to Meranda, but soon he's going to be punished and she'll be trained to deal with the demons that torment her so much."

He glanced at her and gave a smile. "I realize she's fine and things will be made right, however, please understand, she's special to me and we shouldn't have allowed her to be treated badly. The demon pretending to be her mother told me it would be fine. I should have just kidnapped her from that situation and raised her myself."

Morida grinned before she replied. Her voice was soothing and sweet as she talked to him. "I realize she is. How long would it have taken us to realize she and Treidon were destined to be together?"

Hariton glanced over at her and grinned. There was no response. The other Dragon Counsel members stood up then Hariton and Morida stood with them. "The meeting is excused. I'll make sure that Pagues knows Meranda is the one to bring him Gavid's sentencing."

They all walked out of the room and parted ways, going to their own regions for damage control.

CHAPTER 28

L inden knocked on the door of King Ledric's room. He stood waiting then the door opened. Ledric smiled as he stepped aside to let Linden in.

"Things are as ready as they're going to be," Linden said walking to the door. "Ugex and his elves have helped in the poor part of town get things moving over there. Jayidus, Davignon, and our wives have gotten the rest of Herium as prepared as can be."

Ledric gave a nod and then replied. "The goblins will be attacking in the morning. Warn everyone and tell them to be on guard. There won't be as many of them arriving in town as the amount leaving the cave. The shadow elves and the Rangers will make sure of that."

"It's good to hear my family and the king's family have things running so smoothly while I've been away," spoke a familiar voice.

They both turned to see Gervis standing before them. Linden ran and hugged his father tightly. "How's Meranda?"

"She's fine," Gervis replied as he hugged his son back. "What's the word on the rest of the town? And what's this I hear of Ugex being in town? Where is he?"

Ledric responded, walking to the window at the same time. "He's there at the inn around the poorest part of town. I'm sure you'll be able to find him."

Linden watched the pair and then nodded. "He's watching that side of Herium. The shadow elves reported the goblins will attack that side first. He volunteered to take those people who don't trust us to help them into the inn and protect them."

Gervis looked out the window for a moment as Ugex was directing others into the inn for the evening. He looked up to the window and swiftly nodded.

Turning back, Gervis spoke, "We'll be ready in the morning, correct?"

Linden and Ledric quickly nodded and Linden spoke, "We will be. The town has been working hard to get things set up. The people Gavid has hurt have been put up in the inns by Ledric and Ugex. Once this is over, I believe Ledric will help the ones who have suffered the most because of him."

Ledric nodded and sat down. "Those people that would not follow Gavid will get a higher reward. They'll receive a new home, clothes, a new place to work, and food for a long while."

Gervis shrugged and gave a silent reply. "We'll make things right. I'm talking about myself as well. Meranda's happy, but she'll have troubles for a while. What those demons did to her—"

"Demons?" Linden interrupted him. "What demons?"

Sighing softly Gervis turned to his son. "The demons have been attacking and plotting to kill Meranda for some time apparently. Gavid was only part of the plan and the demons wanted her dead."

Ledric was shocked at the news and confused at the same time. "Why would they want her dead? It's not like she was born to kill them."

Gervis looked at Ledric, one that showed otherwise and Linden spoke up. "You mean to tell me—"

He sat down in shock as Gervis nodded then answered. "She was born with the birthmark. She'll be taken into training soon. I wish I'd known what she was. I wouldn't have listened to the crazy ideas that woman claiming to be her mother told me. None of this would have happened."

Ledric sat down and soaked in the information. "Does she know?"

Gervis shook his head and sighed. "Not in the least. She's been through so much already. I don't think she needs to hear this right now. Not yet at least."

Linden stood up and angrily shouted in reply at his father, "She needs to know! Her father shouldn't keep this thing a secret! She's important to our realm! Not just as a Riftrider, but as someone demons fear!"

Turning toward his son, Gervis knew the anger was well placed. Ledric spoke up instead. "Linden you're right, but Gervis has a point. I'm sure she'll be told in time. I'm hoping sooner rather than later. The demons will stop at nothing to kill her."

Gervis nodded and looked back at Ledric. "I know they've called on Macala to help in the process."

"But who will keep an eye on Meranda? It won't be easy, especially if they send her out on missions. You've seen those scars, you've heard the screams yourself, father. They'll do all they can to make sure she's dead," Linden spoke in anger.

Gervis stood up and shook his head. "Look, Hariton and others will be there for her, she has a castle full of guards and

Treidon. They'll do their best to keep her safe. There's nothing more we can do until she starts to get training. Now, if you'll excuse me, I have to go speak to Ugex."

He stormed out of the room and out of the inn. The cold spring air hit his lungs as he took a deep cleansing breath. Meranda certainly had her hands full and he felt sorrowful each and every time facts were brought up about what he hadn't done or what he couldn't do.

Walking up to the inn, Ugex looked up and smiled from one ear to the other. "It's good seeing you again, alive at least."

Gervis shook his hand and together they walked to Ugex's office. Once the door was closed, Ugex looked at him. "How's Meranda? Is she safe?"

Nodding, Gervis looked at him. "Yes, she is safe, for now."

"For now?" Ugex stared at him with a confused look.

Gervis sat down in a chair across from Ugex and shook his head. "The demons will keep attacking until she's ready to combat them."

"Does she have the mark of a hunter?" Ugex questioned and sat down with him.

Gervis only could nod and Ugex let out a long whistle. "I think I remember seeing the glowing on her back, but I could never be certain. It seemed Gavid tried to cut it out at one point. How will he be punished once he's caught?"

Gervis gave a smile, he loved the change of subject. "He's been caught and the plot to take over the realm has been stopped. The Dragons will deal with his punishment. I left knowing I had to be here, before I heard what they will hand out to him."

Ugex nodded, stood up, and walked to the window of his office. "The goblins will be attacking this area tomorrow. I've gathered as many people as I can in the inn. There are a few that are stubborn and refuse to come. Perhaps you could lure them in."

Gervis was thankful for the change of subject and walked to the window, he noticed a few families still out in the cold, harsh climate. He walked out of the inn and to those elves who refused to seek shelter.

Ugex watched from the window and one by one each family came to realize Gervis was still alive and had returned to Herium. They were thankful to hear he would be staying for good this time around and they could come into the inn from the cold.

The last of the families slowly made their way into the building and Gervis walked back to the office. "Ledric has promised them a new place to live, food for a year, clothing, a place to work, and money to get them all back on their feet. He regretted that he allowed this to happen. These people are the ones that wouldn't follow Gavid. Those who are well off agreed that Gavid did no wrong."

Ugex smiled and patted Gervis on the back. "Come, then let us celebrate and prepare for tomorrow morning. We'll show those goblins whose ready. They're totally unprepared for the surprise they're getting."

Gervis stood aside and let Ugex go first then walked after him. Together they talked toward people who had everything taken away from them. The brothers learned that the people knew about Meranda and tried countless times to protect her. He promised, to himself, he wouldn't allow things like this to happen again.

Soon, the nighttime came and everyone retreated to their own rooms to relax for the evening, until the silence was broken by the ringing of a bell to wake the entire town of Herium.

Jael stood at the opening of the cave, the sunlight was peeking over the horizon. He was anxious to get out of the caves with their wealth. He didn't need to return, because his entire tribe would be wealthy for an eternity.

He shifted some of his things as he aid stood by his side with a few more things. The aid stared at him for a moment. "Why aren't we leaving, sire? I thought we were ready? Others are waiting on you to depart."

He turned to his aid and smiled. "Just enjoying the last sunrise in this place. I haven't seen in it so long, I had forgotten what it looked like."

"I understand, sire, but we need to get going before Urdun starts sending out the waves of soldiers to attack Herium," the aid replied.

Jael turned and noticed several goblin men and women, waiting to leave and return home to their families. He took a deep breath and made the motion for them to move out.

He stood aside and watched as the goblins with their belongings on their backs, walked toward the east and home, away from Herium.

After a while, the last of the goblins were returning home had left. Jael walked in the back to keep an eye on the goblins and to walk at a slower pace to enjoy the fresh air. Soon, everyone that wanted to go home was gone, which left Urdun with the task of assigning a leader and then fifty men to go to Herium.

※ ※ ※

Urdun watched as the goblins lined up then gathered up their weapons and armor. He decided the leader would be the first of the fifty and they would be sent out. Soon, the first group was ready and he walked with them to the cave opening. He told one goblin which way to go and he would taste sweet victory soon. The goblin shouted at the other fifty and they were soon gone.

He walked back in and did the same thing for each of the forty groups of fifty and one by one each of them filtered out. Before getting half way, some goblins realized what was going on and skipped getting their weapons and armor, then decided to pick up any weapons along the way to attack. Urdun didn't know how to react to this, but the ones that didn't wish to have weapons or armor it was their choice. This meant more weapons and armor for the rest of the group. As more and more groups were sent out, he realized less and less goblins were going out with armor or weapons. He finally decided they needed their weapons and stopped the thirtieth group and tell them to get their gear or they were not leaving. Deciding that he needed to stand at the line to make sure this was carried out, he asked another goblin to send out only fifty at a time. The goblin gave a nod and was soon at the front of the cave doing as he was asked. This took a long time and he knew by the time they got to Herium, the town would be devastated and overrun.

After hours of sending out goblins he finally reached the end of the troops and decided he would be the leader of this group. He turned to the blacksmiths. "Take what's leftover."

The blacksmiths, covered in soot and ash, looked up at him.

"You want us to quit? Are there any others left?" asked one blacksmith.

"There are none," he replied then looked at the others. "Leave no evidence about what happened down here. Clean it up the best you can. We can't leave clues to the cave's value, in case we do choose to return later."

The blacksmith goblins gave the command to the others to start cleaning up and gathering supplies. Urdun walked to the last group of fifty and saw them prepared to leave.

He spoke to them as they were ready to leave. "By the time we get to Herium, the others should be successful."

"What would happen if they're prepared for us?" one goblin spoke up with concern.

Urdun shook his head. "They'll be defeated by the time we get there. There won't be much of a fight."

Several goblins started to protest, but he raised his hand for them not to speak. "There is plenty of wealth for everyone. I promise you, there will be more than your share once we arrive. Just come with me and we will make sure no elves have fled to get help."

The goblins liked this idea and they charged out of the cave into the forest. They charged out readily and ran through the forest. Along the way, they began to notice that swords and armor were scattered about in the forest. Urdun knew this was armor that was given to the goblins by the blacksmiths.

He turned to his fifty goblins and spoke with care, "Something's not right here. We need to get to town and see what is going on, but we need to be careful about the surroundings."

One goblin looked at him with concern. "Was this all a mistake?"

Not knowing the answer, but wanting to appear confident, Urdun responded, saying what they wanted to hear, "No, it wasn't a mistake, but I think we were set up. Gavid must have alerted them to kill us all off. He must be back in town, telling them what went on in the cave."

"How do we know if he did this?" another goblin spoke.

"We can't be certain until we get to Herium. Be careful, no telling what is in the darkness of the forest," Urdun replied.

As they got closer to Herium, they noticed dead goblins scattered about and cheering in town. Slowly, Urdun approached and peered out of the thick bushes to notice a fully prepared town celebrating the death of goblins.

He turned to his fifty, which oddly were decreased in numbers to twenty and spoke softly, "We need to retreat. The town seemed to be ready. Let's get to Jael and tell him about this. Gavid set a trap for us, I know it. There's no way that this town was prepared for battle without notice."

The goblin who asked questions earlier responded, "So this was a mistake. We should have never come and attempted to attack the city."

Others agreed with him.

"I should have gone back home, at least I would have some wealth from the caves," another spoke up in agreement.

This unsettled the remaining goblins and they agreed with those who had a change of heart.

Frustrated, Urdun snapped in reply, "We wouldn't have known about this. Our scouts never returned and the others vanished into the darkness and left us with no information. Had we known, we would have never come, or left the caves. We have enough wealth, we don't need to attack the towns."

Another goblin spoke up with concern, "What about those who died? Their families need some kind of retribution for their attempts. We can't just leave them with nothing."

Urdun nodded and sighed quietly. "We'll take care of this when we return to our city. Be ever watchful of the things going on around you. The forest is filled with deadly things. Elves or otherwise. I suggest we go in pairs and split up to confuse whatever is out there."

Urdun slipped behind the remaining goblins and walked back toward their home.

CHAPTER 29

The sun peeked over the horizon and slowly touched the town of Herium. The snow covered the ground and the town appeared peaceful, silent until the bell sounded to wake the townspeople to prepare for the attack. Herium came to life, the snow elves rushed out of their homes, running around the town. Mothers whisked their smaller children to the tops of buildings to remain safe, while their fathers and older siblings put on their armor and gathered weapons.

Ledric stood at the window, looking around. They were ready as best as they could be.

Gervis walked amongst the people, gretting everyone. They were shocked to see him there and alive.

"We're ready, Gervis," a voice spoke to his left.

He turned and smiled. "Very well, Ugex. You know about where the goblins were planning to attack, shore that up and make sure no one gets through this area."

Ugex nodded then commanded his troops to go to the fence on the east side of town.

Gervis finished his tour of town and made his way to the top of an inn on the center. He waved his hand then spoke in a normal voice, but the entire town could hear him as if he were standing right next to them.

"Today we're being attacked. I don't want you to be fearful. We're better prepared than they are. They think we're just going to allow them to attack our town and have their way here. We won't consent to it." He paused for a moment and stared to the east then continued, "We'll fight and defeat anyone who tries to take what's rightfully ours!"

The crowd cheered, but not so loudly the goblins that might be nearby could hear them.

Weisgar appeared behind Gervis and walked up to him. "The attack has begun. They're on their way, but the first fifty will only be ten by the time they arrive. The goblins are in such a rage they won't realize what's going on around them until it's too late."

Gervis gave a nod and turned to his friend. "Thank you. How many groups are there?"

Weisgar gave a slight shrug and then replied, "We estimate fifty groups of fifty. Which is twenty five hundred goblins. That was just a small amount of what was in the cave. Most of them were headed home. There had to be well over ten thousand in the cave. The orcs, well you know they weren't really orcs, were they?"

"What were they?" he asked Weisgar, a bit confused.

Weisgar grinned and turned back to Ugex. "Them. They were the ones in the cave watching things for the Dragon Counsel."

Gervis grinned then turned back toward the town. "They had their reasons. I cannot always understand the ways of the Dragon Counsel. Nor the ways of that clan of elves."

Weisgar knowingly smiled. He spoke, "We'll work hard to only have ten goblins at a time attacking the city. The farmers and the children should take care of them."

Nodding, Gervis watched as the sun finally penetrated through the tree line and made things more visible. "Thank you, Weisgar. Please, go back and be ready. If they're on the move, it means they'll be here soon."

Weisgar nodded and vanished. Gervis closed his eyes for a moment and sighed. Things weren't as they had been before, they were different. The truth would come out sooner or later. He knew it. He turned to where Ugex and his clan were stationed, watching only for a moment. Then he looked out in the direction of the cave and wondered how many others had known about all of this.

Soon they could hear the screams of the first wave of Goblins coming in. Farmers on the rooftops commanded the children to start using their slingshots as they began to shoot their bows. The children were hesitant at first until one child actually connected and killed a goblin. The other children saw this as a competition and their confidence began to grow. The first group of goblins was downed by the children and the farmers, but the second and third wave came in faster.

Gervis watched as a few began to penetrate the defenses, but failed to get passed Ugex and the others. That was three waves of Goblins, not even half way. He decided he should get his own armor on, then go down to help Ugex and the others.

Once he arrived, he noticed his sons took position on top of the inn where the children were. Ledric was also nearby, as were his sons and wife. They knew the depleted town would not be able to hold off as many goblins that planned to attack.

He knew he had to thank Meranda for the information she gave him to save Herium. He turned to his sons and asked them to command the children and farmers not to kill the next wave of goblins. There was confusion, but Linden understood.

Soon, the goblins arrived and the elves in the ground were able to attack the ones that scaled the walls with ease. The goblins came wave after wave, but in small amounts each time. The sun reached its peak and the goblin waves were slowing down. Their attacks were meaningless and they were fleeing before they reached Herium.

The cheers came from the elves at the fence when they realized the attacks came to a stop. Herium defended itself with no loss of life. The elves disbursed to their own homes, those who had no homes walked to their respective inns.

Ledric approached Gervis and spoke while others walked passed them. "Glad you could make it. I'm also glad that Ugex and his elves could make it here as well, but I have to ask you a question." Gervis was curious as Ledric walked into the inn. "You did well, but does the town know the truth about Ugex?"

Shocked, Gervis tried to play it off, but he knew it wouldn't get passed Ledric. "What do you mean? Ugex has his own clan. He just came here to make sure we were safe."

Ledric folded his arms and left it at that. "That's your decision. You'll need to tell them eventually. It will haunt you if you don't."

Suddenly, the inn doors opened, Gervis' sons and their wives walked in alongside Ledric's family. They were grateful things ran smoothly.

Maellan spoke up though, still a bit cautious of the attacks, "How can we be certain that was the last of them?"

Gervis turned to Ledric, who spoke, "Weisgar has told me that the caves are empty. The last of the attacks came and the others were fleeing back to their homes."

Maellan was satisfied with this answer. Cadhla looked at his father and was curious. "We'll stay to help these elves get back on their feet? It's going to take a lot of work."

Ledric shrugged and turned to his wife. "That's up to the three of you. I'm sure our kingdom will need your mother and I to straighten out what happened in our part of the region. I'm sure there are other cities that were nearly taken over as well."

Maellan then gave a smile. "Father, I'd like to stay and help as I'm sure my brothers would too."

Ledric turned to Cadhla and Keilan who were both nodding. Keilan shrugged. "I'm sure Cadhla should be here with you since he's the eldest, but that's his decision."

Cadhla hadn't thought of that, but gave a shrug and a smile. "Let's celebrate right now! I'm sure that the night will be eventful and we'll need to reflect on all that's happened or could happen in the region, but we need to be happy for once."

Everyone couldn't have agreed more and they were soon celebrating the night away. They were happy to enjoy each other's company until it was time for bed, then they parted ways.

The town was finally safe and free of Gavid, he would no longer punish them or their way of life. Gervis would make sure the town would thrive again, but it would take a lot of work.

Treidon sat with Meranda and smiled as he admired the tattoo on her arm. "I can't believe you did all of that in the trials. I was stupid to believe that weapon casting wasn't important. When did you get the tattoo?"

She blushed and gently pulled her arm away from him. "I got it last night, when Cirian said they wanted to see me. Although..." her voice faded as she reflected in thought.

He looked troubled and smiled. "Tell me. What happened?"

She glanced up at him. "I had a demon attack me last night. That wasn't something they were expecting, I don't think."

Treidon shook his head. "No, the Elders wouldn't have sent out demons to test you, but then again, who would?"

Shaking her head, Meranda didn't know the answer and stared down at the floor. "I was in pain before he even came at me. I heard a voice in the darkness telling me to fight."

Treidon looked at her. "What did the voice sound like?"

"Deep, baritone, and masculine. I've never heard it, ever," she said softly.

He simply nodded. "Well, at least someone was able to help you through it."

Hugging her tightly, Treidon held her like he hadn't seen her in a lifetime. Meranda placed her head on his shoulder and felt at peace. Her mind didn't wander or race like it had before. With Treidon, she felt whole for once in her life.

There was a soft knock on the door. Treidon sighed softly, stood up, and opened it.

Pagues stood before him with a concerned look on his face. "Meranda, are you okay? After last night, I heard things were a bit—" he paused.

She nodded. "I'm fine. I handled it and passed it. We'll get through it."

Treidon looked confused and he started to ask, but thought it was better to leave it alone. "So what brings you here, father?"

"Gavid is here in the dungeon," Pagues said in a calm fashion.

The moment the name came up, Meranda panicked and began to cry. She ran to the bathroom and slammed the door behind her, locking it.

Pagues turned to his son, "What has her so troubled?"

"Father," Treidon turned to the door and back to his father. "She was tormented by Gavid, she has nightmares of him. Those scars on me were scars on her *from* him. She's so troubled by even hearing his name, she becomes paralyzed with fear. Why tell her this?"

Pagues watched as the tears flowed down Treidon's face. "Why are you crying, son?"

Treidon wiped his eyes and turned again to the door. Although the tears continued to flow, Treidon looked at his father. "She and I are bonded, Father. You know that. We're so connected that her crying shows on my face. I feel her aches and her troubles."

Pagues slipped to the door and lightly knocked. "Meranda, please, come out and talk about this. The Dragons have agreed to his punishment and you need to hear it."

The door unlocked and she slowly came out to listen to what Pagues had to say. He smiled reassuringly then hugged her tightly. He didn't realize how much of a bond she and his son shared. As he hugged her, she cried more. Calming her, he stroked her hair and spoke soothing words until the tears stopped.

He gently pulled her away and looked into her eyes. "The Dragons want you to carry out his sentence. You can do it. We'll be here for you when you're ready, but it needs to be done today."

"I-I just can't," Meranda said sadly. "I can face the ugliest monster out there, even demons, but I can't face *that* man."

Pagues lifted her chin and stared hard into her eyes as a father would. "He's done some damage to you that might never be repaired, but he needs to be shown that he hasn't killed you and you are stronger than he is. That filthy thing down there needs to know he'll never get the better of you. Gavid needs to be shown he's nothing more than the dirt on the floor in there. I'm sure the shadow elves could help you and would be there for you."

She nodded and took a deep, cleansing breath. "I'll do it, if that's what the Dragons want me to do."

"Good. Now get ready to show him you're alive and you're capable of being stronger than him," Pagues said, looking at his son.

She nodded, walked into the bathroom, and washed her face. Soon she was back in the bedroom and they walked down to the dungeon.

As soon as they got down there, she started to have doubts, but Pagues stopped her. "You've come this far, don't stop now."

The guard who was standing watch nodded. "That man in there shouldn't breath the same air as someone as beautiful as you. Scars nor not, your heart is pure, your demeanor is far better than his. Take it to heart that this is what's right."

She shivered. Soon Oriana spoke up, "Are you ready?"

Meranda shook her head, but her words stated otherwise. "Let's go."

Oriana and Meranda vanished into the darkness and reappeared in the cell. Gavid was lying on the bed, unaware of his surroundings.

Oriana gently took Meranda toward him, but she was resisting it. She smiled and touched Meranda's shoulder. "You can do it. Want me to wake him up."

Meranda nodded as Oriana gently woke up Gavid who was sitting up by now and looking around, fully awake.

He spoke loudly and then Oriana moved away from Meranda. Gavid laughed at the girl before him. "You can't be alive, I watched you die in front of me. I saw the bloody sheets. You couldn't even lift a dagger to me. I'm your father for goodness sake. You're a filthy little girl who deserved to die in front of that king. Also, probably by now, your town has been taken over by goblins."

Meranda listened to his words, she was fearful of him. He stood over her and seemed bigger to her. He threw out insult after another toward her. In her mind, Meranda heard the voice of Treidon. *"Do it! You're none of those things that he claims you are. Shock him, like he did you."*

She stood up a bit taller, he finally realized. She turned to the shadows and spoke quietly. Gavid continued to hurl insults toward her, but it didn't seem to faze her.

Suddenly, she reached out of the darkness and pulled out the pin that was used to be in her back. Gavid paled as she began to talk. "You think you killed me, but Ledric and others saved me. You're in Elmwick in a dungeon cell and your goblins failed to take over Herium, thanks to Ledric and my family. Even Lord Siebrein has had a change of heart, but you...you are evil and deserve to die." He shrunk back in fear as she approached him and continued to speak. "I'm a Riftrider. I *will* dole out what the Dragon Counsel has suggested your punishment to be. I won't be haunted by your taunts, insults, or harmful testing anymore."

Gathering courage once more, he grabbed Meranda by the wrist and flipped her toward the bed. He swiftly landed on top of her and pinned her down. She mouthed something then chuckled as she touched his wrist without struggling much. Confused, he watched as she didn't move, but he felt as if the place she touched was turning cold. He looked down at his wrist and noticed it was gray.

He pulled away and looked shocked as he couldn't move it. "What have you done?"

"What I should have done years ago, turn you into a statue," she said coldly as she got up and walked into the darkness then vanished.

On the other side of the door there were screams, then they muffled and stopped.

CHAPTER 30

D ays turned into months and soon wedding bells could be heard around the town of Elmwick. Meranda stood at a mirror and stared hard into it. She was in a beautiful white gown with emerald trim and diamonds throughout. She sighed softly to herself as she missed her family deeply. There was a soft knock on the door and she sighed again. Several women waited on her hand and foot since the day Gavid passed. She was more peaceful mentally, but still haunted by nightmares. She walked to the door and opened it to see Pagues who was smiling from ear to ear.

"Are you ready?" he questioned to her.

She shrugged as he held out his elbow. They walked together to the grand hall and he whispered in her ear, "Your father will walk you the rest of the way."

Meranda beamed from ear to ear when she noticed he was standing in a flowing shirt and emerald colored pants matching the trim of her dress. "You think I would really miss your wedding?"

She gave a shrug. "I never know what might be happening in Herium. Last I knew, everything was okay there."

He smiled as the crowd stood and they walked to the front of the hall. Soon Treidon and Meranda were wed and the town of Elmwick rejoiced.

The reception was a beautiful one. Ledric, Rainah, Maellan, Cadhla, and Keilan were there. Meranda's brothers and their wives were there as well. The evening ended with Meranda and Treidon dancing the night away.

"Think you can stand being married to someone like me?" Meranda said softly.

Grinning, Treidon pulled her closer and kissed her gently. "I don't think I could see a day without you."

The wedding and reception were over and only immediate family remained in the great hall. Gervis approached her and handed her a small gift. "It's to help you with missing home."

She pulled out a necklace with a large diamond in the middle of a filigree metal design. "Bashawn made it for me as a wedding present for you. You can look through the diamond at any moment to see what's going on in Herium."

Standing up, she hugged him tightly. "Thank you, Father. I'll wear it every day."

He hugged her back then pulled away. "We need to get home. Remember, the winter festival is not that far away. You need to come see us."

She nodded and said her good byes to them.

Everyone went on their way, leaving Meranda and Treidon alone. He looked at her with admiration and stood up. "Come on, my wife. Let's go out in the city and just be in each others presence."

Meranda put the necklace on and looked through it for a moment, seeing the town of Herium. She stared at Triedon for a moment and gently smiled. "That's fine with me. I'm happy to be with you wherever you go."

Together, the pair of elves left the castle in wedded bliss, to enjoy the rest of the day in each other's company and to make new memories to replace the ugly ones in Meranda's mind.

"How could you let that snow elven woman send you back here without killing her?" the voice asked in the darkness.

A dark red woman knelt down in a circle before the darkness. "Because we were sleeping, sire. I didn't think that someone would come to her aid and rescue her, nor her family."

"You'll have to find her again and make sure she doesn't find out about her true potential!" the voice boomed in anger. "Use whatever resources I have. We must take over the realm before the end of the spring moon in the next year. We missed this one because you weren't able to get the relic I desired to finish the process."

She winced in pain as she felt his voice booming over her. "Sire, I promise I'll get that relic. I know where it is."

"You better make sure. You should have just killed them all off and taken the relic. Now, we have the danger that the girl will find out about her true potential," the darkness spoke.

"No need to worry, sire. No one realizes the truth of her. I think we took care of that and will continue to do so if I can keep sending the demons after her. With your permission, of course."

She stood up slowly as the voice spoke, "Make sure, I do *not* want her having the knowledge to could stop our plans. Now, go away! Keep attacking her at every turn!"

The demon bowed, turned, and exited the room. Then she spoke to several demons who stood before her. "You heard the master. Go attack the girl. Keep her from even thinking she can stand and walk."

The demons before her vanished, making their way toward their destination. She continued down a long corridor and soon reached a door. She opened it up and stepped into a room with an open portal. She cursed as she watched the images before her. Happiness around the town, joyful images. The demon knew she couldn't walk through the portal without someone calling her out. She took a deep breath and walked out of the room. The time would come when demons would walk the realm freely, controlling it. Hearing the pain and agony from the people would soon be music to her ears. For now, she would have to plot the demise of the girl and her family, until she could truly carry out her other plans.

Index

People

Meranda-The only daughter of Gervis and Anmylica. She has three brothers; Linden, Davignon, and Jayidus. She believed she wasn't important and was mistreated and physically abused as she was growing up. She didn't know her true family until recent events changed all of that. She has a strange birthmark on her back.

Treidon-Son of King Pagues and Queen Morida. He has three sisters; Rasi, Heirana, and Lysiara. He knew there were some strange events happening when we received scratches and cuts to places that he could not explain. Treidon is a Master Riftrider, and was sent out by the dragon counsel to find out the answers to the mysterious cuts.

Gervis-Lord of Herium, father to Linden, Davignon, Jayidus, and Meranda. Was put into a trance state because his so called wife told him it was the best thing. Once awake he realized the damage done and has returned to make sure that the damage is repaired and never happens again.

Pagues-King of Elmwick, former Riftrider, father of Treidon, Lysiara, Heirana, and Rasi. He was in the battle of Terian and helped the Dragon Counsel form an alliance between the Kobolds and the Elves of the continent.

Hariton-Dragon and Dragon Counsel member. Father of Gervis and other elves that roam the lands. Grandfather of many. Helped Ugex and his Aquden tribe to protect the town of Herium from the attacks of the Goblins. Has helped many other tribes and cities, stands at the head of the Dragon Counsel.

Ledric-King of snow elves, region of Yeverdin.

Ugex-Brother of Gervis, Aquden elf, undercover Orc.

Jael-Goblin king.

Gavid-Desert elf, held Meranda prisoner, tried to take over entire Yeverdin realm.

Types of Elves

Snow Elves: each elf has dark hair, their skin is leathery, in shades of dark green, yellow, and brown. Snow elves live at the base of mountains and the snow region of the realm. Their homes are made of a sturdy wood that has magical properties that help protect its occupant.

Desert Elves: Dark skin, eyes, and hair. These elves live in Adobe homes or around caves for shade. They are accustomed to the dry desert heat.

Plains Elves: Light brown skin, lighter red, brown, and blond(e) hair, and lighter blue, green, and brown eyes. They live amongst the windy plains. Their homes are sturdy to keep the constant breeze from blowing them over. Most farmers live in the plains.

Forest Elves: Various skin colors from dark brown to light tan. Hair colors like the tree leaves; yellows, browns, oranges, greens, and reds. Eye colors are blues, greens, and browns. Forest elves are used to living amongst the trees, but someone, in the past, decided that it was best to live on the ground and protect the trees.

Aquden Elves: Albinos of the realm. Their hair colors range from silver to dark gray, their eyes are anything from light blue to light violet, their skin are shades of gray, silver to dark gray. Aqudens are an ancient race believed to be extinct, however, most have blended with the snow elves.

Shadow Elves: chosen not born, given the power to move among the shadows, listening, fighting, and taking people to a destination much quicker.

Blood Elves: Evil race with fair skin, green or yellow eyes, and shades of blond(e) hair. Blood elves live in the forest with the Forest elves, but they are enemies of all good races and seek out ways to harm rather than help.

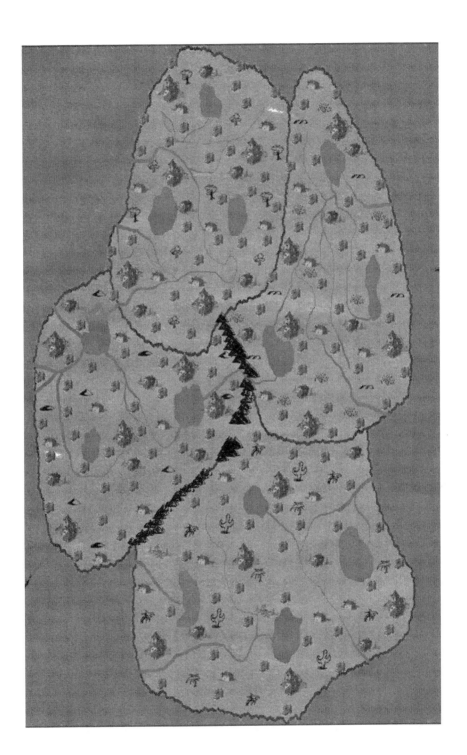

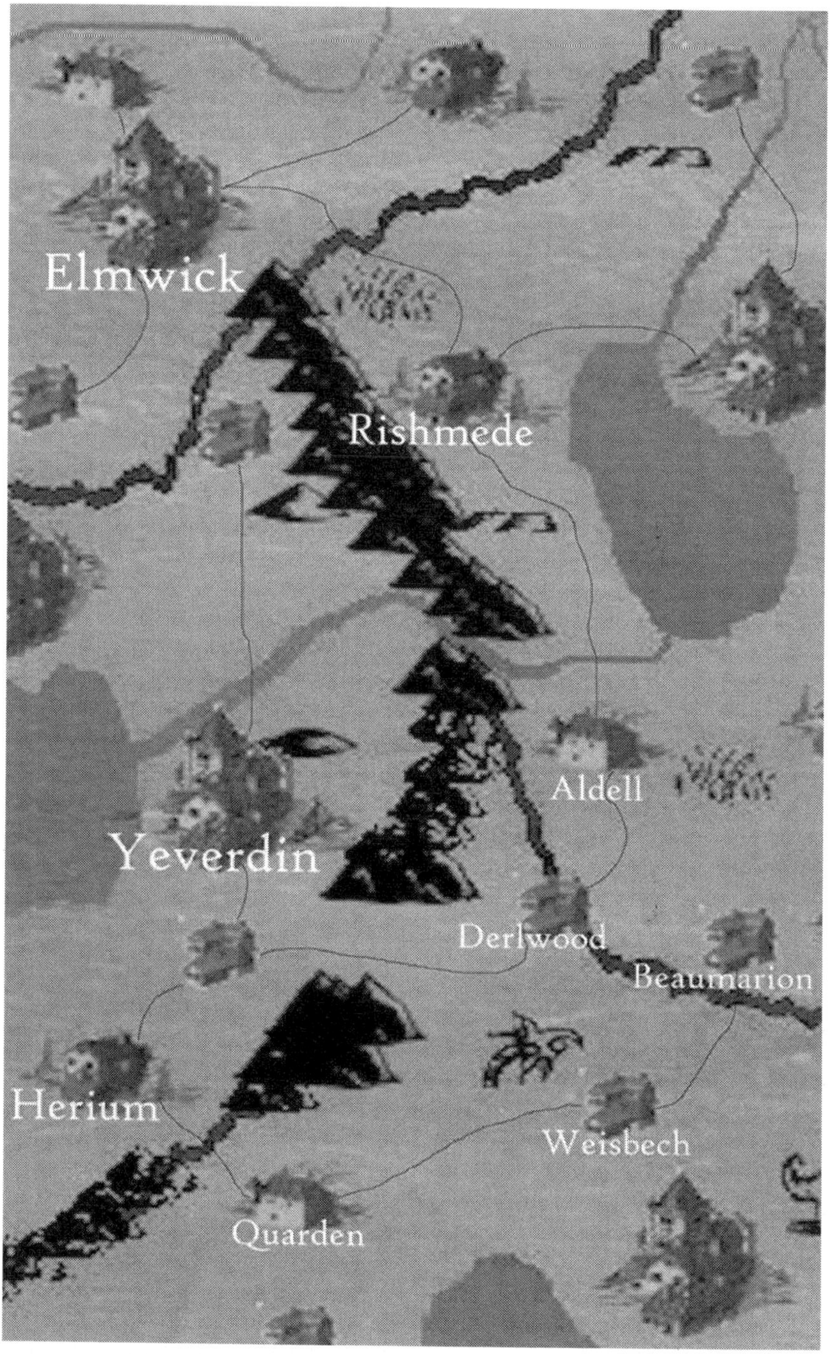
Elmwick
Rishmede
Aldell
Yeverdin
Derlwood
Beaumarion
Herium
Weisbech
Quarden

About the Author

C.N. Pinckard is from Bossier City, Louisiana, where she lives with her two autistic boys. Her own autism spurred her love of reading fantasy. When she graduated from the small rural school she attended, she soon married and began her family, all the while dreaming of the day when she would begin her journey writing.

In the present day, C. N. Pinckard enjoys every minute of working on her Riftrider's Return series as well as making jewelry, bookmarks, and handmade textures to use with photography or cover art.